Righteous,

BUTTERFLY

A *Novel...* Idea

_____

Himaus R Alexander

Righteous, BUTTERFLY A Novel... Idea
Copyright © 2019 by Himaus R Alexander

ISBN: 978-0-578-47621-6

Dedication

I'm dedicating this book with love and happiness, first and foremost to a dear friend to whom just by doing this, I've kept my word. Thank you, Andrea.

To my beloved daughters... my soul purpose.

My love to Wen, Jon and Jess, Mami and Analise.

My beloved sister, my nieces and Goddaughters.

My beloved Mom, the strongest woman I have ever known. She took a whoopin' for us and still makes the impossible happen for both saint and sinner, and I'm not a saint.

My Pop (Stepfather), the coolest motherfucker to walk the planet.

My brothers, and nephews and Godsons.

My Great-Grandmothers and Great-Grandfathers.

My Grandfather (Mother's) and Grandmother and Grandfather (Father's), Aunt Madeline, Ma Yin, Aunt Dolina, Aunt Susan, Aunt Irene, Aunt Lorna, Aunt Frances, Aunt Julia, Aunt Paula, Aunt Ima, Uncle Pete, Uncle Jack, Uncle Bible, Pabby, Uncle Desi, Uncle Fred, Uncle Granderson, Uncle "Boss" Albert, Uncle Steve, Mr. Winston and Godfadda. Christina, Kathy, Nola, Ma Karyl, Rainey, Aunt Mae, Neil, SJ, Quack, Mike, Casper...

RIGHTEOUS!

"... and to you GOD, now what?"

Table of Contents

Foreword 6

Preface 7

Introduction 8

Chapter 1 The Motherfucker Kept Going 'Til He
Died.. 9

Chapter 2 This Is My Son In Whom 27

Chapter 3 A Cute Little Package Like Her............. 37

Chapter 4 Yep, Her Pride Is A Bitch! 44

Chapter 5 Behold The Pale Horse 62

Chapter 6 Are You Proposing? 71

Chapter 7 Where Do We Find Clues For Things
And Things?.. 85

Chapter 8 Summer Fever....................................... 107

Chapter 9 Breakfast In Becs................................. 122

Chapter 10 The Burbs And Katherine Summers.. 130

Chapter 11 Hegira 136

Chapter 12 The Office... 143

Chapter 13 All Holes Are Not A Rabbit 161

Chapter 14 French Kissing In The PTA 181

Chapter 15 Child Of Kate..................................... 190

Chapter 16 No Banging My Teacher 208

Chapter 17 The Hit... 213

Chapter 18 Congratulations On Your Promotion. 236

Chapter 19 How's That For A Trade?.................. 245

Chapter 20 Meet My Mom 264

Footnotes 280

Foreword

"… always."

Preface

During a period of unbelievable bullshit in my life, I was urged by a dear friend to write a book because I wouldn't seek therapy. "Put your experience on paper, since you don't want to talk to anyone," especially anyone who couldn't affect a change in my life. So, having given her my word, six months later I figured I'd create an interesting story interpolating real events with fictional ones with maybe a side order of cult fantasy to go with it. I endeavored to do it in a way and also write it in a way that would present a plausible and likeable story for the reader. "We all need a win, every day as a matter of fact, and when we get it, we need to celebrate it!" H is quoted as saying. I addressed some personal conflicts with a lot of basic everyday bullshit as well, through the lives of my characters, and I will admit, Andrea, you were right. I do feel somewhat better. I still don't agree with this crap, but if my book can entertain you and maybe make you think a little bit... fuck it. Enjoy!

"Whatever God wants, God keeps..."
- Number Two

I'm still here.

Introduction

Righteous, Butterfly tells the story of a man who after a life of disappointment, walks away from GOD when the love of his life leaves him. GOD also walked away but left him with a gift that he eventually discovers he has and discovers how to use and uses to make money. *Lots* of it. Bored now, with just money, he finds five women with the characteristics of his lost love and hires them to run his wealth. The youngest of the women he's chosen, soon embodies her the most and he finds himself drawn closest to her. She becomes the biggest threat to all, including his reason for his feud with GOD in the first place, when after a decade, the love of his life and seemingly GOD, unexpectedly returns.

Chapter One

Amanda was in her office reviewing bank statements on both of her monitors and on her desk and in both hands, running H's entire operation under one tight fitting umbrella, which he determined was her. All activity involving the collection, exchange or movement of every penny in and out of H's pocket, Amanda Rosado knew about, yet something wasn't adding up. She wasn't your typical status driven, power-hungry, COO figure head, delegating to subordinates while posing behind an immaculately kept desk in a picturesque corporate office playing boss. She was modest and kind and somewhat insecure, but very hands on. Maybe because she was a woman and or maybe because she really *was* the boss. She kicked ass personally and delegated only when she needed to.

She called out to Maureen, "Mo?"

Maureen came into Amanda's office in a beautiful tight-fitting skirt and buttoned blouse holding her pen in her teeth to answer her call. Maureen didn't sleep on H or with him, but she did hold him down.

"Yes?"
"Hey, is Ana still here?"
"Yeah, she's in the kitchen."
"Homework?" Amanda asked, hesitantly.
"You mean, *'Men At Work'*- shit all over the place?"
"Lord," Amanda exclaimed, "can you get her for me, please?"
"Sure."
"Thanks, Mo."

Maureen took the elevator down to the 11th floor to RH LLC and to the kitchen, which was located near the entrance, to fetch Anastasia who sat isolated at the table with her books all around her and with her headphones on, lip syncing a song. Anastasia wasn't her favorite. Not sure if it was her or just her authority in the company, but since her promotion, Maureen has kept it short and sweet and cordial with her, and Amanda's peeped this. Anastasia could usually be found in H's office when he wasn't in, or here, her next favorite place and unofficial office when he did, much to the chagrin of all those who wished to hang out there. When Anastasia was in the kitchen, the office fasted, and everyone drank spit.

"Ana," Maureen called while waving to her and opening the fridge door.

Anastasia, who was wiggling her head, caught Maureen's stare and asked, "What's up?"

Maureen, tending to a snack replied, "Amanda wants to see you when you get a chance."

Anastasia took off her headphones and followed Maureen back upstairs to Amanda's office, knocking on her door as she walked in.

"Hey, hun, got a minute?" Amanda asked, pointing to the seating in front of her.

"Yeah- sure, what's up?"

"I've been going through some of your boss' bank statements, the real obscure ones, and found something odd in an account I need to ask you about. Maybe you know something?"

"Ok?"

Anastasia took a seat in one of Amanda's comfortable armchairs, relieving the ass cramp she got in the kitchen.

"Girl, I don't know why you don't just sit in his office or sit in the conference room or at a desk?"

"I like the kitchen," she said, whining.

"You must like your ass hurtin' you too," Amanda remarked, leaving Anastasia to work it out on her own and get comfortably seated, briefly, before continuing. *"Grimmy* has a squirrel account that hasn't had more than nine thousand in it since he opened it, way back."

"Ok?"

"He sees a teller every month or so to make deposits into this account."

Surprised at this news, Anastasia responded, "Really? Why not just transfer?"

"You *see* my point."

"Yeah, that is odd. Why so little?"

"My guess is your little squirrel is trying to keep his nuts under the radar."

Anastasia chuckled, "Well, that would help me out a lot but I'm still not following?"

"Come here. Look at this." Anastasia reluctantly stood up and went over to her and Amanda said, "See that amount right there, that's the deposit. These series of amounts are all paid out every month like clockwork. Look here- here," she continued to point, "as far back as I've checked, and here, the same amounts are all paid in checks."

Anastasia asked, "What are they for?"

"That's what I'm hoping you can tell me. There aren't any copies of the checks in the statements. All I have are the amounts, but-" she proclaimed victoriously, "I did find *this* out. Look." She brought up an email on the next screen and asked, "Hun, do you know these people?"

Anastasia read the email, which contained a list, and the list were names of his old girlfriends. Realizing she recognized them, Amanda leaned back in her chair to chat with her a moment.

"Ana, I'm not trying to be nosey when it's obvious whatever he's doing he's trying to keep it a secret, but he's still writing checks? I'm also not trying to ask you to share any information held in confidence with him, but do I need to be concerned with this? And do I need to tell Becca?"

"Between us," Anastasia asked, cautiously, "if I say it's cool, could you get past it?"

Anastasia knew the information Amanda had wasn't serious enough to involve Rebecca, who was usually informed of any developments that threatened his fortune, his safety or in general disturbed his peace of mind, the latter of which was her primary responsibility. It was a bullshit account with bullshit money in it by H's standards, but none the less, she didn't know what the fuck it was for and hoped it was voluntary, which might be worse. Shortly after her graduation and things had calmed down, Rebecca, at H's request, sat down with Anastasia to discuss her future in the company now that she was going to college and the company was strong and functioning profitably. They were both very pleased with her as his consultant, the official position that he hired her for that quickly changed to his personal assistant. In this role, she relieved a lot of the day to day burdens from Kate. But now, H wanted her role increased and permanent. Though she was given her freedom in the company, Anastasia was hindered in her ability to govern because she was constantly being overseen by someone. Kate, Amanda and Yvette were present in Amanda's office when Rebecca changed that, speaking with Anastasia at length about her new official title at RH LLC and what she personally expected of her in this position.

"Anastasia, I am naming you H's Executive Assistant," Rebecca said, sitting next to her in one of the two armchairs facing Amanda's desk.

In compensation to her for her present 24/7 availability and attention to him, doting on him hand and foot as her cute lovable adorable self, Rebecca also made her an officer in the company. She gave her the authority to act as necessary on his behalf without oversight except where legal implications came into play.

"H is to be kept insulated at *all* times," Rebecca stated *firmly,* resolute and unmistakably clear. "As his Executive Assistant, you will make sure of this more than anyone else here."

Anastasia replied, "Yes, Rebecca."

"I'm giving you *power,* Anastasia, and lots of it. Do not fuck this up. He is our money and I will not tolerate excuses."

Anastasia listened intently as Rebecca spoke, scribing in detail her every instruction in her mind and immersing herself in every possible amount of joy the freedom of it represented and had to offer.

"Make sure that nothing and no one interferes with him. Not family. Not friends. I don't care who it is. If you run into a *sensitive* situation or need advice, you will notify me immediately. Other than that, hun, I'm trusting you to handle it," she said, placing her hand on Anastasia's knee. "And, you'll continue to report to me about everything concerning him."

This part of the deal didn't surprise Anastasia. Rebecca was read in on everything and everyone in the company. There were no secrets once they left your mouth.

"Are you up to this?" she asked.

Anastasia, thrilled with excitement over the opportunity to be officially included with them, the only four executives in H's firm, immediately jumped at the chance, "Yes, I am!"

"Good!" Rebecca said, smiling at her young debutant's excitement and enthusiasm. "Congratulations!"

Anastasia surprised Rebecca with a hug where she sat. The girls had never seen her display this amount of affection for anyone besides Kate before and were even more surprised by Rebecca's response. *Ms. Prim and*

Proper hesitated slightly but embraced her exuberant ingénue tight and was deeply affectionate towards her.

"Aw, sweetheart you're very welcome. I'm so proud of you!" Rebecca stated as Anastasia held her.

"Well, that was surprising?" Kate quipped, sitting with Yvette across from them on the couch.

"I know. I'm sorry! Sorry-" Anastasia said, overwhelmed with emotion and apologizing to Rebecca as she released her.

"Oh, no, hun, don't be. I'm happy for you! You've earned it. You deserve to be happy."

"I am," Anastasia responded, wiping the tears from her eyes. "Thank you."

"Thank *you,* Anastasia. You're coming along very well, sweetheart. Enjoy it!"

"Careful, Becca," Kate said, "you're sounding a little like a *real* mom. Don't want to kink that cast-iron bra of yours."

"Whatever, I don't care. I am so proud of her! She's growing up so fast!" she said, lovingly fixing Anastasia's hair.

"That's right, Kate, she is. You need to share," Amanda insisted, with her head in some paperwork.

Yvette shook her head, "Y'all just too fuckin' cute! That's a grown ass woman y'all talkin' about. For real!" she added, sitting sophisticated with her legs crossed in her corner of the couch as they all laughed in the moment.

Rebecca retorted, "At eighteen? I couldn't do half of what she does, not with *my* mother!" grinning privately with Yvette who smirked.

"I don't care. I'm the only one allowed to spoil her! She's mine!" Kate declared, amidst the laughter as they sat and celebrated the formal induction of their new business partner to the firm.

When their emotions were all satisfied and they were done hugging it out, Rebecca composed herself batting away her tearing eyes and announced, "Anyway, as I was saying, Anastasia, this will be your new salary effective immediately," Rebecca said, handing Anastasia an envelope with an offer letter in it for the amount of $250,000, "with a three million dollar expense account from RH to more than cover any issues that may arise."

The offer letter was a formality really. It was Rebecca's way of fostering Anastasia's independence and supporting her individuality among them, though they had access to each other. Her new salary was no secret, nonetheless, she happily appreciated the gesture. The expense account however did seem excessive, but she kept that question to herself.

"Anything above that," Rebecca said, pointing at the envelope, will require Amanda's approval."

Presently, Anastasia already performed her new official job description and practically for free but with Kate's supervision, assistance and bank roll. But now with her very own autonomy, she could do it alone and *her* way. In other words, by default, Rebecca may have made Anastasia the baddest bitch in the company because while they each governed over his stuff, Anastasia solely governed him, having intimate knowledge of almost everything about him, and therefore also his stuff. The girls knew about Anastasia's feelings for H, which they allayed as best they could and the distraction that accompanied it. So, by giving her this position and with this amount of power to serve him, Rebecca served her own purposes just as much. Still, Anastasia was disturbed by not knowing why H was paying out this money every month and hoped she was making the right call containing it or it would most certainly be her ass. Baddest bitch or not, Rebecca Rubin was not the one to fuck with.

"Are these payments planning on stopping any time soon?"
"I doubt it," she replied, sullen from the mystery before her.

Needlessly reminding her of her job, Amanda asked, "Is he in trouble?"

Anastasia replied, "No, he's not."

Amanda inquired further, "Then this is all personal?"

"Yes, it is."

Amanda thought about that while Anastasia thought of the potential implications and wanting to solve this mystery privately. She was turning to walk out, determining her wants irrelevant, when Amanda asked, "You didn't know did you?"

Anastasia stopped and shook her head, "No, I didn't."

"I appreciate your honesty, hun," Amanda said, gracing her with a comforting smile. "Between us then. I'll leave you to your business."

Anastasia thanked her and returned to the kitchen and to her papers in front of her and her headphones off to the side, trying to figure out how to approach H about this.

"Hey, boss, Amanda and I were snooping through your shit today and found your hush money account that you use to pay off your ex-girlfriends every month, for whatever reason. To my knowledge, you're not still fucking them. You didn't by chance knock any of these bitches up, did you? Because I can't figure out why you payin' all of them except for curiously enough, two of them. So, what's up with that? And you've been doin' it in a way that we haven't caught until now. Why boss?" she thought. "Yeah, I'd cuss me out too."

At the very least, she saw this as an excuse to go hang out with him, so she packed up her books and called for a car to his apartment.

"You see the craziest motherfuckers on the subway, man. It takes all types you know?"

"Who was he talking about?" Kate asked.

"I honestly don't know. He lost me. He was venting and I didn't want to interrupt. He was running out of shit to do and places to go. I'm worried he's gotten to the point where he's outgrown a lot of shit and a lot of people. 'I feel restless sometimes, staying in my *tomb* when I'm not in the office,' he complained to me once, saying that he didn't *'fuck around as much'* because I *'watched him like a hawk and protected him like a pit bull.'* But he said he had noticed he had found some *peace* with us, in occupying his time focusing on his relationship with each of us."

Where trading was concerned, Vetty was getting really close to H, poking and prodding him about the *'Carnival,'* which was one of the few reasons she would dare to venture downstairs to *Gen Pop* and hang out when he was in his office. She was also spending a considerable amount of time with him at his apartment.

"As close as y'all are to me, y'all didn't know me back when it was just me in a one-bedroom apartment with a bullshit job and the love of my life. That's funny," he said, laying on the couch telling me his story, *"she was the love of my life but I wasn't the love of hers. Boo hoo? Ha ha!"*

"My stomach tightened up when he said that. I felt everything he did."

"What girl was this?" she asked, as I took a breath and tried to condense a lot of info into a concise segment for her. Kate tended to lose her shit the more info you gave her, so I'd learned to give her only the highlights and be picky even with those.

"Her name was M," I answered, "and she broke his heart"

"Life, it was all so simple then…" he sang to me. *"I went to work, I came home and I passed the fuck out. Rinse repeat. Yeah, I desired shit like everybody else and believed in shit too that someday, you know, something could happen to fuckin' amaze me."*

"Like what?"

"Like willing my dreams to come true, babe."

Anastasia inquired further, *"Tell me about it."*

"You don't want to hear my shit," he said, abruptly dismissing her inquiry.

"Yes, I... do. I'm serious! Boss, please? I've heard what, countless stories from you in one friggin' jigsaw puzzle of a life? Today, I want it straight, no detours, from beginning to end connecting all the dots. You're mysterious, I get that, and I get you. It adds to your," Anastasia smiled flirtingly, *"appeal. But I need your complete rags to riches story. Shit, you made me one. How could I not be curious about yours?"* She postured herself lying next to him on the couch, then looked him in his eyes and reminded him saying, *"You owe me."*

H exhaled and smirked at her. He was in and she was calling one in, as was most of the world, and with all things considered, he knew he was getting off easy.

"Come on, tell me. What was it like for the savant trading genius prior to me filling the void in his tumultuous life?"

"Oh, you fill my void, huh?" he asked.

"Yes, I do," Anastasia replied, staring seductively at him, then awkwardly whispering, *"Isn't it about time you fill mine?"*

H reflected while smiling cautiously at Anastasia sitting next to him. Vulnerable as her gaze was, it intensified on him. Her big beautiful brown eyes were so innocent and alluring and inviting, acknowledging her surrender entirely to him when he *"severed,"* as Rebecca put it, freaking her out when it first happened.

"I can look at a chart, and... and put my money in," he said, *"a shit load of it, where it needs to be."*

"See the future?" Anastasia inquired.

H snickered, *"Visit."*

Anastasia discovered Rebecca's best kept secret on her own and confronted her, eventually agreeing with her that it should be kept that way and shouldn't be revealed to the rest of the girls. They agreed to down play it and run interference when it should happen, so he didn't come off looking too weird. H felt bad that Josh sweated him thinking he was getting insider information. He was certainly rich enough. But Rebecca didn't need the headache or the scrutiny, so they occasionally had him miss one, a small one, to make it look good. H could see the future as if he was momentarily there. Depending on the intensity of his *sever,* his memory was sometimes affected causing him to forget the moments leading up to and during it. Anastasia put her cup of ice cream down and leaned over and stole a kiss, then tapped him gingerly and he returned to her.

"Sorry, babe," he apologized.

She smiled copiously while caressing his face and said, "It's ok. You were saying?"

"I remember when I use to lay on my bed and think of all the shit I was gon do once I came through," he started.

"Came through?" she asked, settling down next to him. *"What does that mean?"*

"Succeed," he replied, as Anastasia laid her head on his arm prodding him to tell her the story of his beginnings.

"I'ma keep going until I got no more breath. On my tombstone they gon write, "That motherfucker kept going 'til he died."

- Asay El

"For instance, simple shit. Like, I had one pair of glasses," he pointed, *"one, and I took care of that motherfucker more than I did my phone."* Anastasia laughed hysterically at his plight and he asked, *"You*

19

laugh?" Smiling at her as she rose up to face him and folding her arms on his chest, he questioned, *"Really?"*

She answered, *"You're serious?"*

"The struggle is real!" he replied. *"Shit, what you know about that? I hadn't had my eyes checked in years! Fuckin' book will blind your ass!"*

"Oh, my God, you sound like Mel!" she said, laughing at him.

"When I asked him why, he became dejected... and this is when he first told me about her."

"Some time ago, I met a girl and I fell in love with her from the moment I laid eyes on her. She was the most beautiful woman I had ever seen in my entire miserable fuckin' life. For me it was love at first sight. Straight up, no bullshit. I had died and had gone to heaven. She was that unbelievable and that impossible and that miraculous a chick for me to pull, that she proved to me immediately that not only was there a God, but that God actually, finally, gave a fuck about me. You dig? Some nigs had their burning bush, sun and moon standing still, their sling shots and glory on a tree. But me, I had her, and I was good with her. It was like I rubbed my lamp, named my price and God copped it. She was the one. Was it just my imagination, once again... to have a girl like her was truly a dream come true. Feel me?"

"I laughed at him and the way he would always seek to amuse me when he spoke to me. It was also interesting to me how everything surrounding his life plays a part in the events happening to him. Nothing is ever insignificant to H. Every thought, every word or action... the direction the wind was blowing, had some deep metaphysical meaning to him and he couldn't rest until he revealed it. He sang to me and I continued to listen."

"No stories. No prayer warrioring or jumping through hoops. No 'Jesus take the wheel,' none of that bullshit. I'm not sure if you know this but to hear these

mindless fucks tell it, God got us all like hamsters locked in a cage runnin' on a fuckin' wheel, and shit."

"I laughed endlessly at his blasphemous insight."

"What I got was just, 'Here, son. Hold this. You're good! I got you!'" H said, pausing while still reflecting on his memories as he spoke, *"Thou art my Son; this day have I begotten thee.' You know what I'm sayin'? Have you any idea what that feels like, Nana? A dream come true?"*

Anastasia paused to appreciate his sentiment and more importantly to her, to appreciate him.

"Man, I thanked God every day. I used to lay up in bed and watch her like TV, and shit. I'd fall in love with her over and over again like while she slept and the way she would smile at me when she caught me... I was nervous around her so much, it flattered her. I'd ask her, 'Say word? Baby, you really with me?' And she'd laugh and kiss me as proof she was, and I'd be good. M had the most beautiful smile. You remind me a lot of her. Y'all born only a couple of days apart."

Anastasia stared at him in her surprise and responded not just with her eyes, *"Why were you so insecure?"*

"I knew I deserved her and what I mean by this is, I didn't question how I got her. That was all God and I didn't debate that. You dig? That wasn't my argument. What I did question however, and I'm not gon front was, was she for real with me? Dig, M was way the fuck out my league, babe," he said, staring through the ceiling in his living room. *"I wasn't kidding myself. She was gorgeous, sexy, sensual, kind, comforting, genuine, loving and compassionate and... and eternal. But her flip side, man..."* he paused while he chuckled about it and just sighed. *"Truthfully, being with me it was woefully obvious that she was slumming. I ain't have shit, Na. I was just getting back on my feet, but she never, not once*

made me feel that, and for that I loved her even more, you know?"

"How did you two meet?"

"Her aunt hooked us up. She dug me and been singing my praises for a while, and shit. M and I hit it off though I wasn't sure why," he said, putting his ego aside as he concentrated on an answer, *"but we did and with everything that I had been through, receiving her to me was prophetic."* Excited, yet confused by the events as he experienced them, H said, *"Turned out to be more like pathetic."*

"He was embarrassed by what he had admitted only to me and I hadn't experienced that with him before. My rock had a chip in it and had shown it to me and I was fine with it."

"Still, for once in my life, I was the happiest motherfucker on the planet... cheesin' and shit. So, now that I had the girl of my dreams, and was obviously in God's good graces, or so I believed, I needed to be the best possible everything, you know, for her, right? So, here I am thinking the hook up gon continue, I'm workin' hard, bustin' my ass tryin' to deserve her love and giving her every reason to want to stay, dreaming she's gonna build with me, and then," he said, starting to chuckle uncontrollably until it was all out of his system, *"shit. One day we spoke, I mean a deep, deep conversation, God, with everything groovy, and we put a plan together for us and she said she was down, and I know I was down, shit, I was the motherfucker that came up with it and the next day, poof,"* he said, animating the word with his hands, *"she was gone. My hopes, my dreams, my prayers, my dollars, my God, all of it, everything just came up short and bailed on me and M left me for the next motherfucker, and she never... looked... back."*

"I stared at him only to realize that the ceiling he had been gazing through this whole time had suddenly closed just like that opportunity in his life and he asked me, 'What was I gon do, Na? Seriously.'"

"I'm so sorry, boss."

"I watched him catch a tear from his eye with his thumb and wipe it on his shirt and he replied, *'Yeah, thanks. Yet, you know for whatever reason, I still believed. Can you believe that? I still continued to believe, and I still kept- the faith,'* he said, sniffling and chuckling lively to himself in disgust. *'I thought our break up was temporary. I swear to God. I was like yo, stop playin', man... for real! You couldn't tell me otherwise. This was GOD, sweetheart, and I know GOD well! What, fuck me over like this? And for what? Come on now! You know what I'm sayin'?'* He sniffled and exhaled completely, and I snuggled in closer to console him with my arm around him and after a long pause he continued, *'Well, needless to say after a while, that brutal reality finally settled in,'* he said, giggling his ass off and infecting me to do the same. *'See, but don't touch. Touch, but don't feel. Feel, but don't... enjoy! And if you do decide to enjoy, better enjoy that bitch quick, bruh!'* H sighed. *'Anyway, I gave up or so I thought, and dealt with the fucked up days, the bitchin' about waking up, the endless disappointments- it seemed I was on a roll and shit,'* he said, becoming more and more disgusted as he reflected, *'the rejections and the begging of Her Royal Holy fuckin' Highness to just kill a nig dead already and be done with it 'cause it was painfully obvious at this point, you know? It dawned on me that 'Yo, they're really not going to do shit to help you, man?' She wasn't gon do shit to help me!'"*

"I looked to him and scolded him, *'No digas eso! Wait... she?'"*

"He looked at me, smiling as if I wasn't paying attention and said, *'You're gorgeous, you know that?'"*

"I responded, *'Um, you've told me. Hold on! Get back to she!"*

23

"He got really quiet like I do when I remember something I thought I had buried deep down and it resurfaced."

"I begged her to stay, Na, and I pleaded with her to take me back and make us work. Make us work,' he whispered, *'our fuckin' plan.'* He started to drift then caught himself and continued, *'But, she did what she felt she needed to do, and that was the end of that.'"*

"Ouch," Kate criticized, "that was cold!"

Anastasia remarked, "No, *that* was fucked up! And there was this other girl, a real blur, actually, he called *Siren,* who he only brings up every now and again. She really mind-fucked him, literally, much like you do. She told me she turned his mind into fucking pudding."

They laughed and it released the tension and as if understanding exactly how it could be done.

"Oh, that's a classic," Kate said, hysterically. "I can see how he would put us together! Oh, my God?" She then seemed to have gotten lost in a thought and daydreamed for a while and asked, "He loved M *that* much, huh?"

"... I met a girl and fell in love with her from the moment I laid eyes on her."

I answered, "Yes."
Kate then asked, "And what do you think?"

"When I lost M, I lost my trust in them." H explained to her, *"Failing on your own dime is one thing, right? But when you're coupled, you know, that shit leaves you wanting to save face, even desperate and I got dissed, man, and I just don't eat that shit well. I would've sold my soul for M and she knew it. My word is all I got,"* he insisted. *"She deliberately made it so I couldn't keep it."*

"Boss," Anastasia suggested, *"maybe it was all just a test?"*

"I hate that fuckin' word."

I stared attentively at him and watched the way his lips moved and the rhythmic rising and setting of his chest. I laid close enough to hear his heart beating. I felt his frustrations and the desperation in the words he used, the cusses he chose and the inflections in his tone. I thought about what my life would be today without him. What would I be doing right now? I'd probably be in my room at my mom's dreading life, fearing the unknown and wondering where the fuck happiness was for me too and why couldn't it find me, much like he did. It's like he said, *truth.* Kate stared at me for the longest and it unnerved me. I felt like I was being mind-fucked and I couldn't help but feel that she knew what I was thinking, so I looked away and when she stopped it, I continued.

"I believe he thinks he did, and he hasn't gotten over that and hasn't gotten over her, since."

Kate accepted my answer, confirming my suspicion.

"Was Siren before or after M?"

"That's the thing. It sounds like they might have been together right about the same time? But Kate, he wouldn't have cheated on M."

"Maybe she thought he did and that's why she left, or maybe she was just a bitch like you said," Kate surmised.

"Well, whoever she is, I'm never letting her ass near him again." Anastasia sighed, "I think he's afraid of her.

"Really?" Kate responded, grinning as she got up to refill her ice cream. "You do that. Want more?"

"Sure."

Kate took both bowls and went into her kitchen as Anastasia recalled privately.

"We keep coming back to these fucked up precepts, man, and they blow, and that's the truth. You dig? That's the fuckin' truth! I'm done with that shit, Na. No more!" he said, sighing and squeezing me closer to him.

"So wide can't get around... my mother's tits."

Chapter Two

This Is My Son In Whom
"The Birth Of Yvette Williams"

It was Thursday and the day I take my favorite run to Brooklyn to see my oldest friend on the DL, Ms. Joliet Lewis, for our scheduled brunch, which included tea for her and orange juice for me and fresh baked corn bread for us to go with her great wisdom counseling session. Next to my Godfather, Kenny, her insight for its fairness and objectiveness I valued like no other. Ma was impartial and just in her assessment of what I presented her, and her views came with a built-in woman's perspective, which was paramount. She invited me to discuss all my concerns and divulge all my secrets, which at first was kind of nervous to me since I've done some things, but I held her absolute trust, she assured me. I took care of her most prized possessions on earth; her beloved granddaughter, Yvette Essie Williams and her beloved ward, Rebecca Abigail Rubin. Ma loved these girls like she birthed them herself. When they needed nurturing from parents too immature to face responsibility or too career driven to pay attention, she was the sun and the moon and the stars to them transcending color, creed or divine visitation. They shared a resilient bond between them that life tested and even shook a little bit but was incapable of breaking because of me and yet she had felt was in fear of jeopardy since me.

"Two women cannot love the same man, not in the way they love you, H," she quarreled. "Those girls have met their match if you messin' with their hearts now, you hear?"

Ma scolded me for what she took as a slight by me potentially driving a wedge between *Vetty* and *Becs* because of their attraction to me.

"Ma, I started with Becs and my loyalty is to her. I've given it to her."

"Then you needs best stop fuckin' Essie!"

"Psss! Vetty ain't sweatin' me."

"Yeah, you keep tellin' yo'self that and don't you suck yo' teeth at me boy!" she barked, rolling her eyes at him. "You think competition with them is new? They been at it since they were kids! Dependin' on who they around determined the winner, it seems. Around white folks, Rebecca shined and around black folks, Essie, but my gran'babies *never* let it get too far! You ain't smart playin' 'em against each other! You'll get your ass kicked by Essie or chewed out by the ghetto-est white girl ever," she said with a scowl and then she laughed at me.

"Oh, you know? No secrets between y'all, huh?"

"None… until you." I acknowledged her concern and promised to correct my transgressions and she continued, "Now, eat yo' cornbread and don't interrupt," Ma Jolie said, propping herself up in her lounge chair and adjusting her shawl that was thrown over her legs. "Hear an old woman's wisdom. You can take it with a grain of salt or a spoonful of sugar, makes me no never mind, but you gon take it with you and best understand it! You have managed to surround yourself with five of the most beautiful, strong, capable, smart, savvy and sassy ass women I know, that are incapable of holdin' their tongues. They know themselves, which is to say, they know their troubles and they are behind you supportin' you and taking care of you and each in her own way lovin' you. Now, all that and then some you got, as opposed to you hangin' on to just one good woman." She leaned over to me and asked, "Raisin, is this money really the blessin' you wanted?"

I found myself at odds with that question, particularly with the way Ma Jolie posed it. The simple answer was 'yes' but the more involved answer was not so 'yes.'

"Seems to me it's made you lazy, so lazy you don't even bother to work for yo'self or choose to commit to one of them heart first."

I wasn't lazy. I was supervising, even better, observing. In fact, I preferred the term *delegating* even *bullshittin'* to lazy. But I was working and acting according to the precepts of my vision in giving each of the girls their autonomy in my blessing to govern as they saw fit within it. Yes, I had a God complex and I had the right to it. I came true before they wished and in that fact everyone was secure. What the fuck would you think?

"Think about what you know about these women and then imagine that that's only the surface. The first woman brought you to the second woman who brought you to the third woman and so on and so on, and now you got five women and you ridin' 'em like yo' own personal harem carousel. Everybody smilin' and havin' a good, *good* time, gettin' dizzy with bliss and they revere you, but yo' ass is like the fatted calf. As I recall, in the end that calf got sacrificed to their beliefs, now didn't it?" She paused to look at me and asked, "Do you know what they believe in, Raisin?"

I listened intently as she spoke.

"You see, I know what you know about them and I know what I know about them. They know more about themselves than our knowledge of 'em put together. You know I got your secrets right here, don't doubt that," she said, tapping her temple, "and I hold their secrets deep down in here," she said with her right index finger on her chest. "And buried beneath all 'em secrets," she said as her eyes widened on me, "be my own."

"Is this your way of telling me, don't let my noodle get me in trouble, Ma?"

"Aw, shuga, we done passed that shit. We workin' on damage control now," she said, chuckling as she said it. "You don't like being serious, do you? But baby, you got to be a little bit more careful to get on back from where you came. You thought about her much?" she asked me while sipping on her tea with her saucer resting securely on her lap.

"Who?"

She replied, "You know who the hell I'm talkin' about."

I looked her dead in her eye and answered, "No, Ma, not since Becs."

I lied.

"Why do you ask?"

Ma asked, "You think she know?"

Shaking my head, I replied, "I don't see how she could. I don't think there's any way she *can* know. I have had zero contact with the woman. I would even venture to say that she doesn't even know I exist much less remember me. Why?"

Ma fixated on the space between us and inquired, "What happens if she does?"

The thought struck me as far-fetched as fetch could get. Like science fuckin' fiction fetch. I hadn't really thought about the shit, man.

Angrily I responded, "Seriously? Ma, who left who? I received it and she passed on it, and really, I don't think it was her *right,* maybe just her opportunity? No different than her choice to bail on me and take her shit down the block."

Ma corrected me and said, "That's not what I asked you and you bein' awfully defensive. And, she ain't pass on it. You never told her. Same way you never told Rebecca. You just gave it to her. You the one chose."

I conceded to her because she was right, which is why my ass was here bright and early on a Thursday morning seeking answers to the questions I had. Today her answers came with a little bit of ass whoopin'... and a side order of smack me.

"I felt Becs deserved it, Ma."

"Why, because she got her ass beat or because you say so? Which of 'em ain't yo' vengeance talkin'?" she asked, staring at me and then she answered for me, "I thought so."

"Ma, I'm sorry. I don't take being dissed well. Apart from you, she would be the only other person that could conceivably help me now. Ma, if M knew this, all *this*, she'd want what's hers and I'd be in for some *shit*."

Ma had a reason for this question, and I wasn't sure if I should press her for an answer. I hadn't thought about M since the bar with Becs, the restaurant with Kate, the pool with Nana, when I hired Vetty and now with Ma, to be specific. For somebody non-fuckin' existent I sure thought about her ass a lot? Specifically, everyday too motherfuckin' many. Did that mean something? She had her head down with her gaze focused in her tea like she was seeing the future floating in there in vignettes of prophecy and alchemy. I inquired of her juju.

"What you thinkin', Ma?"

Ma Jolie sighed. It was a thing she did when she processed information she received. It was like she was making line by line comparisons and surmising at the same time and when her tally was done, she would share that view.

"Raisin you ever hear that old sayin', *'Nothin' out here for you, you gon miss?'*"

"Yeah, I remember hearing that a lot while I still caught ass. That and $2.75 will get my ass on the bus."

She laughed and called on the Lord for strength to deal with me and then returned to my ass whoopin'.

"I believe it is *yo' choice* who you choose and from what I see, you've chosen well. Each of 'em be very unique in their qualities and their strengths and you that glue, that center, that reason and that purpose for 'em. Yes, maybe it was only supposed to be one and you done gone and divided that one into five. Hell, if that ain't genius, then I don't know what is? But that just bring you right back to your trust issues and you refusin' to choose one woman over the other, but instead securin' five of 'em that will always need each other. Life's a bitch when it come to *'choice'*... ain't it?" She smiled at me and asked, "So, what you solve, huh?"

I shook my head as Ma managed to turn my life into a fuckin' R&B song.

"Are you complimenting me, Ma?"

"Boy, you know you too damn smart for yo' own good, yet you might actually know what the fuck you doin'." H smiled and she rebuffed him, "Don't smile at me! I still think you carryin' a little bit too much concern over what folks out here think about you though, and that shit needs to stop. You rich, shit! You ain't gotta answer to nobody? Fuck these thirsty ass motherfuckers! Nigs always got shit to say. Let 'em go get theirs. Work on your issues," she said, mumbling sarcastically to herself, "startin' with you ain't exactly choose the most unattractive women in the world to surround yourself with, myself included."

"Now, Ma, you know if I was just a little bit older, you and me, we would do some things, hmmm?"

Ma Jolie cracked up. It was such a pleasure to hear her laugh. I made her day. She was so free since we met, with no concerns or worries or problems pertaining to this world. Much like with my mom and all the older folks I retired, I saw to it that nothing offended her tranquility. Her girls made sure her every want was satisfied and that was simply for her love and her sacrifice for them.

"Raisin," she said, placing her hand on mine, "What you driven to do is so admirable, baby, and so prophetic, you got me believin' in it too. But, to choose Rebecca over M disturbs you way too much, you hear me? What's that sayin' they got, *'Image is everything?'* A powerful black man with a white woman at his side is a hard sell for you ain't it?"

"Only because it's a harder buy for them."

"Because a white woman come across as yo' savior?"

"Yes, Ma."

She quipped, "Especially the way you gone and fucked it up."

"Yes, Ma, I know. Thanks for reminding me. I still stand by it though. I know I am right. I will not have her gettin' ripped apart."

"You sure love her that much, don't you?"

"Ma, I love them all."

I fought with the frustration I felt not being able to presently justify my decision and the pending backlash I could receive as time went on. I had been driven by my instincts on every decision I've made since that day and second guessing myself was not a habit I was looking forward to adopting, so my decision would stand and all that I was building with it. Still, Ma Jolie was assisting me in reconciling in my mind the guilt I carried for the way I chose one woman over another and my determination to continue to do so despite a growing need to revisit that decision around me. I grappled with the fact that they had secrets, she had secrets, hell, I was the only one without secrets since I told them all… maybe. But their secrets did not shake the trust I had in them and they made sure of it. In that I was secure. I looked into Ma's eyes and I recognized her soul. It was the same soul I had seen all my life in so many women *in* my life, including Becs and M.

"So, why do I still feel like shit?"

"That's on you, baby. I been told you put that thing down," she reminded me, pointing her finger at my shoulder. "I do have a bad feelin', well let me not say *bad* before I go make mo' trouble for myself," she said, tapping my hand again. "Boy, you gon have to make some hard decisions soon. The thing is, the only person seein' it as hard will be you."

"Fuck me!" he thought, *"...Again?"*

Ma looked me in my eyes and said, "Come here Raisin, let me tell you somethin'."

Ma Jolie spoke with me at length of my position and about the choices and options she saw at my disposal. She also bequeathed upon me her wisdom and her insight and warnings and forebodings and most importantly her blessing. She shared with me her take of my gift and what she felt it meant, all the while urging me to focus and allay my guilt and regret, which she saw as an impediment to my success. She was the closest available understanding I had to the source, which she often reminded me was my choice and she knew everything about me even more than Becs and more than M, which again she stressed was my choice.

"Rebecca will not bend, you need to know this, and Essie will defend her as she always has, and the rest of 'em will probably follow."

"Yes, Ma."

"So, when she comes, and I feel she will, you'd better hope to God you firm in your decision or she'll have yo' ass."

I paused as I absorbed her foreboding, "It's not hers Ma and it has always been mine to give as I see fit. I know I am right with the choices I have made."

Ma explained, "True, but boy you still thinkin' about the money, but that was just the distraction and the smoke screen. Please don't lose sight! Raisin they'll eventually figure it out and when they do, there will be trouble. She will want you, they will *all* want you and if she's angry, *all* hell will break loose. Most women don't like to play fair, especially when it comes to matters of the heart and what they claim as their own. And as far as these girls are concerned, each of 'em feel that you their own, especially yo' darlin' *little princess,* Anastasia,"

34

she said, pointing her finger at me and eyeballing me with her warning. "Don't even get me started on *Lil' Miss Thing.* She might be the worst outta all of 'em. One more pussy in that litter gon set somethin' off, believe me!" Ma took another moment to calculate some more, then spoke, "Still, it can't be helped. Fuck it. It is what it is."

"What? Good job, Ma. The sum total of all that shit is, 'Ah, fuck it'? This is my life here!"

Ma pleaded her case to me but in the end, I alone had to reconcile my issues and make the best call available to me. I had money and lots of it and employed five of the most beautiful women in the world to me and the most powerful one of them was white. They willingly devoted their minds and their bodies to my every whim, no matter how selfish my request and believed in me as much as I believed in them and loved me perhaps even more than I could ever love them. They trusted that I had their best interest at heart, which I always did, even if at face value it appeared to everyone outside of us that my interests began and ended with my dick. Being with me made them the highest paid whores in the world and they didn't give a fuck.

"Raisin, I believe we do control our destiny and that we do have say in what happens in our lives and we ain't just passengers on a ride to nowhere bitchin' and complainin' along the way. Pay attention to those girls and to yo' signs and to yo' gut and mind yo' mouth and your choices you hear? *Think,* boy!"

"Yes, Ma."

And with that instruction, Ma concluded this build's calculations of my ongoing dilemma and left me with a brand-new bunch of questions that needed answering. Maybe next Thursday?

"You ain't just yessin' me to death, are you?"
"No, Ma."

She smiled and her eyes sparkled, "Good. You full?"

I laughed as I reached for the plate on the coffee table in front of us.

"No, Ma," I replied, staring at her with a grin. "I'm just gettin' started."

Chapter Three

A Cute Little Package Like Her
"The Birth Of Anastasia Movado"

"Hi, Coral, it's Celeste."

H's mom hadn't heard from her in years and here she calls wanting to stop by to catch up. A voice out of the blue. But when your number hasn't changed in decades, a call like this was to be expected. When she arrived, she sat in the breakfast nook near the window in the kitchen while his mom stood at the hot stove continuing her thing. It was a hot Saturday and with guests expected, cooking needed to get done while they spoke.

"So, how's H? How's he doing?" Celeste asked Coral, eagerly.
"My son is doing very well, thank God. He's got a successful business in the city, some investment, trading company or what have you, and making a very good living at it."

No matter how much H explained to his mother specifically what he did for a living, her description of his occupation would always be as abstract and convoluted as such. He was the CEO of a private investment firm, but it didn't roll off her tongue like "*Doctor* or *Lawyer* or *Indian fuckin' Chief.*" Perhaps she should just simply say, "My son is filthy fucking rich and doesn't need to work at all," but that might be considered vain. So, their conversation continued with his occupation incorrectly presented until his mother's phone rang again and it was Anastasia informing her that she had arrived with the papers for her to sign. She came in through the driveway, which was the entrance to the kitchen and was customary on weekends, especially on hot summer days, and greeted his mother.

"Hi, Ma," Anastasia said, giving her a kiss on her cheek as she came in, and relinquishing a brown paper bag with some pastries she'd picked up for her and a folder of paperwork.

"Ana, I want you to meet a very old friend of mine, Celeste. Celeste this is Anastasia, my son's Executive Assistant."

"Hi, Celeste, I'm pleased to meet you," Anastasia said, offering her hand.

Celeste shook it and replied, "Likewise."

Anastasia remembered the name and remembered the story that went with the name and gazed at her suspiciously.

"You mean, *Hatchet Woman, Death Vader, Pee Wee Executioner, Big Tiny Bi-*"

"Shut up, Mel!" Anastasia barked. "Why you startin'!"

Mel continued, "It's what I do. You see this woman here, don't let her fool you. That's a mistake. You see her here all cute and adorable, a little mini me, but watch out! Oh, what sharp teeth you have grandma!"

"That's not true!" she said, smacking at him to shut up.

Mel was H's youngest brother and the closest of them to his heart and the family comedian. He was the only one who did not need to work and was taken care of, no questions asked. He was terrible with money and a work in progress with his responsibilities but received a weekly check with more than enough to blow and still have left over until the next one. He held Anastasia's flailing arms back and continued.

"You see this one, be afraid. Anyone and I mean *anyone* that she doesn't like around my brother, they disappear," he said, making the poof motion with his hands. They all laughed as Mel explained, "You see my brother is very *successful*," he said, making it a point to stress the second syllable, "and paid out his ass and you know the poison-"

"Shut up, Mel," Anastasia laughed, half wanting him to be quiet and the other half of her dying to hear his depiction of events surrounding her. "Don't listen to him. I'm not that bad."

"Notice she said, 'not *that* bad'. This is true. There's a woman that works for my brother that is her mentor that I know for a fact," he paused for dramatic effect with his index finger, "has a bloody shovel in her back yard!"

"Oh, my God, don't listen to him. Mel, stop!" she implored, bent over and laughing hysterically.

"Celeste, I can tell you stories of poor unsuspecting women who fell victim to *Little Miss Sunshine* right here."

"Oh, my God! Ma, stop him!"

"Me?" H's mother said, defensively, "Leave me out of this my dear."

"They didn't know any better," Mel continued.

"They did!" Anastasia insisted.

"They just wanted, you know, a little help. They made my brother feel *good,* you know, and they wanted a little *help,* but when *she* got done with them?"

"Don't listen to him, please, Celeste."

"One left the state..."

Anastasia pleaded in vain as Mel continued to inform Celeste of the peril she faced becoming involved in his brother's life today.

"That other one got committed-"
"No!" Anastasia barked.
"Dead ass!"

At this point everyone is in stitches from laughter.

"That's not true, Mel!"

"Oh, yes, it is! You know that!"

"Ma, stop him! She didn't get committed! She had a breakdown, a'rite, and needed *time* to decompress!"

They laughed some more.

"Anastasia engaged in psychological *murder* on that poor defenseless woman!"

"Defenseless? Psht! What? That… trick? Excuse my language. She tried to extort money claiming she was pregnant for him!"

Mel added, "She not pregnant no more!"

"Celeste, I had nothing to do with that," Anastasia stated adamantly.

"The baby gone," Mel quipped.

"Not my problem," Anastasia retorted.

"Not your problem *anymore* you mean."

"Oh, my God, Mel!"

"But, truthfully, I love her and what she does, because she protects my brother and keeps him safe because he *is* a soft touch," he stated firmly. "But what she is capable of you would never expect from a cute little package like her."

"Wait, did you just compliment me?" Anastasia asked, appreciating him.

Mel smiled at her and replied, "No."

Anastasia cracked up and her phone rang.

"Hold on. Hey, boss. Nothing. What's up with you? I'm at your mom's. Yep, I needed her signature on some paperwork for Amanda. Uh huh and Mel is bothering me. Yeah, he's being funny at my expense. A'rite, I'll tell him. Ok, I'll see you in a little bit."

His mother asked, "He's coming?"

"Yes, he will be here shortly and I'm blocking the driveway. Mel," Anastasia asked, flirtingly, "can you move my car, please?"

"What, you can't move it yourself?"

Anastasia barked, "Oh, my God, you're such a prick!"

"See? You see the teeth?"

"Ughhhhhhhhh!" she uttered in frustration. "Your brother said, 'To stop bothering me!'"

40

"Give me the keys," he demanded, looking at Anastasia after acknowledging he had made his point. "The Benzo?"

"The *new* Benzo," she said, correcting him. "He picked it up for me this week."

"Yeah? Of course, he did. Same color?"

"Yes, but this one has gun metal rims and it's the AMG," she said, smirking at him.

Mel, while pointing at Anastasia turned to Celeste and said, "You see the privileges she gets?"

"No, that's on *your* brother! He insists on trading in my car every time a new one comes out. Not me!"

"Why, may I ask?" asked Celeste.

"That's just the way he is and how he takes care of us, that's all.

Celeste still curious questioned, "Us?"

Mel answered, "The Five. The five most dangerous women you ever want to meet. They run my brother's business, and do practically, in fact, they do what they want, how they want and whenever they want and are *ruthless* when it comes to him and mini me here is *one* of them."

Anastasia smiled, appreciating his depiction of her immensely and responded, "Celeste, I was in class when H took my car from the garage and brought it to the dealer and switched it and then came to pick me up. When I got out of class, he was leaning up against it, holding the keys that he had gift wrapped in a purple ribbon for me. When I saw him, *aye Dios mío, él era tan lindo!"* Anastasia cooed.

Mel said, "You got that man wrapped around your sharp little… finger."

"Do not."

Mel retorted, "Poison."

"Go move the car, Mel!" She shouted, then batting her eyes at him said, "Please."

Mel retorted, "I'm not him, you'll move it yourself."

Anastasia warned, "I'll stop your check."

"What?" he responded, as she stood firm before him with the evilest of grins capturing his and everyone's undivided attention.

"Like you said, I'm not a nice person."

"You know I believe you," he said, looking down on Anastasia from his five-foot-nine vantage point. He turned to Celeste and whispered, "She got power."

Anastasia smiled, "Ma, tell Mel to go move my car, please?"

His mother commanded, "Mel, move the car!"

He looked at Anastasia, "You think you cute? You tell my mom on me? I'm a go for a little ride first and test the brakes!"

"Mel!" she shouted, chasing him out the door. A short time later as they were reflecting and recovering from his silliness, Anastasia announced, "He's here."

"He is?" asked Celeste.

"Yes," Anastasia replied. "Mist makes a distinct sound."

Celeste quietly whispered, *"Mist?"*

Through the kitchen window the rear engine lid came in to view as H reversed into his mother's driveway. Anastasia used the distraction to further scrutinize Celeste, who now had her back turned to her while peering through the window to marvel at the unique lifestyle event. She searched for any ulterior motives or secret agendas that may be given away, since to her knowledge, Celeste had been a distant memory, not just to H, but to his mother as well. It had been quite a long time since Celeste introduced H to her niece, M, when she brought her to him one night in this same kitchen sixteen years ago. As Anastasia thought about it, she also deliberated over her decision not to warn him of Celeste's visit, which she typically would have, but weighed his potential reaction to it and decided she could absorb the blowback, if any. Not to mention, it would provide her the opportunity to deal with this problem permanently, her way. She found herself now being the one doing the peering and anticipating as she counted the footsteps she heard as he drew closer. First,

42

she saw his hand on the screen doorknob and then his eyes as they met hers. And as H entered the kitchen, it was her as always that caught his attention.

"Hey, babe," H said, shrouded in his hood.

"Hey?" Anastasia replied, but did not approach him. Instead, she respected his mom to be shown love first. But when he was done and he returned his attention to her, she hugged him, and in the presence of his mother, did not deny herself her right to his affections as well.

He kissed her, "What y'all up to?" then turned around and saw Celeste and froze.

"Hi, stranger," Celeste said. "How are you?"

"So, when she comes and I do feel she will, you better hope to God you firm in your decision or she'll have yo' ass."

Chapter Four

Yep, Her Pride Is A Bitch!
"The Revelation Of M"

"What do you mean you're not going to be here? Where are you going?" Celeste asked.

"Kevin is picking me up."

"Ok, but why are you leaving?"

"I didn't tell you to invite him here," she said, reminding her aunt of who was at fault. "Who said I wanted to see him?"

"M, why are you being so fucking stubborn? I'm only trying to help."

"By setting me up?" she argued.

"Who's setting you up? I'm merely reacquainting, you with him. Your pride is such a bitch, you know that?"

"Listen, that guy is *your* friend, ok. Not mine. If you like him so much, then why don't *you* reacquaint yourself with him?"

"That guy?" Celeste questioned, "Did you forget his name now?" M glared at Celeste who insisted, "Had you listened to me about 'that guy' you might not be in half of the shit you're in right now! H takes care of his own and you had him first," she said, very kindly.

"Ok y'all, calm down."

I had had enough of their bitching back and forth. Celeste wanted to hook them up again and M was runnin' scared as usual.

"Trish would you please try to talk to that girl? Please?" walking away momentarily and then turning right back around to add, "He's on his way here, now. Just *talk* to him."

"No!" M barked.

Celeste warned, "I'm telling you, you'll regret it if you don't stay. I promise you!"

"I agree, M," I chimed in. "It couldn't hurt."

Celeste added, "M, every time you haven't listened to me when I've given you sound advice, some dumb shit always happened. So, I'm begging you, please, don't be too stubborn for your own fucking good? Please, trust me on this?"

M paused and I seized the quiet opportunity to counsel her, "M, what could it hurt to hang out for a little while and say 'Hi?' Shit, he's coming all the way over here. Who knows?" I said as I winked at her with a smile.

Her pause continued. Given enough time it could potentially take root and become a moment of clarity for her, but no. Almost as quickly as the moment had arrived, then it was gone as a car horn blew.

Seemingly snapping out of her daze, M reported, "Kevin's here, I got to go. Tell H I said, 'Hi,'" she said, already beginning to sound regretful as she took her pilgrimage out the door to Kevin's BMW.

"Fuck!" Celeste yelled at the top of her lungs and slammed her hands on the kitchen table.

"Like I said, given enough time..."

"At least she said to tell him, 'Hi.'"

Celeste looked at me and was furious. I guess I could understand why, after all, she did go to a lot of trouble to arrange this reunion at her house for her niece. But slamming her hand on the table like that was a sign of desperation.

"What the fuck was she so desperate about?"

M got in the car with Kevin and paused again. Subconsciously, she may have still been second guessing her decision to discard sound advice in the presence of only good advice and leave. I've seen enough movies to know when some shit was hovering and about to happen, and I got the feeling that some shit

45

was about to happen right about now, and it most certainly did. In the distance was this roar of what sounded like a car engine as it was racing down the block approaching them from behind. Kevin looked for it in his rear-view mirror and then his side mirrors. That sound, whatever it was, was commanding itself a whole lot of attention. Squinting a little bit, and still shuffling between mirrors, it still wasn't there and then suddenly it was clear as a ghostly apparition, as if appearing out of nowhere pulling up alongside them violently surreal and in slow motion. It navigated flawlessly and parked blocking Celeste's driveway in front of them. M's heart dropped in her chest and so did her body into her seat. Her gaze fixed on a matte grey *Lamborghini* parked in front of her. She kept watch as the driver door lifted open and a figure *very* familiar to her, made his grand entrance and slowly stepped out. She sank even further down into her seat. Celeste and I were just as mesmerized with him at the front door with M held hostage by pride in Kevin's car. The three of us were bearing witness to a highly improbable reality and almost instinctively seemed to confirm it by muttering our own version of these same four words hypnotically together.

"Shit, she fucked up!"
M said, "Shit, I fucked up?"

H was swiftly propositioned by the hottie across the street as he shut his car door. He smiled and waved at her, so as not to be rude, but she asserted to him that she was being very serious with her offer and that he should be as she so *ghetto-loquently* put it, "bringin' his ass over to her side of the street and quit bullshittin'!" With all this entertainment occurring around him, he was unfortunately distracted from the very person sitting in the car in front of him that he had traveled all the way from Queens to Brooklyn to see, and walked right past her.

"M? M? M!" Kevin called to her as she sat beside him and appeared visibly shaken. She seemed to realize that her aunt's words, that were uttered just moments ago, laid standing on the verge of haunting her yet again if she continued the path that she was presently on. It was a *run-Forest-run* moment of clarity. Right now, she could choose to get out of the car and out of her stubbornness and out of her pride and go in the house and make nice with H. Right now, at this proverbial *'if I could do it all over again'* moment, she could recapture her past, right here and now and right a wrong. Kevin continued, "Do you know that guy?"

Clarity was still in play as she watched the screen door open and Celeste's arms wrap around H and the door slowly close.

M returned, "Huh?"
Kevin repeated his question, "Do you know that guy?"
"Um, no... I don't. Let's go."

Kevin started his car and they drove off.

I watched them through the window as Celeste greeted H, ushering him inside and I thought, *"Yep, her pride is a bitch!"*

The whole ride over to Kevin's house, she could sink no further into her seat or be more blatantly foolish and prideful. He spoke to her, but she heard and understood nothing. She was a shell of a beauty that needed a shine yet would do nothing to soothe her own soul. Tears abandoned her because she didn't feel sad. She wasn't scared and she wasn't sorry. She was just empty. She played the moment in her mind over and over again repeatedly. Each time imagining a different variable to the movie. She imagined her not sinking into her seat and no hottie across the street. She imagined her finding her voice and H noticing her by choice. She imagined one last appeal by Celeste in her zeal, but in every scenario that she shifted the blame, the verdict returned the same. She could provide no justifiable excuse as to why she alone couldn't have saved herself. At Kevin's apartment she had more problems. She was shit for company, thinking about what was going on back at her house. She lost her appetite and Kevin's advances were pissing her off. This was a good thing because her feelings maybe had returned to her. He was too close. You saw it on her face. His every touch violated her. She felt dirty and used. She felt angry and abandoned. She finally felt just enough to rise out of the bed.

"I can't do this," she exclaimed.

"What?"

"This!" she said, pointing emphatically at the bed and throwing the sheets off her and grabbing for her pants.

"M, what the fuck happened?" he asked.

Chuckling she retorted, "I know what's *not* going to happen!"

She zipped her pants and put on her blouse. She fumbled for her shoes and like a traffic cop threw her hands in front of her when he tried to come near her.

"Don't touch me! Don't you dare *ever* fucking touch me again!"

Tears streamed down her face. He asked her to tell him what was wrong in vain. She refused. She grabbed her bag and stormed out with her eyes filled with tears and called Trish, who was engrossed in conversation with Celeste, Uncle Gerald and H, when her phone rang. She excused herself and stepped away from her seat on the couch to answer.

"Hello?"

"Trish, I'm sorry… but I need your help!"

"M- What's up? Hey," Trish whispered, "are you crying?"

Whisper or not, my alarm must have aroused attention in the room, and I saw H look up.

"Where are you?"
"I'm around the corner at Kevin's and I can't do this shit anymore." She screamed through the phone, *"I can't!"*

I tried to calm her down to make sense of what she was saying but couldn't. So, I turned and made eye contact with H and mouthed to him that it was M and that she was crying, and he immediately excused himself and stood up and walked towards me.

"Where is she?"
"Trish, who was that?"
"It's H."
"Oh, my God, Trish! No-no-no-no, no! Don't tell him!"
I put my hand over the receiver and turned to him and whispered, "Will you go get her?"

H nodded.

"Trish! Don't tell him! I-"
"M, where are you?" I demanded. M hesitated and I listened and waited. When she was more accepting of her predicament, she told me, and I informed H.
"She's on E 43rd and Ave D."
H responded, "Cool."
"I fucking told you not to tell him!"
"M, stay where you are, he's coming to get you."
As he was walking towards the front door, and without looking to confirm my acknowledgement of his instruction, he said to me, "Trish, stay on the phone with her until she's with me, please?"

That was how he did it I guess and the way he got things done? H seemed very linear to me. Very point A to point B. He desired and then he delegated and then he waited to receive. At this moment, I was no different to

49

him than an employee on his payroll. There was a problem to solve and he was solving it. He respected my needs and required that I now respect his, and then he was out the door. Celeste and I followed him as he left and stood at the door where we had been earlier. As he descended the steps, he triggered the driver side door, which was fully lifted by the time he hit the curb. He stepped in, closed the door, started the car and pulled off. I returned to M who was still bitchin' on the phone.

"Ok, he just left. He's on his way. Now, what the fuck happened?"

"I don't want to talk about it, Trish. I'm tired of fucking up," she said, *"I'm sick of it! Every fucking thing I do is wrong. Nothing works out. My life is just fucked up!"*

"M, listen to-"

"I should never have left," she screamed through the phone. *"Celeste was right, I've made a fucking mess of things... again! I'm sure he hates me."* M sighed, *"Why did you send him?"*

"Bitch, can I talk now? I didn't *send* him. He heard me talking to you."

"He did?"

"Yeah? I'm in the fuckin' living room, of course he did? He dropped everything, well... us, to go get you. I couldn't stop him if I tried."

Celeste grinned and shook her head.

"Lord, forgive me."

"Isn't that the kind of man you said you want? That special someone who would stop the world for you?"

"Funny!" M said and was silent for a moment. *"Stop the world,"* she chuckled, *"you sound just like him."*

"He kinda grows on you, don't he?"

"Yeah." I heard her still sniffling but chuckling over the phone, then she quipped, *"He's fucking hardheaded too."*

50

"You would know."

"Whatever. Here I am, I haven't seen this man in what, sixteen years and he's running to my rescue?"

"Shit! Bitch you lucky. I don't even know why you complainin'. Be grateful!"

Just then, M turned her head to listen in the direction from where that familiar roar was coming from and before she could finish the thought, he arrived in front of her for the second time today. She gazed upon him once again and this time she had all the time in the world. Most importantly, she was taking advantage of her clarity.

"Trish, he's here."

"Dayum? What that nig do, fly? Ok, listen… stay on the phone with me until you're *with* him.

"Why?"

"I don't think this man is a fan of people deviating from his *explicit* instructions, you know, 'Do- Do not do'? He wanted me to stay on the phone with you until you were *with* him and that's exactly what you're going to do! And plus, I might need a favor?"

M laughed at Trish, probably because she was new to the "H experience." H got out and leaned on the roof of the driver side of the car and gazed into M's tear-filled eyes as she laughed some more because her Knight had come.

He smiled and called to her, "Hey?"

She smiled and replied, "Hey, right back."

He shook his head and asked, "There's never a dull fuckin' moment with you, is there?"

"No, sorry." Staring at him curiously, she asked, "What's with the pale horse?"

"Mist?"

H shrugged his shoulders and she followed, "I see. Can Trish hang up the phone now… please?"

H raised his voice as he came around the back of the car to M on the sidewalk and said, "Thank you, Trish."

51

M added, unquestionably distracted, "See you in a little bit," and hung up.

Standing in front of her, she appeared to realize that she hadn't been this close to him in over a decade. She processed the last time she saw him. How he looked, how he smelled and what he was wearing, and her last words to him. She processed every feature of his face and compared it to her memory. She stared intently into his eyes that were radiating joy and remembered how kind they always were and his smile and how it warmed her. She wanted to touch his face and to process the reality of the moment, when he spoke.

"May I take you home?"

Losing the battle with her tears again, M nodded and buried her head in his chest and cried uncontrollably. Now, crying in public might catch you a few bystanders, you know, some sympathy and maybe some laughter or make you the star of someone's *Snapchat,* he thought to himself. But crying in public next to a half a million-dollar sportscar, illegally parked in a bus stop, that's a motherfuckin' crowd condition.

"Hey, look at me." H held her head in his hands and focused her gaze on him and stated, "Whatever it is, no matter how bad you think it is, it ended just now. You hear me?"

He searched her face for an acknowledgement beyond her tears and found it when she whispered, "Ok."

He then smiled and said, "Good. Now, baby, we got to go."

He took her by the hand and rushed her through the developing crowd like a celebrity to his car and held her hand as she maneuvered into her seat.

"I've never been in one of these before," she said, while laughing.

Agreeing with the statement and looking directly at her he replied, *"Righteous."*

M stared at him passionately. He had made her the envy of the onlookers and their pics and videos and so many women passing by. Her Knight had returned to save her, and all the townsfolk would testify.

"Here's to us discovering more new firsts together, huh, baby?" he asked, and she nodded eagerly, and he gently shut the door.

She watched him get in, shut his door, hit the ignition and put his seat belt on. He had parked illegally and pulled off illegally too.

"Boo," her nickname for him, "you've got yourself an attention getter?"

"You or the car?"

"You would think that wouldn't you," she paused, "that I was talking about myself?"

"We didn't *just* meet, did we?"

M smiled genuinely, and it felt good to him.

"You know I don't usually see things the way other people do. If I had a choice of eye candy, with you as an option, it would be you I'd eat... it for damn sure wouldn't be this car."

"Thank you," she said, seductively and stared, taking all of him in. He always complimented her the right way and always knew exactly what to say and do to make her feel like *the* most important person in the world to him.

He caught her staring from the corner of his eye and asked, "What?"

"I'm sorry about all of this, H."

"No problem, baby."

"Babe," his nickname for women he liked. *"Baby,"* for those who *really* liked *him*. This term wasn't exclusive to her, nonetheless when he called her baby, it

was still just as personal. It began with her and she couldn't remember the last time a man called her that and it meant anything real. She thought about it and felt for her birthday present and said, "I'm sorry about getting you involved back there."

"Not a problem. It's in the past. Can we leave it there?" he suggested.

"Is it?" she probed. "Is everything always that simple for you, H?"

"Not everything. Just the simple shit."

H was trying not to get upset with her, but she was testing his resolve. He was putting up a good front seeing her again, but after all this time, he still wasn't ready, and he didn't need to deal with her self-deprecating mind-fuckin' bullshit right now.

"After all these years, couldn't she have made a better choice... in small talk?" he thought.

"Can I ask you a question?" he asked.

M answered, "Sure."

"Could you have done something today to change the course of events that transpired just now?"

"Yes. I think so."

H nodded his head and asked, "Do you know what that something is?"

M replied, "I have an idea, yes."

H continued, "Ok. Did you know ahead of time that this shit, just now, could've gone south?" She hesitated and he glanced at her and asked, "M, you knew that what you were doing could cause this shit just now and you did it anyway?"

She sat speechless as H indicted her.

"You saw you apologizing to me and me coming to get you and finding you in a pool of your own tears, and you figured you'd still run with it?" She just stared at him and he declared, "Yeah, just the simple shit!"

"Why are you upset?" she asked, calling him by his *first, middle* and *last* name, his full *government,* which she only did to provoke him. "What do you want from me?"

"Oh, no, don't you dare! You don't get to take the high moral road, M! You don't get to still play the victim after all these years!"

"Victim?" she asked. "Is that what you are, H, my victim?" M snapped, "Is that why you came back?" Heated and provoked she asked, "What? Did you figure you'd impress me with your money and this, this… *car,* and maybe rub it in my face how well you'd recovered from the *ordeal* I put you through? Is that it? Is that *simple* enough for you, huh… victim!"

That was my cue to just drive and shut the fuck up. M had a sinister strategy in any argument. She didn't care so much about winning, which she did anyway, as she cared about backing you into a corner and determining your hand for whatever her end game was. That was her thing. She read and picked minds. Then she would revel in the paradox she created, knowing you would never challenge her, because if you did, then she would wipe her ass with you. Since she placed the odds insurmountably in her favor, the issue usually ended in a stalemate where you knew she was right, and she showed you compassion and didn't gloat. She was so fuckin' sexy when she did that shit, but I swear to God it angered me to high fuckin' heaven. The fact is, I only have two cars. My other one is a Range Rover. Anything else you see me in, I borrowed. Even after all these years, we were still seeing way too much and saying way too little. I parked my *impressive* car in front of her house and got out to get her door and her gaze never left me. The scissor doors were enough of an excuse to be courteous, but she could read my mind and knew I was still pissed. She knew every fuckin' thing about me and everyone. God was doling out her psyche whoop-ass as she took my hand and stood up. The warmth of her touch, her familiarity, her vulnerability, her physical presence, they all challenged every rational emotion in me. What did I expect, for her to apologize and beg my forgiveness? If she did, there would be an angle. Was she supposed to at least meet me halfway with some sort of act of penance and make it all worth my while? I would have loved that, but if so, that could be a set up. I thought I was ready for her. I thought I had her out of my system, but how do you prepare for an omniscient woman on earth? I thought I had overcome 'stupid,' but realized she could never be that simple, watching her stare at me.

"Are you *cumming,"* she paused, "in?"

M knows only one definition and one spelling of *that* word. She watched my lips tremble fighting back the smile that would unmask the sheer pleasure I felt in reuniting with her. She gazed into my eyes and released my thoughts so that they were once again my own, and as I had taken her by the hand when I rescued her on the sidewalk, so she also took me by my mind and rushed me through her thoughts. She replayed the events of the day, which she had shrewdly orchestrated into place. She showed me how she had summoned me to her on her terms, abandoning me only to test my faith. She showed me how she presented the challenge before me and my gallantry in her service in sworn fealty to her will. I saw how in conflict I resisted the temptation to disrespect her Goddess presence, and as a reward for my loyalty, how I had earned the right to serve the whim of her seduction. This she would promise me for as long as we both shall live.

"GOD, she's gorgeous!"

M kissed him goodbye and after he drove off, she put her key in the door, but it was already unlocked. Trish was there and Celeste was in her room and Uncle Gerald excused himself after he had determined that she was ok.

Trish stood up from the couch and said, "You fucked up, you know that?"

"Yeah, I know," M replied.

"You my girl and all, but you really fucked up. What is wrong with you?"

"I know."

"No, you *don't* know, M!" Trish said, sucking her teeth at her.

"That guy," Trish sighed, "H came all the way over here to see you. He ain't come to see Celeste, and for damn sure didn't come here to see my ass and you couldn't pay him the *courtesy* of being here?"

"I fucked up-"

"Yeah, whatever! Listen I'ma say what I gotta say and I'm out. M, I know the shit you been through and I know it's been hard on you but you gotta stop this bullshit you on. You've got people around you that give a fuck but you're not listening when they try to help you. H seems like a genuinely good guy."

M confirmed Trish's opinion and agreed, "He is."

"The money and all that- Celeste ain't stupid, keepin' that shit to herself. But paid or not, this man who I ain't never met before today, and who I was so impressed with that I asked myself, what could possess you to not be here to see him? That man really cares about you! I heard his story about what happened between the two of you and it hurt me. For real. How could you? And even after all of that, that nig still care. You so fuckin' lucky!" Trish said, chuckling. "What you figure, he still ain't have nothin', so he wasn't worth your time? So, you ran off with that fool," she said, dismissively with her hand, "because you thought *he* did, and you was wrong again, weren't you?"

M defended her actions adamantly, "No- no, that wasn't it!"

"Dead wrong!" Trish dug in.

"No," M screamed, "I thought he'd rub it in, ok!"

"His money?"

"Trish, why else would he come here?"

"Really, that's what you got?"

"Yes, really. I didn't want him to see me like this!"

Confused, Trish asked, "Like what?"

"A fucking failure, Trish!" M screamed back.

Trish laughed a long good laugh and remarked, "Girl, please. Take that dramatic actress shit down the block. See that's the thing- I'ma tell you something about *you.* See? It's always about *you* and your vanity and what you gotta have and where *you* need to be and that's the shit that made *you* run with that other fool and got *your* ass... ragged, and you still ain't learned nothin' yet!" Trish said, laughing some more.

"What would you have me do, Trish? Hang out and play the victim divorcée or maybe the materialistic cold-hearted bitch! Ooh, I know! 'Hi, H. Sorry I passed on you and married that other guy that I thought would give me a much better life than you ever could, but it's ok, because I for damn sure paid for it. And oh, by the way, I'm so glad to see you and how everything appeared to have worked out just great for you in your life, boo, because my life has been absolute *shit* since I left you! But, hey, let's relish this moment, shall we? I caught hell, so obviously I must have been wrong and since you're fucking richer than God, of course you must have had to have been right. Can you ever forgive me?'"

Trish stopped laughing and shook her head. She and M have been friends for a while. She helped her get her back on her feet when she came back to New York. Since then, the two of them have been *like* sisters.

"Shut the fuck up!" Trish snapped. "You think so very highly of yourself and so very lowly of everybody else, don't you?"

"No, I don't. What are you-"

"Yes, you do!" Trish barked at M, infuriated and frustrated with her vanity. "You think everybody is just waiting in line for that glorious opportunity to fuck high and mighty you, don't you?"

"I never-"

"Please! M, spare me!" Trish stepped closer to M and put her hands on her shoulders in support and said, "Listen, girl, you grown and I can't tell you what to do with your life, but that shit you on," Trish made a circular motion with her hands arounds M's body and continued, "I strongly advise you to get off it before it gets your ass *really* dogged out where nobody's interested in helping you." Feeling that talking-to-a-brick-wall feeling overwhelming her psyche she paused and exhaled. "And for the record you ain't foolin' me. The real reason you didn't want to see H today is because you're in love with him and have always been."

M's eyes widened at the thought of any truth to Trish's statement.

"And I'm willin' to bet you realized that shit way before you got married, too, but you did it anyway. You knew H forgave you because you know him and there was no reason for you to feel *embarrassed* or like a *failure* because he'd always been real with you."

M snapped, "How do you know?"

"How do you *not* know?" ripped Trish. "Ain't you the 'Mind Game Queen? 'Nigs like him don't change. I don't care how many zeros they add or subtract from their bank account. If they *was* fucked up broke, then they fucked up rich. And if they were good men broke, they are still good men rich and H, is beyond that now! Tell me you don't see the only thing he ever cared about was you and what made *you* happy and that's why y'all made *that* plan."

M froze and her eyes widened more as Trish finally broke through and compelled her undivided attention.

"Yeah, he told me," Trish said to M who was visibly concerned as she never told Trish about that.

"What did he tell you?" M demanded, urgently.

"That plan was for you wasn't it and to benefit only you and all he wanted out of it was... you! But then you stepped off and left him hangin', didn't you?"

M's jaw dropped and her lips parted slightly, and she angrily repeated herself, "Patricia... what did *H* tell you?"

"Yeah, that decision blew up in your face and got you to thinkin' God don't like ugly, so you've been out here punishin' yourself ever since," Trish exhaled some more, then shook her head as M simmered quietly. "You are so fuckin' lucky. In fact, let me correct that. You are so fuckin' in love! You should've seen him today when he left here to get you. Woo, girl, I wish I had me a man like that! Hmmm!" She got in M's face and enunciated, "One that was still in love with me too, after sixteen fuckin' years!" M moved away and Trish dug in, "One that I loved back. Bitch, I don't know why you hidin' it. We all see it. You need to accept it and find a way to forgive you and move on because he has." She sighed and grabbed her bag and headed for the door, then stopped and turned, "Yeah, you wanna know what he told me?"

M's gaze never left her.

"I see you lookin' at me all evil. He told me y'all were going to get married? Young birds. I didn't know that, and that he was saving up for the ring? And one day y'all had an argument, but he didn't say over what, and that he called it off?"

"He...?"

"Yes, *he*. He said it was all *his* fault." Trish opened the door and said, "See? Cute guy. Can't lie for shit though. You need to fix that."

It's a cool thing I don't get those migraines like you see in the movies and your mind gets sucked out your fuckin' head. There was absolutely no reason for that fight. M knew better. She just didn't care. Yet, even that assessment is inaccurate. I just met the woman and she sabotaged the reunion. I don't get that shit. Granted, half the shit she said was true, but damn was I supposed to Uber to her fuckin' house? Come on, man? As a rule, I try to be about right now and fuck the past, but this woman is in my fuckin' head, kid. I'm tryin' to make sense of her, along with everything else I've got going on. I was crazy for her the moment I saw her years ago, but that was motherfuckin' years ago, man? She was like a hit and pining for a woman in my past logically sounds like trouble, but the emotional aspect is what makes us human, *and* fuckin' stupid. When I think back to that lynchpin event that brought about the reality I live today, where she's not by my side and she doesn't have my last name, it would have to be that conversation I had with my mom right before I made the phone call. Another headcase. Now I've got money and lots of it and all the conveniences that it affords, and I don't want to be one of those people that say, *"Money can't buy you happiness!"* which is the dumbest shit, money or not, that I've ever heard in my entire fuckin' life. Those motherfuckers ain't got no imagination. I'm happy! Fuck that! Yeah, I got chick issues, but you name a motherfucker who wouldn't want to be in my position. I also don't want to be one of those that say, *"The love of money is the root of all evil"*. Really? Those are another set of assholes. Lose that brain chain! Notwithstanding, there is a substantial part of my life that still carries *regret,* and I struggle constantly with it, but that ain't got shit to do with my money. I do what most rich motherfuckers like me do. I dull the pain in tits and ass and wild the fuck out, and shit. Still, anybody paying attention to me can see through my shit and my girls pay very close attention to me. At the end of all of this, the narrative is probably going to read that God did me a fuckin' favor. Unfortunately, that's not how it feels right now.

"… sooner or later you just gon have to accept it."

"Yes, Ma. Maybe later."

Chapter Five

Behold The Pale Horse
"The Birth Of Rebecca Rubin"

In the beginning, I, who am also your brother and companion in tribulation, and in the kingdom and patience of GOD, was in the isle that is called *Queens,* where I live, and for the testimony that is my life and I too had a fuckin' vision. Yeah, about that, I couldn't make it happen for years, until one day I did. My name is H, and this is *my* story.

I was in *Righteous Spirit* on the fifth day and was consumed by a great light and in that light, a great hit and great wonders about me. And what I saw I wrote in a book and gave it to… my lottery retailer. I woke to see the voice that spoke to me one Sunday morning and being woke, I saw that I had won the lottery jackpot two days in a row. I saw that I had won over s*even hundred and nine million dollars…* much more than I had in my motherfuckin' pocket. Here's the thing.

I saw it comin'.
I saw how I received it.
And I saw how much.

"What I didn't see was when?"

Just in telling my story, I'll probably piss some people off. It is what it is. Still, I'm concerned how it'll be received by my family and friends first, if they're not made a priority in the events. You know how that shit go. Money makes enemies, and lots of money makes it time to move? It was time to move. The fact is you never really forget family. Blood is thicker than mud and I take care of my own, answering to a higher power and all that, but family ain't always there for you and don't always understand you and make you happy. Where they do, I will mention it. Where they do not, I won't… as much. It is said that *"a man cannot truly be all he can be without the means to provide and be a good provider"*. Cool shit. Well, I was given enough to provide for many and for several lifetimes and I planned to, starting with me.

When I checked the tickets and realized I had won, I fell on my knees and wept. Yes, I wept- I wept a lot and I thanked God. I wanted to thank God, and I was grateful to thank God. You know what I'm saying? I can't tell you for how long I was on my knees, or for how long I wept, but I was on that floor for a while, kid, and when I was done, I was dizzy. It had finally happened. I had asked for apples and got apples. You know? Usually you ask God for apples and get oranges, and then nigs will tell you to *"Shut the fuck up and be grateful,"* I guess because it's still a fruit? Fuck you! That's not what the fuck I asked for. I'm sorry, I don't get the concept of being happy for shit I didn't ask for? If you had put your money on the counter and got some shit you didn't want and still had to pay for it, you'd be tight now, wouldn't you? The whole concept behind GOD is the realization of that direct line to the impossible, if not highly improbable shit. That *"need just a little help, that push, to get you over the edge"*, type shit. If God can't do that, then what the fuck you got *them* for? I couldn't keep explaining away failure and disappointment simply because it was my deity. You dig what I'm saying? If God was a nig on the street giving you stories, you'd have been cut your losses. It's sick to me how folks have just committed themselves to failure. Somebody out there sold you some shit that don't work, so get rid of it or as they say, *"get your fuckin' money back"*. It's your right. Right? We gave the goods, but we didn't get the service. No problem. We got beat. But, to keep holdin' on to this motherfucker? Figuratively speaking, I suppose getting your money back is the equivalent of taking back control of your mind. Fool me once...? You explain to me why *you* can't do that? Please, explain to me why it's a sin to *think?* Oh, that's right! God gon get me! Really? Well, ain't you already catchin' ass, nig? I know I was. What the fuck else was gon happen? I took a real long hard look at my thoughts and was delivered from the strivings of the people *and* made the head of the heathen, nig. That right there validated quite the number of suspicions and then some, for me. I'd been getting oranges for a good long fuckin' while now and besides drinking it, it felt good to be done with it. I have earned the right to pop shit, and I wondered what else I earned? Anyway, dehydrated and with face cramps, I kept the news to myself and fell asleep. A few hours later, when I regained consciousness and my manhood, I called the only lawyer I knew personally, and requested an immediate consult.

I enjoyed the trip out to her spot in Bed Stuy, getting off at the Utica Avenue Station on the A Line. I walked out and caught that frigid air strolling down Malcolm X Boulevard to Halsey Avenue, recalling the circumstances for which I had ventured this way and to this neck of the woods the first time. The air smelled fresher. The concrete didn't seem so grimy and you know the shit that you always say that you can't wait to get the fuck out of, for me stood on the verge of finally giving me up? *Thank God.* This however was the new upcoming Bed Stuy. The site of recent, more further Anglo gentrification. Speckled now with boutique haberdasheries, free Wi-Fi nooks, realty offices and once a Starbucks gets here, them block parties gon end and nigs will be outlawed in the community. They'll still be a church though. Nigs *love* Jesus. Brooklyn brownstones are awe inspiring though, with their tall slender stance, rich in classical architecture, craftsmanship, tradition and family history. White folks don't seem to care too much about that though, our family history that is. They kick us some bullshit ass money and black folks sell off and then are off to the car dealer with their exploits. It's a fuckin' shame. Truth is we wouldn't sell if we had money to keep it. We'd fix our shit, pay the taxes and insurance on the motherfucker and beat their ass if they dared ring our doorbell making us an offer. When was the last time a black man stood on their stoop talking about, *"Hi my name is John, and I would like to buy your fuckin' house?"*

"Fuck outta here!"

Granted a good portion of black people are fuckin' embarrassing, honestly, but that ignorance could be corrected with proper role models, economic inclusion and political influence. Yeah, I know we already have it. You may know that, and I may know that, but the nigs that seem to represent us collectively as a whole and seem to find themselves on TV, don't. I gotta get my *'Jonah: You go save those motherfuckers if you want to your damn self'* t-shirt. Still they be my people. What the fuck you gon do… Jonah? Anyway, it had been a while since I graced these steps, I thought, as I arrived just short of frozen. She had herself a beautiful spot here, bought as a piece of shit and renovated into a work of art. It felt good to be back and not on a humble again, you know what I mean? Her doorbell rang ding-dong, how appropriate, and after the sound of the pitter patter of her little feet and some dead bolts disengaging, she opened her door.

"What's goin' on, babe?"
"Hi!" she said, enthusiastically.

Don't you love that shit? All women seem to hit that same note with the word "Hi." It don't matter if it's you or their girlfriend or whether they're really glad to see you or not, so I try not to take the shit in the way that makes me feel bad. I greeted her with a kiss on the cheek and a hug.

"Thanks for seein' me on such short notice."
"It's ok, come in. How are you?"
"You're about to find out."
"Good news, huh?" she asked, as she closed the door behind me.
"I think so."

65

Arika Monique Bennet is a beautiful, jovial mild tempered sister and a straight shooter. She was recently married and seeing me today out the good graces of her blessed heart. She would do what she said she would and thoroughly complete it. I've known her to be fair and honest with me and she's looked out when she didn't have to. I consulted with her before on setting up my firm a year ago and she was more than helpful. She was the best direction I knew of to take to get my money correctly, but I didn't necessarily want to have to involve her too much, so she could properly advise me.

"She took your call nig, so what you sayin'?"

"I'll keep my stay brief. I don't want to take up too much of your time, but I need to bend your ear."

"It's fine. What's up?"

"First things first, I need to hold you to attorney client privilege. How do I do that?"

She laughed and asked me for a dollar.

"Arika, this ain't no bullshit! I'm good for it!" H said, stressing his need for her help. He gave her his American Silver Eagle coin that he walks with as a good luck charm and told her to hold it for him and that he'd be back for it.

"The usual?"

"H responded, "Yes, please, and a private place to talk?"

We sat in her kitchen as she assured me that she was alone, and she handed me a glass of orange juice, which I chugged down, then placed the empty glass on the counter and began to share my good news with her.

"So… what's up? The suspense is killing me!"

"Arika, Friday night, I hit the Mega Millions Jackpot for three hundred and fifty-nine million dollars."

"You did what? Oh, my God! H are you serious? H?"

"Yes, I'm serious."

"Oh shit? Congratulations!"

She hugged me like she hadn't seen me in years, like just now, but only *better.*

"Thank you."

"Now I understand why you were being so mysterious," she quipped, smacking my shoulder and hugging me again. I'm so happy for you! I thought you really fucked up or something!"

"Nah, but it's good to know you care though?"

"I'm just kidding!"

"I know, but I'm not done yet."

"What? You did?" she said, pulling away from me almost fearing the worst.

"Hold on now, that was Friday."

That look of *'what the fuck now'* furrowed her brow as she said, "Oh kay?"

"Last night I hit the Powerball Jackpot for another three hundred and fifty million dollars."

Her eyes widened and the hysteria began. Arika lost her fuckin' mind, so much that I had to plead with her to calm the fuck down before somebody called the cops.

"Oh, my God, oh, my God, oh, my God, oh, my God, oh, my God…"

I had to interject, "I think God's good, babe?"

"Both? Oh, my God, you hit both? Are you serious?"

"Yes, I'm serious!"

The joy she experienced was incomprehensible for anyone without the winning ticket or knowledge of that person. I was able to view my reaction through her eyes and it was cool. It took her quite a bit of time and several bear hugs to calm down. At least she remained conscious. Neither of us believed it had ever been done before and it wasn't. The question of how I felt was immaterial. I was over half a billion dollars richer and I needed to get my money. We had already determined that I was the sole jackpot winner in both instances, as it was in the news, so I needed direction on how to claim the money, eliminate any exposure and maintain my anonymity. She informed me that although she was an attorney and a damn good one, the legal work I needed wasn't her forte. In conversation, I mentioned a name and so it began.

"Do you know her?"

I urged Arika to sit and I proceeded to explain to her that *that* name was given to me in a *vision,* which was part of the same series of visions that culminated into my wins and today's events. I explained to her that even our conversation now, I'd *seen.* I went as far back as I could, short of Bellevue, explaining and answering every question Arika asked me and on certain things, swearing her to secrecy. She didn't wince as much as I thought she would.

"Oh, my God, H, where are the tickets now?"
"I hid 'em. My girls will know where to find them if anything should happen to me."
"Ok, you need to keep this, *all* of this to yourself," she ordered me sternly. "Have you told your mom?"
"No, not yet. You are the only one so far that I've told."
"Ok, tell your mom and your daughters," she instructed, "Who else is closest to you?"
"I gotta tell my sister."
"That's fine," she said, approvingly. "Just keep the circle of knowledge tight as this will aid us in maintaining your anonymity."
"Ite."
"In the meantime, I will get in touch with her and see what I can arrange. This is *so* weird?" she exclaimed. "You knew this would happen all this time and you said nothing?"

"What was I supposed to say? H asked, reflecting on the memories he had all around him. He worked here during the renovation and left prior to its completion. Prior to his visit last year, he had only been back for the housewarming. "You would have believed me? Tell the truth?"

She replied, "No, not a chance."

"I rest my case, pardon the pun. I've been livin' like shit and I have lost *everything.*"

"Yeah, I heard."

H paused a second while thinking about how he could now put all that shit behind him, and it made him smile.

"I was a fuckin' joke- I barely had my word left."

"Well, now you have a whole hell of a lot more and by your story, this is pretty long overdue."

"You ain't bullshittin'!" he said, and they both laughed.

"My God, H, I am so *happy* for you!"

"Thank you," he said, with relief, "I appreciate it."

Keeping his word on the length of his visit, when she was done advising him, her richest client ever, Arika offered him a cab and a check to hold him over. But he couldn't vibe in a cab no matter how cold it was. He turned her down, but she would only accept one prideful choice from him today. Only after she watched him endorse the check image, was she cool with him walking. He would always remember that.

I left her to feel the impact of the street under my feet, which was my conduit to the ethereal, my comfort zone and the source of my power. When you spend enough time out here in the struggle with a weight on your head keeping it down, for me, when my feet pound that ground, that was in defiance and that shit became my sustenance. I do firmly believe that God don't dig buildings, not these anyway. You ain't gonna find shit up in there except pimps and more problems.

I returned to my tomb, so fuckin' grateful that first, it didn't have bars and second, any restrictions it did have were only economic and were being removed as I thought about it. Everything cost money and it cost you every time you leave your fuckin' house. So, I learned to minimize that experience proportional to my pocket. I could afford to hang the fuck out now, but I chose instead to put on some *PARLIAMENT* and chill.

> *"When Gabriel horn blow better be ready to go!"*
> - George Clinton

"Good afternoon, Rebecca Rubin speaking."
"Hi, Rebecca, this is Arika Bennet. We haven't-"
"Arika? My God! Hi, how are you?"
"I'm good and yourself?"

We spent the better part of our conversation catching up. I was flattered she still remembered me, and it was good to hear she was still around because I was about to return the favor.

"Listen, I've got to meet with you," she declared. "We've got an urgent issue to discuss."
"Is everything ok?"
"Yes. I've got a huge client that could use your expertise."
"Really, wow? Thank you!"
"When are you available?"
Rebecca replied, *"How about now?"*
Arika responded, "Perfect."

Chapter Six

Are You Proposing?
"The Birth Of Rebecca Rubin"

"Hey? Wow? Arika, it's good to see you!"

"It's good to see you too! You're looking good!"

"Thank you! It's been a while, huh?" Rebecca questioned, recalling the last time they saw each other.

"It certainly has." Arika agreed, as she sat with Rebecca catching up in a small coffee shop with free Wi-Fi, distracted customers on tablets, smart phones with headsets pitching the next, best and greatest idea.

"So, what's up, girl? The suspense is killing me!"

"What I am about to tell you must be kept between us, please?"

"Yes, certainly." Rebecca assured Arika, propping herself up in her seat and giving her undivided attention.

"The client I have for you just won the lottery."

"Wow, good for him! How much?"

Arika replied, "Seven hundred and nine million dollars."

"Seven hundred-?" Rebecca caught herself exclaiming her surprise and regained her composure dialing down to a very enthusiastic whisper, "What? Arika, are you *serious?"*

Arika sat there nodding her head like a bobble head doll waiting for the shock to subside in Rebecca.

"How's that possible?" Rebecca whispered moving her chair in closer to hear the details from an elated Arika with a secret to tell.

"He won two of them consecutively. Mega on Friday and Powerball the following day, Saturday."

"My God, that was this past weekend? No one's claimed it- them. You're telling me it's the *same* person for both?"

"Yes," Arika grinned and Rebecca salivated.

"How did he do that?"

"He played numbers he received in a dream."

"A dream? Did you say a dream?" Rebecca inquired hesitantly. "Are you fuckin' kiddin' me?"

Arika looked at her shocked. Rebecca didn't strike her as the cussing type?

"No, I am not." she stated trying not to laugh. "I couldn't believe it myself. You want to know what else? He received *your* name as well, which is another reason why I'm here."

"Me? Do I know this guy?" Rebecca inquired.

Arika replied, "No."

"You say *'he received.'* Is he psychic?"

Arika responded, "I've known H for years and I don't think so. He's been through some stuff and trust me it's a modern miracle he's survived them, but the paranormal, even for him, is a stretch."

"Oh, my God, Arika, I never expected this." she said, keeping her voice down. "Well, it sounds to me like he's got an in with the *miraculous?* Two lotteries back to back? My GOD!"

Rebecca took a sip of her mineral water to regain her focus.

Arika asked, "Are you alright? I know it's a lot."

Rebecca was dazed by the news she had just received, and her curiosity was piqued, and she answered, "Yes, I'm fine. Now ok, so what does he need from me?"

Arika sipped her hot chocolate and explained, "Specifically, he needs to claim the money and have its source buried as deep and as far away from him as possible."

"I can understand that," Rebecca responded, emphatically agreeing with the request. "I can do that."

"I know you can," Arika confessed, "which is why we're speaking."

Rebecca asked, "Have you told him to keep his mouth shut?"

"No need. I had to convince him to tell his own mother."

"And you believe him?"

"A liar he's not," Arika stated. "It could have spared his ass if he was."

Rebecca was humorously impressed, "Wow? I like him already. Rich and follows instructions. *Definitely* someone I can work with."

Arika asked, "So, you will meet with him?"

"Yes," Rebecca exclaimed, "Are you kidding me? Absolutely!"

"Good, I'll set it up," Arika responded, pleased that Rebecca was on board. She was also fascinated with how amiable the encounter was, just as H had described.

"So," Rebecca asked, inquisitively, "tell me more about H?"

"Let's see, I met him through my husband, who…"

Arika began and what was supposed to be a quick meeting between colleagues turned into a business brunch through lunch filling Rebecca in on her new client, H. When they were done and nothing else was left to share, they agreed to another meeting immediately to make introductions and finalize the arrangements.

"Like I said, anytime tomorrow will be fine," Rebecca said, putting her bag on her shoulder as they rose from their table to leave.

"Good. I know a place we can meet. I'll call you," Arika said, and got in a cab and left.

The morning of the meeting I rose out of bed and chilled as I usually do until the house was clear. I then shaved and showered and chilled until it was time to leave. Arika had set the meet for 12:30 and wanted me to meet her first, so we could chat. I arrived at her house and waited in the living room while she got ready. The house had come along nicely, since I was last here. I was grateful that the work I had done had put me in her good graces that she was going out of her way like this for me

73

when I needed it most, if you know what I mean. In truth without her paychecks at the time, my ass would've been dead, so I just said, 'thank you', and left it at that. We Uber'd to the city, I guess that's how you say it, and she told me about Rebecca along the way. Arika informed me that she was a shark, and a big one, who left the fast track to *find* herself at the cost of her career. Her family had money, so she wasn't hurting, but the move she made, not too many folks could follow. In fact, most folks would've killed to be in her shoes. When we pulled up to the bar, Arika reminded me that I was the client and if I didn't dig anything about her or what she could do for me, I was to speak up and not hold back. She reminded me that she was there only for support and if I needed privacy, she would not be offended. I expressed to her that I understood.

"You ready?"

I took a deep breath and replied, "Yes, ma'am."

"Oh, and you look good by the way," she said, encouragingly.

"Thanks, babe."

I got the door and we went in. The bar was a cool place, an old English type joint with lots of wood paneling and high back seats around tables dimly lit and a funky vibe. I was diggin' it. Arika looked around and further in just off the center of the bar I saw her wave to her. We walked over and Arika leaned in and hugged her and introduced us.

"Rebecca Rubin, I would like you to meet H. H, Rebecca."

"H, it's a pleasure to meet you."

"The pleasure is all mine, Rebecca. Please."

I motioned for both of them to sit and I sat at the end directly opposite her.

"Congratulations! You've accomplished a miracle by any standard! How do you feel?"

"Thanks, I feel vindicated. Is it callous of me to say that I would prefer not to be in the company of some folks and most situations in the near future?"

"After everything Arika has told me about you," she said, staring at her and recalling their conversation, "no, I don't think it is at all."

The bartender came to our table and took our order and she left. Arika ordered a beer, Rebecca ordered a mineral water and I had a glass of orange juice.

"She's told you my *story?* I'm not sure I would've recommended you hearing it. Were you sober?" I joked and she laughed, and I loved her smile. She was genuine, unhappy but genuine. "But we will get back to that. Tell me, what's your strategy to collect the funds?"

Rebecca described her clear and concise strategy that would secure the funds and infuse capital into an entity I controlled that would make me gradually richer over a given period of time with a plausible back story to spin.

He looked at her and responded, "Wow, that would be *lovely!"*

"You'll also be in a position to alleviate your tax burdens shortly and I've been made aware of certain restitution concerns you'd like addressed?"

"Yes, please."

"These can be done as well, anonymously or not. The decisions are yours."

"Cool! Well, you've answered all my requests *exceedingly* to my satisfaction, Rebecca. Thank you!"

"My pleasure, H."

Seeing that it was a lovely time to bring it up, he said, "Now, regarding the elephant in the room?"

She looked at me cautiously almost as if I were being cross-examined, "You asked for me by name?"

"Yes."

Rebecca asked, "Why?"

"I'm not sure, but I have my suspicions." I answered, dreading a complaint.

She quickly inquired, "Which are?"

"I need to do something *for* you or *with* you but I'm not sure what or which or both, so I am going to need your help figuring it out."

"How can I help?" she asked intrigued more and more by the vague answers I gave.

"That's what you have to tell me, Rebecca Rubin." I asked, "What can I do for you?"

She pursed her lips and said, "Well, you can hire me to represent you, if that's what you mean?"

"I'm sorry, I thought I did that. Congratulations!"

She looked at me and Arika joyfully, "Thank you, H!"

"You're very welcome. I have the utmost confidence in you, but that's not it."

"Then I'm not sure I understand what you're asking me?"

"What I'm asking you to tell me is, how can I *benefit* you by being your client?"

"You mean my fee?"

"No, I don't care about that either."

She stared at me confused at first. I was asking her a rather unusual question that seemed to cross the boundaries of attorney client etiquette and venture into her personal life and she was very uncomfortable with that. When her eyes shuffled back and forth between Arika and I, Arika got the hint and excused herself.

"Oh kay, well, I can see that you two have *a lot* to talk about, so I'll leave you to it?"

I stood up to let her out. She leaned into Rebecca and hugged her and then me where I stood.

"Please call me later?"
"I will." I assured her.
"Thanks again," Rebecca waved.

"I'm sorry. I didn't mean to put you on the spot like that," I said, sincerely.

"No, it's ok," she said.

"No, it isn't. It's hard. I'm just meeting you and coming off weird. You know what I'm sayin'?"

She laughed and assuaged my guilt somewhat by saying, "Given the circumstances, it's a fair enough question albeit a loaded one."

I gazed into her eyes and said, "In my life I've found, the only wrong answer is the deceitful one."

She stared at me some more and asked, "H, am I reading you correctly in that you're asking me about my *personal* stake in this arrangement?"

"Please forgive me, Rebecca, but yes, I am."

She laughed, "I don't see what that has to do with me representing you as your attorney?"

The bartender returned with our drinks and we had one extra.

"That's just it! It has nothing to do with you representing me as my attorney. I want to know, what can I do for *you* Rebecca for you representing me as *you.*"

Rebecca stared at me curiously and was reluctant to open up and I can't say that I blamed her.

"Ite, dig. Consider it from my perspective if you will. I've just made over half a billion dollars off some numbers I received in a dream, the same dream that gave me *your* name, *'Rebecca,'* and prior to today neither of us had never even heard of each other. Am I correct?"

Rebecca nodded her head in agreement.

"Yet, here we are brought together to form this here perfect union, forgive me I'm not tryin' to break into an old Negro spiritual on you, but aren't you just the least bit curious why?" he asked Rebecca, who got her head tapped and gazed into his eyes. "Think about it," he said,

77

"Seven hundred million dollars and a name, all so you can *cash* the check?"

She looked away from him, pondering what he was saying.

"Rebecca, I'm not tryin' to get in your business, babe, and I'm not tryin' to get in your skirt. I *am* however, tryin' to figure out the meanin' behind all this shit, pardon me. You dig?"

Rebecca smiled. She had piercing brown eyes that glimpsed within her a well of warmth, love and tenderness that called to me every time I gazed into them because I'd seen them all my life in the women around me, though never on a white woman before. My comfort level was there beyond my built-in rudeness even though she was white because her soul I recognized. And it was crazy to me that this was all that stood between a life of 'have' and a life of 'ain't got shit.'

"Packaging?"

I sipped my orange juice and took in the scenery of the bar while I too pondered what I was saying. It was a cool spot and not too busy. Arika had chosen well. Everyone in here seems to be about something, even something serious. When I had soaked it all in, I resumed my focus on her.

"You know, anything you say to me I must hold in the strictest of confidence since technically, as my attorney, you would be sworn to protect my ass," H joked. "It wouldn't be in my best interest to make your life hard. Not to mention, we do have a binding agreement that no matter what you tell me, we will still complete the terms of this arrangement."

"You haven't signed anything."

H pointed, tapping on his chest and stated, "Check your heart."

Rebecca laughed and to the list of qualities I sensed through her eyes, I would also need to add hope. I begged her to please let me be her therapist, even if only for my sake. She sighed and finally agreed.

"Ok, H, I have no idea what you're looking for but since you've been open and transparent with me, the least I can do is pay you the courtesy and reciprocate? Are you ready?"

Rebecca went on to tell me every sordid detail of her life since college to this point. Her family, work, loves, you name it. She got so loose on me I think she must have figured at this point I had to have been a Hail Mary anyway, or whatever the Jewish version is. It was deep, because she finished her mineral water and started on Arika's brew. She told me though she came from dough, she was broke as shit, which was still richer than most *and* my ass prior to last week. She confessed to me that she hated her life and that she didn't know how to fix it, short of turning tail and going back home. She told me that when Arika spoke to her about me and about the circumstances regarding her involvement with me, for the first time in as long as she can remember, she was eager to work. Rebecca bared her soul to me, and I listened attentively because at some point we would finally be getting somewhere.

"Since at this point my professionalism has gone out the window," she said, finishing her brew, "I'll answer your question like this. You're right, H, there *is* something you can do for me."

"Thank you, God! I didn't have the heart to tell her she hadn't taken me deep enough?"

"H, I want *power* and lots of it, so much so that I crave it!"

The look of dread that she gave me from realizing what she had just admitted to me, maybe under the

79

influence of alcohol, mirrored the impact of her revelation on me.

"Oh shit, that's her?"

She looked at me as she stopped, embarrassed and vulnerable and I held her gaze.

"Hey," I said, and she was unresponsive, so I reached out again. "Rebecca, it's me you're talking to, ok?" I said as if it was supposed to mean something. "I'm cool with this. I need for you to tell me *all* of it. Please?"

She thought about my plea for a minute and I think she accepted the chance when she chose to continue.

"H, you are my biggest and only viable client that can give me this. You represent an enormously golden opportunity for me, and I could live off you, quite frankly, forever," she said, shrugging her shoulders as she held what was left in the beer bottle in her hands, tilting the neck towards me. "I want to come and go as I please and I want to be in charge of my life and my choices. You see, I've been everyone's fragile priceless artifact for as far back as I can remember, and I just wanna get the fuck outta this goddamn box!" She grinned and placed the bottle down and said very emotionally, "You wanna know what you can do for me? Gimme that!"

She clenched her fists and closed her eyes and then she was silent again.

"Rebecca?"
"I'm sorry," she said, "I- I should be going now."
She dug into her purse for "drinks money" when I put my hand on her arm and said, "Wait."

Rebecca looked at me almost as if I had violated some code of conduct rule or acted out some cultural taboo, which I suppose I did. I just placed my hand on a white woman, man, and a Jewish white woman too. What the fuck? Yet, it felt intimate and sensual and she was aroused by it. I saw it in her eyes. I also saw there was no way she could ever allow herself to break free of those restraints placed there by her or on her from generations of indoctrination no matter how much she may have wanted to. Still, if she were to allow herself to break free beyond just handling my money, being with me physically would represent the *exact* type of out of the box freedom and power she was craving. She needed me to stop, but she really didn't want me to. I took my hand back and again asked her to stay.

"I gave you my word," I asserted, "money or not, that's still worth *everything* to me. This right here is just us and between us. You and me, straight up." I found myself enthralled in her gaze yet lucid enough to do what I needed to get done. I became overwhelmed with conviction and said, "You want power, I can give you that. You want to come and go as you please and be in charge of your life, I can give you that too. Every bit, every detail of every nuance, all of it. All that I have is at your disposal."

Her eyes widened drawing me in deeper.

"Be careful what you ask for, nig!"

"But, you gon help me protect it," he said, pointing at her as he leaned back in his seat, "grow it and keep it… and, I must make *one* demand of you."
   "Demand?" she asked.
"Not negotiable."

"It was a vibe he gave off when he said it, sitting across from me and staring me down with authority. He wasn't asking, and it transcended the monetary aspect of our arrangement. It was curt, direct and compelling. Arika, it hinted to me of much more behind that gaze and

81

that smile of his peering out from that hood and hat he had on..."

Rebecca wisely conceded and acquiesced with her eyes when she looked at him and whispered, "I'm listening."

"I know the most important thing I want in this life, but I'm not exactly sure how to get it and regrettably my money can't buy it."

"What do you want?"

"Trust," he answered, and she listened intently as he explained. "With what I've just received, I'ma have me lots of friends, lots of pussy and lots of opportunity for bullshit. I imagine through all that, I may find myself *maybe* a handful of honesty, and that's where I need you. The next thing I want is for you to help me build somethin', though I'm not sure what... yet. I need to be able to trust you. Come hook or crook, sink or swim, come high, swing low, I will need to be able to trust you and have you trust me. I'm asking you to understand that we might be the same, you and I, and how you feel about your privilege is probably exactly how I feel about my lack of it too."

She laughed and I joined her.

"Seriously, I don't want to employ *a people whom I have not known* and have them *serve me.* I don't want to be their *boss.* I want to be more. I want *us* to be *more.* Right here. Right now. You and me- a family."

Seductively, she asked, "Sounds to me like the job of a wife. Are you proposing?"

I thought about it and I replied, "And if I am?"

Rebecca's eyes widened at the thought and she sobered up.

"Becs," he said, and this was the first time he called her by that *name,* and she held his gaze, "I don't want to fuck up my money, God. I want to grow it and the best way I know to do that is to give everyone with me a stake

in it, so they're working for themselves and building for themselves and benefitting our *family*. You feel me?"

She nodded, "I feel you."

Rebecca chuckled and H enjoyed more of her smile as she blushed, embarrassed by the expression.

"So, can I *trust* you, Becs?"

Rebecca nodded again emotionally and answered, "Yes, you can, H."

"Shit, again?"

H was right, as he stared at her with more of that authority in his eyes. He was awake and had been so for a while, but it was as if he had just lifted his head off his bed, working feverishly to comprehend the meaning as Rebecca continued to hold his gaze. She had succumbed to his will, all of it.

"You want power?" he asked, as if reciting his vows to her where she sat blushing before him. "Here it is. Apart from my daughters, you answer *only* to me."

Rebecca looked at him in shock and disbelief and felt herself faint as she still held his gaze, which she feared would consume her.

"So, what's up? You gon help me get my money, or what?" He asked, teasing her. "Please?"

She said it as if understanding for the first time what the word meant or maybe it was the first time, she had really meant to say it to a guy, this guy, and for this same reason, "Yes," and then her vow, "I will."

"We doin' this?" H asked, offering his hand.

Taking his hand, Rebecca gave him a smile that came from perhaps the fruitfulness of the hope she'd so desperately clung to and replied, "Yes."

"Cool!" he celebrated, rubbing his hands together as he folded his arms on the dark hardwood table and drew closer to her, closing the space between them. "I now pronounce us *Righteous. May I kiss the bride?"*

Chapter Seven

Where Do We Find Clues For Things In Things?
"The Birth Of Rebecca Rubin"

I received the first of many wires to come in my account this morning. This one was in the amount of *ten million dollars.* Becs chose to surprise me and that she did. I was checking my emails and saw my account balance and fell on my knees and gave thanks to GOD, both, and got to work. It was February and colder than a motherfucker and she invited me to come by her place, but I didn't give a fuck! As a rule, I'm good to go, so short of the apocalypse and white folks walkin' around lookin' at me with the munchies, she was seeing my black ass today.

Becs had herself a low-key studio apartment in a low-income high rise on the lower East Side. Everything around the motherfucker was low. Nothing that I would've expected given the story I was told, but sometimes you got to ask yourself, *"Where do you find clues for things in things?"* I was cool with it. It added to her style. We took some hits and were getting back up.

My Uncle Jack once told me, *"If you fall down ten times, get up eleven!"*

Man, Uncle Jack, I've fuckin' lost count. She was standing at her apartment door at the top of the stairs when she buzzed me in. I walked up to a woman who broke down in my arms while I just stood there strong, holding us both up. If a hug could've knocked her up, then she was about to have twins. You dig? For a moment, even a stolen one, her conflicts took a back seat and she held me tight, expressing to me her sincerest appreciation and gratitude for the freedom I had given her. It was like *she* had won the lottery and maybe she did? I was given two gifts, my cash and her. The cash part seemed simple, a whole lot simpler than me trying to solve the complex mysteries of Eve.

"We all need a win, babe, every day as a matter of fact, and when we get it," he said, holding her, "we need to celebrate it!"

When her hang-ups returned, not too long after, she slowly released me and wiped her tears from her eyes. I knew the feeling, but I was all cried out and a good thing too. I might have set us back a few years. We sat and we consoled each other of our unresolved emotional concerns, or what most people call regret, and for me had all but faded away or so I thought and for her was yet to be addressed. For now, she was free, thanks not to daddy or fiancé's money but to me, a stranger and what I freely shared and gave her to own. Free by that which she earned with no strings attached, except to secure that the only low we ever see after this shit was a sweet chariot coming forth to carry us home. I pulled out a 'shit list' that I had made many a moon ago for just this occasion, that we had fun reviewing as we sat together in her comfy 1-bedroom joint with the project heat. She had a list too. We discovered that you've got your folks that you write a check to and you leave them *good*, and then you've got your other folks that you simply say, *"Just meet me at JFK."* I have me just such a folk, a brother out in the struggle wearing the mask and holding it down. The rest of them would have to meet us there. I made it point to see Arika before my flight and personally deliver her finder's fee *and* retrieve my dollar. She was having dinner with Becs later to celebrate.

Becs booked a handful of rooms in Vegas, and for me a nice suite. I didn't need to be too high, just in the right spot strategically and she made it happen. I could afford to get whatever I wanted but first I just needed to enjoy what I had. I didn't have many friends before my winnings, and I wasn't looking to improve my numbers or my position either. But by the end of the *build,* every head I requested was in my room, along with their own

86

heads, so the brainstorming could begin. I heard every idea, every thought, every concept and theory and every proposal these men and women could create. We took them all and threw them up against the wall to see which ones would stick. We had money but what we didn't have was power, so we didn't have respect. When folks don't even consider considering respecting you, then you need to break everything down and rebuild it from scratch. Face it, God wasn't going to do it because God's ass wasn't down here in the fire. But we were. So, we could take this here God money and break north or we could reinvent the wheel for some power and some respect. We chose respect. I talked Star out of breakin' out to Canada, for now. With all in agreement with the plans we drew up for a new wheel, Becs cut a check for all the ideas that stuck increasing everyone to make it happen. I sent everybody off with my explicit instructions on how to function and then settled in to answer what to do with my idea still stuck on the wall.

"So, what you gon do, man?"
"Shit, Black… hope to fuck this shit work!"

"You've got to go from failure to failure without losing enthusiasm."
-    Les Brown

"…or your goddamn mind."

I finished the winter out in Vegas and got on a plane back to Queens. Becs gave me an address to go to from JFK, in the heart of the art district, directly across the street from MoMA in Long Island City. I hadn't seen her in a while and given the mysterious instructions coupled with the decadent and impressively perverse behavior I had just engaged in out west, you can imagine my thoughts were less than pure. She insisted I stay on the phone with her after I copped the key from the front desk. She rode with me on the elevator and out into the hall and listened to me turn the key to open the door and enter my brand-new apartment that she bought me. We walked into the smell of paint and polyurethane in a spacious and modern 3-bedroom condo that she had freshly painted, and the cherry wood floors refinished. As I walked through it my feet made crunching noises on the craft paper that was rolled out for the delivery of brand-new appliances that she had installed. My new apartment came with lots of amenities, like remote operating electric blinds on amazing full height windows with a view of the city to one side of the apartment. She also bought me a blow-up bed in the master bedroom that was well made with a note on it that read:

"I promise to be over in the morning with breakfast and we will go furniture shopping!
Love always,
Rebecca"

"Say word! Wow? Babe, you did this?"
"Yes."
"Thank you."
"You're welcome. You really like it?"
"Are you kidding me, I love it!"

The next morning, I left my door open when she said she was on her way up. She knocked and peeped her head in, and I caught and welcomed a familiar sight.

"Check you out?"
Rebecca responded, "It's nice isn't it?"
"Yeah, man."

"Was she talking about the house?"

"How are you, babe?" I asked as I hugged her tight, rocking her gently in a dance. It had been so long since we last saw each other, and I missed her. I was back in town and honestly it was a good thing she thought to get me this place. I would've had to hotel it or crash at my mom's. I didn't even think about it. I think I had gotten a little spoiled by her looking out for me. Becs had anticipated my every need and supervised my every move. 'She was *that* girl,' I'd heard that expression out west, that was leading me in the direction I told her I wanted to go. That girl had done some shopping for herself too. She stood before me wearing a beautiful Prada spring dress with low heel slip-ons and a pair of designer shades on her head. Her bag was Dior and her class was first.

"Fashion sense? Nah. I asked a question. She loves to talk."

"You look good, Becs!"
She blushed when I complimented her and her eyes gave way to her lingering lack of comfort around me, but she smiled pleasantly and said, "Thank you, H," then paused and said it again, "Thanks."

The extra 'thanks' I imagined was for her. I was a man and whatever her issues were with men in her past, we were grouped on the same team, but hopefully in time she could learn to appreciate me for my own game. I'm not sure what else was going through her mind, but I knew what was going through mine, goddamn. Becs was one sexy woman. She was voluptuously sexy. Crash your car or break your neck when she's walking the street sexy, and she knew it. She downplayed it though and around me she gave me the impression she feared it and how I could possibly affect her and how she handled it. Most women want men looking at them in their eyes and not their tits and I did that with her. I think by the time we get to know each other better, still with our clothes on now, she will be a lot more expressive and freer with that little hoe inside her because of it. I don't mean it as a bad thing. I was attracted to her and I knew she felt the same way about me because she still looked at me the same way she did when we first met. She was amazed, intrigued and tempted. Maybe confused. My horns were showing underneath my skully. Some things
89

just can't be helped. She fought with how obvious her attraction was and how I was the type to make nasty things happen. I'm black and I said it loud.

"I'm a perv and I'm proud!"

My perversions were contagious too. If there ain't shit on TV, let's fuck. Ooh, a commercial break, let's fuck. I'm bored we're fuckin'. And if you're hot, well I'm always horny, so then we're absolutely fuckin'. I don't think it's only a guy thing either, except for maybe we just cut through all the bullshit and go straight to bustin' a nut. Still, Becs remained tight. There wasn't nothin' going on up in there. If she wanted to play prude and bullshit herself, then I don't know what to say. I have more than made her life heavenly comfortable and a dream come true. Now after all that, was I supposed to only receive a fuckin' handshake? *It's a perspective. You ain't got to agree.* I believed that she was working on trusting me and being more comfortable around me, though. She still seemed all types of *pocketbook* timid when I came around and shit, so she needed to start there. There's nothing like a full-grown woman with no apprehension about dropping her drawers to give life a sense of, inhale for affect, perspective. I didn't have time for games and was way too paid for them too. I didn't care much for social norms and religious dogma that proved to lobotomized humanity's intelligence, especially black folks. I had one boogie, baby. One basic fundamental operating directive. Simply put:

"I do not fuck with anyone in any way I do not want to be fucked with myself."

You wanna give your God the glory, go ahead. Everybody needs a hobby. But this precursor right here, I solely defined as the *basic* tenet of love. And if let's say one day I unleashed the freak in her and caused her drawers to drop, *"... and with ego in charge I charged into what seemed to be the quickest way into her womanhood,"* then she could scare the love right out of

90

me. The irony? I was wearing the t-shirt. I continued to stare at her, enjoying my *Hardcore Jollies,* until seconds before awkward kicked in and then asked, "It's been a while, huh?"

"Yes, it has." she answered, agreeing with me while making the kind of eye contact that starts with a drive by and ends in a park.

"Please, come on in, babe. Make yourself at home. My home is your home."

She walked in feeling no need to reacquaint herself with the apartment but obligingly focused on me and my reception of it.

"I want to thank you again for this. I hadn't even thought about a place. On my way in I was thinking I would crash at my mom's or something. I was totally unprepared. You hooked me up."

"You're very welcome, H."

She was thoroughly satisfied with my reaction and I noticed the shopping bag she still held in her other hand, so I asked as I pointed at it with my chin, "So, what have you been up to?"

I looked into her eyes and she lifted her right arm and said, "First things first- you have to eat breakfast. Come on." She moved in the direction of my semi island kitchen and said, "I kept it simple. I remember how your appetite is in the morning."

I followed her keeping my line of sight on *duh- her- risin'* or me risin'. Yeah, I was hitting on my fuckin' lawyer.

"Do you see her leavin'?"

Becs put the grocery bag on the counter and took off her Dior and placed it off to the right side of it. Then she took out some napkins and opened and placed them in front of me where I stood opposite her. She then opened another bag and took out a pint of orange juice, which she shook for me and gave me with a smile.

"Refreshment?"

"The suckle of the *Gods,* babe!" I said, taking it.

"Really now? You like that shit that much, huh?" She giggled at my exuberance over the thrill of drinking orange juice and asked, "Straw?"

I smiled and said nothing as she peeled off the wrapper while avoiding my gaze as she did it and put it in. She caught my eye for an instant to confirm I was staring and then her eyes drove away. I took one top quarter of my buttered bagel that she put before me and traveled with it as I basked in my new apartment, then I inquired of her after my review.

"You obviously put in some work. What made you choose this spot?"

"Value," she said, walking around the island and joining me looking out onto the Manhattan skyline, "and the view."

I couldn't argue there. The view was nice.

"I kind of got an idea of your tastes," she said, looking at him as she made her way back to the kitchen and suspecting he felt that she was referring to his appreciation of her. "I took a chance you might like this. Not too high, but high *enough?"*

I smiled as I looked at her and replied, "You should take more chances more often. It may not hurt you at all or be as bad as you think."

Rebecca lost her smile but through his gaze she found it again and ordered, "Come here and eat your breakfast."

While I made my way to her, avoiding the invisible furniture in the living room, I saw her pick at my bagel surgically with her fingers and place a morsel in her mouth. This I took as her apple. I joined her and she sipped on my juice and then offered me some, which I took to mean a kiss under her tree.

92

"I know the cliché, but how was Vegas?"

I grinned mischievously and replied, "Decadent," while her eyes locked in mine, "than a motherfucker!"

"Oh, my God, H? Any trouble I should know about?"

I nodded happily and she laughed when I suggested, "We should get furniture first. Word! *Big* furniture!"

I love her eyes when she smiles.

"Again, how's life since we last met if you don't mind me asking? Forgive me, but conversation short of anything personal, especially between us, just seems too ordinary and I don't want that."

She looked at me and her eyes wandered momentarily, and she took a chance and said, "I bought my new apartment while you were away."

"Say word! You moved, huh?"

"Oh, yeah," she stated emphatically.

"A condo?"

"No, a co-op."

"Where, downtown?"

"No, on the upper east side." She smiled as she finished when she saw the look on my face and said, defensively, "What? H, I'm sorry I'm a *little* spoiled. I can't help it!"

"Yeah, I figured. It's cool... still funny as shit though, you know?" She laughed and I said, "But listen, Becs, enjoy your come ups. Don't even sweat that shit. Congratulations!"

"Thank you."

"How long since the housewarming?"

She replied, "It's been a few weeks."

I asked, "Are you happy?"

She smiled completely satisfied and replied, "Yes. Everything's perfect."

"Perfect? Well, shit? I can't fuck with that. Can I ask how much?"

Becs was open with me when it came to finance. Perhaps it was her lawyering thing. I had a lot of finance to concern myself with, so this was not an out of line question in her mind.

"1.1 million," she said, and her eyes sought my approval, which was new to me and she appeared to relax when I gave it. Literally.

"Ah, I ain't tryin' to be in your pockets or nothin', but your fee is spent?"

"Ooh, yes, just about. Yes!" she said, cynically with her lips pursing and her head nodding and all.

I nodded too, finishing my breakfast and said, "I can imagine. Cool. Cool. My gift to you. Cut yourself a check."

Rebecca was taken by surprise by what she heard. It really hadn't sunk into the extent that it should have by now who he was. They had known each other several months now brought together by unusual events and circumstances and they had acquainted themselves considerably speaking constantly throughout his jaunt in Vegas. H had told her to as he put it to just, *"Take care of it, babe or I trust you, babe,"* and she did just that for every request he made or for whatever she needed to secure his fortune, but she never thought once of procuring any monies that weren't justly expensed or billable. She bought and paid cash for her apartment reducing her worries and budgeted her monthly maintenance based on her projected income to afford her lifestyle. Truthfully in the back of her mind if shit ended badly, again based on her not grasping the seriousness of her circumstance with H, she would simply sell the bitch. But H was serious. He really considered her his partner and she could spend as much as she needed to make herself happy and him happy and secure both their futures.

"H, you don't have to. I didn't mean to imply anything by it. I was only answering your question," she argued.

"Thank you, counsellor, but you and I are building together, remember?"

She looked at him still surprised but didn't answer.

"Do you?"

Rebecca nodded and H said, "Listen, Becs, if this is not alright with you or if you're having second thoughts about our arrangement, I will cut you a check right now to keep you straight well into the afterlife, and we can part company today. I know I didn't exactly give you much of a choice when we first met, but I'll give it to you now if you want it."

"H, I'm trying. I really am, but you do realize how you sound to me, right?"

H chuckled, "Yeah, I know. I do hear myself... standing here. I sound like a fuckin' quack. But you realize what I've given you?"

"Yes, I know," she sighed heavily, "and I'm still wrapping my mind around it. You *dreamt* your wealth," she said, recalling cautiously, "and me, and now you're offering to share it with me. Who does that?"

That question was "Rhetorical 101", and one of my emotional concerns. I didn't even fuck with it.

She asked, "Am I," then paused and changed her mind, "What happens next?"

I looked her in her eyes and said, "I don't know."

"Yes, I do."

"Listen, I know we're still getting to know each other better and hopefully not forcing it, because if we are, then I might as well just end this shit now and say fuck it. I would love to continue to press you for answers-"

"Answers? What answers, H? What makes you think I've got the answers you seek? You're the one with the fucking vision!"

She stepped back and leaned up against the sink and I admired her body language and its beautiful expression. I could tell she was struggling with this and

95

with me. My horns were out again and not being entirely forthcoming with her wasn't helping.

"Ok, maybe not answers. Perhaps ideas?"

She stood there blank.

I asked, "You scared?"
"I'm fucked."
"Yeah?"
She lifted her head and looked at me and said, "Can you be serious, please?"
"Forgive me." H said.
Rebecca put her head back down and grinned and continued, "I have enjoyed so much since I've met you, you don't know!" she told him. "Not just the money, but my life." She pushed herself off the sink and walked back to him and placed her elbows on the counter and spoke up to him, "Even with my father's money, there were always conditions, you know? What I had to do. The image I had to keep. What God expected from me to be pleased. Where I should be with my life right about now. But with you, I don't have to do a damn thing but whatever the fuck I want to do every fucking minute of every fucking day. We're not even in a relationship. Imagine that? What's that all about?" she said, stopping as if suddenly remembering a thought. "Oh, I know, you don't know, right, H? But see, I believe you do."

Rebecca pursed her lips as she finished, capturing my attention and working up my appetite for more. Her eyes became very inquisitive as she continued.

"I believe you know a *whole* lot more than you're telling me. Perhaps you think I can't handle it, so you're sparing me or maybe you've got ulterior motives for your secrecy or you just suck at lying."

"Or maybe- I ain't superstitious or nothin', but you ever find sometimes you run your mouth, then all of a sudden your shit fall apart?"

96

I asked, "And how do you propose that could benefit me if let's say I did?"

Rebecca answered, "See, that's the thing. To be honest, I'm not sure. On the surface you seem like a great guy. You do what you say, and I trust you. You make *that* easy. And it's not necessarily sex that you're after, though I could very well be flattered, I *won't* be bought." Rebecca appeared unnerved by the look he gave her and stated, "No, you're driven, and I think I play a big role in that drive and an even bigger role in whatever agenda you're on." She searched his face for signs of stress anticipating it as she spoke, "And yes, I do believe there's some divine inspiration in what you're doing. You don't seem the type to discard or disobey who or what has just given you seven hundred and nine million dollars, am I correct?"

H nodded.

"So, what's nagging at me is, what if God or whoever or whatever wanted something you were not ready or able or in a position to give. What then?"

I thought about her question, which I had asked myself a thousand times, comforted in the faith that I was on the right track, because I hadn't derailed or suffered any loss to date and I gazed at her still searching for that truth in me and I asked, "What you're really asking me is, what if I needed you to give me something you weren't willing to give," I stared at her and it was written on her face, "like yourself?"

I didn't think that beating around the bush was Becs' style but I had maintained the upper hand since we met, and it looked like she would continue to let me.

She answered, "Yes, like me."

"Becs, you can't *make* anyone do anything they don't want to do," he reflected. "Not happily anyway."

I was getting a nagging feeling that by the time this plan was complete, I might have to have bribed a decent size village of motherfuckers into obedience, my damn self.

"The means justifies the… way?"

"Am I supposed to just go along with you? Do I get to know what you're doing? How am I to know that what you tell me is the whole truth?" she asked, emphasizing *'whole'* in her question. "What if I say no? What if I leave you?"

"Wifey, you mean you'd pass," I asked, sarcastically, "on the opportunity to ride off into the sunset with me, makin' *Halfrican* babies and livin' happily ever after? You?"

"I love how unencumbered you are with me in your imagination," Rebecca quipped.

"It's a *gift.*"

"And yes, me. I'm serious. What if? What would you do if you needed me to say yes and I said no?"

I replied decisively, "God ain't your pimp, babe. You gon fuck who you want."

Becs believed me. She just didn't believe *all* of me. She chuckled as she stared at me and then she laughed. Maybe I had successfully bullshitted her or maybe I had softened her up to put out for a divine cause for my benefit. Either way, I needed her to stay, and more importantly, I needed for her to need to stay. Just asking her wasn't going to cut it.

"History has shown that God isn't one to tempt or to fuck with?"

"Yeah, I've heard… always had issues with that," he said. "And by your sentiment it would appear you aren't one to be fucked with either, Ms. Rubin."

"Maybe I'll just tempt?"

"You're good," she said, grinning and seemingly impressed with how glib he was with all of this.

"Everything about how I was raised and my lifestyle, screams at me that this-"

"That this is right, but it can't be possible Black?" H concluded.

Becs shuddered when he said it and asked, "Excuse me? Where did that come from? I'm not a-"

"Racist? No, but you're a separatist."

"A what?"

"A separatist. I'm not even sure if that term exists. You know, we cool as long as you're in your corner over there and I'm in mine over here. I can be around you but not with you because you can't afford to break on through to the brother side. You could and would believe all of this if it was *his* story and not *my* story. You're privileged. White and right. Even *your* religion says so, I'm pretty sure? You're fuckin' chosen, right, if I'm not mistaken? On a black continent! Y'all done discovered a bunch of shit *already* existing? Your parents have raised you in *absolute* truth. You've got the money and power to prove it. Fuck, some of your best jokes are black. Shall I go on or do you get the picture?" She said nothing, so I continued, "Now here I come, I roll up on you, a nig from the hood. I seem nice, but then I lay this prophetical shit on you. And though I back it up mind you, *big* time, you can't help but say, fuck this! But hey, I'm just a man. You're the woman. Feel free to break me down and hand me my ass whenever you'd like. I wouldn't ever want to win an argument with you!"

"That's not how I feel," she said, critically observing me, "at all."

"Really? Well, it's how you act. You're nervous when I'm too close to you. You got *'Clutch My Purse Syndrome.'* You cautious when I'm behind you and though you should be, I only bite during sex," He said, displaying a brilliant smile. "I think you like me, but you fight with leading me on. Yet you seem to enjoy my company, like how we are now, but still me over here and you over there. You're very sexy and you know it, and you know that I know it, but you understate it around me, quite unsuccessfully too, I might add."

"You've got me so wrong," she said, still observing me with her eyes surveying every square inch of my body within her sight.

"Really? Then correct me, God. Please?"

"You think I'm fucked up, huh? Calling me a racist," she said, squirming when she spoke.

I corrected her, "I did not-"

"Interrupt you... when you were talking, now did I?" she said, firmly, with her flawless manicured fingers rhythmically tapping on the granite countertop, patiently awaiting my attention before continuing."

"Naked."

I nodded and she went on, "A *separatist* or whatever the fuck made you think you could climb your dick like a fucking flagpole and criticize me like you *know* me. You don't know me! You assume you know me, and you judge me maybe by my vanity you misconstrued as a privilege or my power trip that I errantly convey as prejudice? I ain't scared of you or intimidated by you! You can't handle this," she said, waving at her fine body to me. "None of this! You should thank God that you can stand bein' so close to this! And if I did, for whatever crazy ass reason, decide to give you a piece of this, you might just lose your fuckin' mind and hurt yourself, bitch!"

"Ouch?"

"You're right, I do have issues that weigh heavily on my character, but they're not with you or in any way concernin' you. And yes, I do have ongoing regrets with that, but, no matter which way I may present at present, be rest a-*fucking*-sured, Mr. H, that I am not a racist or separatist or prejudiced or any other 'i-s-t' you feel you can so easily accuse me of, and I am very insulted and pissed about *this* right about now! You think your money affords you the right to voice such defamin', insidiously anti-Semitic and inflammatory opinions of me? Whatever your problem is, you need to back the

100

fuck up off me with that shit! Your lawyer or not I will fuck you up and leave all your money hollerin' for help for your black ass! I will let this shit pass this once, but if you- Don't you ever come out your mouth at me like this again or I swear to God the next vision you see will be of the shape of my ass that you so wishin' you can fuck, walkin' out that fuckin' door."

"Ooh?"

"Have a good *fucking* day."

Her eyes were aflame with anger when she looked at him and grabbed her bag to leave, and he cut her off as she did, "Becs. Rebecca, wait!"

"What!" she griped as he stood in front of her.

"Thank you. You're right. I do know more. Please don't leave. I-"

Becs looked at me, cocked her shoulder and slapped the taste out my mouth.

"Who the fuck do *you* think *you* are sayin' shit like that to me?" she asked, with her pistol finger waving in the air looking for another opportunity to strike.

"Ow! Shit? Goddammit woman!" he uttered under his breath, "I had to know."

"Fuck you! Had to know what?"

"Ah! Ok, ok. Calm down! Please, hear me out... M-o-t-h-e-r fucker that hurt! Shit? Ite, let's say I don't believe you're fucked up?"

"I'm not, you... fuck!" she hollered, pushing me.

"Fuck,' I can live with. It's less fight worthy than 'bitch.' Well, so much for tempting?"

"You've still got fucked up ways-"

"And how the *fuck* would you know? This is the first time I'm seein' your ass in months! Oh, 'cause I ain't walk up in here and fucked you? I see how you lookin' at me!"

"I never claimed to be blind, but no, because you won't admit that you're *uncomfortable* with me being close to you, probably, *probably-* from being fucked with."

"Like you doin' now?"

H drifted and muttered, "I believe you're even more special to me now. You've shown me who you are?"

She questioned him curiously, "Ni- Are you makin' this shit up as you go?"

"Hmmm?"

He caught her gaze and said, "I'll admit, I know you genuinely do give a fuck about me, and you should, but I also know that *that* scares you. That's what I'm sayin' is fucked up."

"Well, ain't you just full of yourself. Oh, the stress I must endure just to please your dumb ass!" she said, handing me my phone, which was on the counter and continuing. "Here, call 'em and get your money back. Your PHD is bullshit." She looked past me to the door indicating that I was in her way and said, "Excuse me!"

"Yeah, maybe, but I still want you to accept it and accept me! I know I'm fuckin' with your life, but I'm also vastly improvin' the motherfucker too!"

"So, *you* own me now?"

Rebecca stared long and hard at H and he reciprocated. Her eyes, answering every question his thoughts could ask, entertained another slap as he scoured the infinite for the right words to stay that impulse. He found one.

"No."

Then they stood silently before each other, both reflecting, both calculating and both feeling froggish, and H leaped.

"Listen, what I said wasn't fair-"

"Motherfucker it wasn't right!" she hollered, expanding the lungs in that beautiful busty chest of hers.

He continued, "… and it wasn't *right,* but maybe the best bet for you is to take some money and go. My life wasn't easy before this shit and money may not necessarily change that." Rubbing his index finger against the skin of his other cheek and pointing at her, H said, "You ain't gotta see none of this."

Rebecca conceded, "You're right, *black* man, I don't. But the *mere fact* that I *am* here- still, seein' you through all of it, should have already indicated somethin' to you."

"What, that I make a good *pet?* "

Frustrated and angry, Rebecca remarked, "You're a fuckin' asshole, you know that? Might even be the whole ass!"

"And you might have gotten a little turned around in the projects. You misplace your religion?" H asked, as she felt him staring through her. "Maybe more?"

She hesitated to speak, distracted much like he was, and instead returned to staring at him for the longest with her eyes again locked in his. Standing silently before him while reviewing her findings, her voluptuous body tempted him.

> *"Eat this from me, and from a tiny tree…"*
> -   FUNKADELIC

Rebecca's right hand stood guard daring him, but he was done pressing it. He had gotten what he was after. She grinned and stepping in kissing close, whispered, "You like them a lot, don't you?"

"I had drawn her face on the canvas of my mind and was painting her while my eyes enveloped her twins resting snuggly on those lungs and between her arms. I admired every inch of her taking artistic liberties. Becs was the right height, the right weight, the right proportion of saint to my sinner and that dress contained

103

her about as well as-" she interrupted my fantasy speaking sternly.

"My eyes!"

H woke and looked up and nodded, and she smiled. She tilted her head to see from her five-foot five-inch perch how red the side of his face was from her slap and took pleasure in a job well done.

"What is it about them?" she inquired.
He fell back deeply into them and answered, "They give me a familiar feelin'."
"And what feelin' is that?"

A lot had transpired just now and perhaps not just over breakfast. We still had a full day of shopping, I would imagine, to get through, plus an attitude over time I hoped would subside. I confess, I deliberately pushed her. I had to discerned more about what made her tick. I learned she definitely was no push over, not anymore, and she had grown teeth and her bark came with a bite. I'd also had enough time in Vegas to discern this much about my vision. Our happiness lay in the two of us being together not apart. It didn't matter who we were fuckin'.

"I owe you a huge apology for just now. That wasn't me. Becs, when I look in your eyes, I feel confident and secure and encouraged to accomplish the day... but the packaging isn't familiar."

Rebecca stared at him curiously.

"It's the heart the counts and you've got heart. You've also got integrity and honor and strength," he said, holding his jaw, "to back it up. You gon need it. Yeah, Becs, I do want you. Have you seen yourself in the mirror lately? What the fuck? I won't apologize for that, but it's not the forefront of what you mean to me. I don't know *all* that lies ahead for me, God, but I do know

104

I *need* you. I'm confident with you. I'm secure with you. My bullshit got more meanin' *with* you. If I haven't fucked up irreparably, and shit, or set you back with your own personal issues, I'm askin' you to please forgive me."

H took a deep breath feeling the violin shit waning as Rebecca continued to stare at him. Like a nut he was cummin'. He just wasn't there yet, and she felt it.

"And now that my heart is out in the open, please allow me the opportunity to conduct myself in a professional and respectable manner with you and ask you to please continue to represent me as my attorney and close... i-s-t friend?"

Rebecca smiled but her eyes never waived.

"I promise that movin' forward, I will refrain from disrespectin' you and I will conduct myself in the least intrusive or what was the word you used just now, *'intimidating?'"*
She answered, "Yes, intimidating."
"I will conduct myself in the *least* intimidating way possible. No more unwanted sexual advances and innuendos, I give you my word. *Righteous."* He then recaptured her stare and arrived, "Becs, I'm scared as shit, man."

Rebecca drew closer to H, submitting to him and placing her hand on the side of his face. Her pristinely manicured thumb caressed his cheek as she lovingly accepted the confluence of his hopes along with all his doubts and his fears onto herself.

"Of what?"
"I don't wanna fuck up my money, God, you know what I'm sayin'? Fuck this whole shit up and fall on my ass *again?"* he stated chuckling nervously but serious as hell.

Staring into his eyes and supporting the weight of him until it was all out, she wiped her kiss on his bruised cheek and smiled, "Welcome to *my* world."

Chapter Eight

Summer Fever
"The Birth of Katherine Summers"

I met up with Mai at her branch on Seventh Avenue. I was just getting my game going and she was helping me work through some business. We were in April and holding a fair collection of properties, and what P was putting together based on our Vegas meet, was going to benefit her a lot. I hadn't noticed it, but I was being observed when I left. I was on my way to see Becs who insisted on steady updates on my exploits. She needed to bill me for something, so it might as well be conversation. Plus, there was no fuckin' way I was going to be in the city and not drop by. Rebecca Rubin wasn't having that shit. At the desk of one of the banker's she was hitting off, was a woman inquiring of my accounts, which is illegal, fuck… immoral, but done anyway. She was told that she needed to speak with Mai, so she did.

"Hi! Mai, right?"
"Yes," Mai replied, "how may I help you?"
She smiled, "Hi, I'm Kate Summers."

Kate Summers was an investor, Barbie dolled prim with an aura of energy and determination mixed in with an insatiable quest for cash targets. She was highly motivated, and laser focused and meticulous in her planning.

"Hi, Kate. How may I help you?"
"I couldn't help but notice your friend who was just here," she said. "Have you got a minute?"
She motioned to the chair in front of her and Mai sat back in her seat, crossed her legs and obliged, "Sure, how can I help you?"

Kate sat and ran her game and Mai listened attentively. Kate had a proposal for me that could only

107

be delivered through Mai and potentially would benefit the both of them. Mai sat and listened. You had to hand it to her, Kate was good. Whatever she was selling, Mai thought that I should be buying and arranged a meet.

"Leave me your number," Mai requested, "and I'll have him call you."

Kate rose from her seat and shook Mai's hand, which formed a covenant in her new plan, and I was the fatted calf. I was still making my way to Becs when Mai texted me to call her. She wanted me to come back, but I had already hopped the train, so I told her I would meet her at her place after work. Becs doesn't like me on public transportation and keeps bringing it up why I still haven't bought a car for myself though I did personally buy my oldest her Jeep Sahara and a Range for my sister. She wants me to move to the city for my protection, and sanity, not too fond I bought the house back, and where I can be closer to her and where she would have a much better chance of convincing me to Uber. But I love my new condo in Long Island City. I'm high staying up high and I love the iron horse. Ain't nobody fuckin' with me here, man. My little one visits on weekends and any free time in between to check on me and has helped make my transition to wealth gratifying. Now that I have finally gotten what I want and what I have fought for and what I feel I deserve, it's interesting to see the folks I thought would be around me today aren't necessarily here and the new faces I do see, *truthfully,* make me nervous.

"They wonder why we weedheads don't dig crowds? 'Cause that's where the paranoia kick in."
-    Griot

But hey, I'm digging the movie and writing the script, you know? Now it's my time to live and to go about enjoying that living. Vegas was a warmup and I wasn't going to allow myself to cool down.

Later that evening at Mai's I took my usual seat. She had some bad ass furniture and whenever I would visit, she'd insist I have her favorite seat in her place. It was just her thing with me. I honestly don't think she did it with anyone else, that's how much she dug me.

"I met an admirer of yours today, H," she started, "and she had *much* to sell, I mean say."

She laughed.

"Hmm. An admirer?" I chuckled, "Who the fuck is that?"

Mai was my girl, my little sister from another mother. We worked together back in the day and got pretty close and I valued our friendship. She stayed in the grind while I left to get rich.

"She's a girl."
"Ah huh?"
"She's a very pretty girl."
"Ite Prick James, get on with the story."

She laughed and ran it all down to me and I have to admit it sounded pretty fuckin' good. I asked for her honest take on it and after she informed me of all her concerns, she still wanted me to do it.

"Cool enough," I said, "I'll call her."

Mai did her little jump for joy. She was on the south side of five feet, tryin' to make it across the border, and Vietnamese American. Why she dug me the way that she did, you'll have to ask her, but me breathing seem to make her happy, so I was good.

"H, you know what," she said, *"I'll* call her, and I'll send you the details."

"Whatever makes my baby feel good?" I added, "I might have a caveat or two though, babe, when I talk to her. Cool?"

She looked me in my eyes on her tippy toes and kissed my cheek, "Whatever it is, I know you've got my back. I'm good."

She hugged and kissed me, and I walked out and heard her door close and lock behind me.

I entered the eatery at the address Mai gave me and looking around I immediately noticed the hottest fuckin' blonde chick I have ever seen in my whole entire life perk up and completely lose interest in whoever the fuck she was on the phone with. I'm thinking she had me by about an inch with her heels and had the body of a model as I perused. Her hair was long and straight, and she twirled a lock of it around her left index finger while staring at me and reading my mind. I knew this because when I thought of how fuckin' hot she was, she smiled and when I caught that thought, she laughed. Was she psychic? I don't know. What I did know was that she was hot, sitting at her table alone and inviting me in for a swim in her aqua blue eyes. With every step I took closer to her, her eyes grew wider and laser focused. I hoped to GOD that she wasn't a mind reader because there was no way I could keep my thoughts clean.

She looked up at me and called, "H?"

Her expression dared me to deny it. She could've called me Toby and I would've copped to it. She offered me her hand to shake without getting to her feet, and I took it. She motioned to me to sit and put both of her arms on the table crossing them, swelling her chest up to me and introduced herself.

"Hi, I'm Kate Summers," and while tilting her head up so that I might appreciate the mole artistically placed in the curve of her neck continued. "It's a pleasure to meet you."

I grinned and replied, "The pleasure is all mine."

I couldn't explain it really, not now and not then. There was only one other woman I'd felt this psyche assault from, and I hadn't thought of her in forever and she was long gone. Kate however was right here in front of me and much like her predecessor she spoke more with her eyes than she did with her mouth. She led, boldly, aggressively and with cunning. She had what she wanted from you the moment your fool-self laid eyes on her. You saw her as a prize you could afford, a trophy you could wear and a pleasure deserving of your status, but she was none of those. You saw a quick fuck. She saw a quick way to fuck you up. This chick was broken from what I imagine was nothing more than an endless litany of men trying to hit it and not caring to appreciate it or who she was. They copped her beauty for stupid and her consent as their privilege. And as a result, she'd heard it all, believed it all, and fell for it all and would no longer be impressed at all. But when your dumb ass still believed she could be that's how she'd fuck you and leave your ass looking for that pussy in the daytime with a fuckin' flashlight. I however had an edge. You see I'd done this type of stupid before and I wasn't looking to do stupid *and* dumb too, so I focused on her nuances, her reactions, her edits and her plot twists. I laid eyes on her and I saw the set up begin with the way her lips touched when she swallowed. Then the manner in which her tongue wet her lips right before she smiled. I followed as she directed my attention to those same wet lips with her eyes, drawing me into her soul and subduing me. Terrified now that I've been discovered, I quickly raise my line of sight to escape only to realize there is no escape and she caught it all. For the final act of her silent seduction, she lowers her eyes and curls a lock of hair to seal my fate.

"Thanks for cumming," she said, smiling at me. "Please have a seat." The waiter approached and she ordered drinks for both of us, "He'll have an Orange Juice, right?"

I looked at her a bit surprised and replied, "Yes, thank you."

She had done her homework on me and was relishing the win. I could see it on her face and read it in her body language. The game had just started, and she already had points on the board. If I were to have any objections to anything she did, I could quickly skew things in my favor by disagreeing. Somehow, I don't think that possibility was in her plan. Any indiscretion committed on her part would quickly be compensated to me with a generous batting of her eyes.

"H," she said, cautiously, "that's a very beautiful name. Unique and very unusual. Does it have a meaning?"

"Thank you and yes, it does," I answered relaxing into my chair as I explained, "however given the nature of our relationship I'm not yet at liberty to share but I'll say this," I paused, for dramatic effect, as I've seen in movies, "Its meaning is quite enjoyable in summer."

Her eyes widen and try as she could, she could not hold back her amusement with me and revealed the most beautiful smile. I'd caught up to her now and was on the board too, and I still had the ball.

"Hmmm, very intriguing," she flirted. "You must share that point with me... soon perhaps?"

"*So close*," I thought.

"I sure hope I get the chance to," I said, and I meant that shit.

She laughed and broke her hypnotic gaze with me to divert her attention to the couple sitting across from us. I stared at her intensely as she fought hard to deny me the satisfaction of her pleasure. I had her backpedaling. She called a timeout by fixing herself in her seat. Then she composed herself and approached me with the purpose for our meeting.

"As I'm sure you are aware from Mai, I'm very interested in partnering up with you to help you develop your investment business."

"Yes, I heard."

"You have come to my attention, by a few sources, as a person looking to break into various avenues of investments and investment vehicles, including real estate. I feel with my intimate knowledge and experience, I'm in a unique position of expertise to enable you to make a swift and profitable impression in the market."

"Yes, she filled me in. She was very excited when we spoke. *You* made quite an impression on her."

"Thank you," Kate responded. "Did you know she's very protective of you?"

"Is she now? Well, that's good to know."

"Yes, and as tiny as she is, I must admit, I do fear for my life having an audience with you."

We both chuckled at the thought of it. Again, she was so close to being able to get anything from me.

"Also, good to know, but tell me, *Kate*, how exactly do you plan to do this and why come to me?"

Kate went on to describe in detail my current position, the market share, availability, profit margins, strategies based on her analysis, her take on knowledge of target sectors, you name it. If I didn't know a little bit about half the shit she was talking about I'd think this woman, this white woman, was just spitting out jargon to impress a brother because the prevailing thought would be that I didn't know shit anyway. But she wasn't gaming me at least not on this. She didn't talk down to me. She wasn't speaking in circles or trying to coddle me. She wasn't trying to impress me as much as leave an impression on me. Kate knew her shit and was being

113

honest with me, so far. I watched as she became more animated with every word she spoke. She grabbed a pen and used the napkins as her scrap paper, illustrating her strategies and resulting analyses. She took me through each scenario she could think of pointing out the pros and the cons to purchases and sales with the risks and the rewards. This woman was brilliant, and I was being schooled. I thought I was her captive audience in her bedroom, but that bedroom turned into her classroom quick and I, the teacher's pet, wanted so much to give her my apple and a whole lot more.

As if reading my mind again, she suddenly paused and said to me, "You're staring."

"*Fuck, she can read minds!*"

I asked, "Are you just now noticing that?"

She smiled and let her gaze fall and as she did, she gave me a glimpse of her with her guard lowered. That was my in.

"I'm sorry, was that too much?" she said, with a serious tone.

Her change in emotion caught me off guard. We went from trading quips to her suddenly taking offense over a stare.

"I-," she hesitated very noticeably, "I would really like the chance to work with you, H." She petitioned me, "There's *real* money to be made here. You and I, if you'll support me on this, I know I can make it happen."

The waiter returned with our drinks. Hers was a Cosmopolitan and mine was a breakfast drink. I lifted my glass in a sincere attempt at an apology for the misunderstanding.

114

"Please forgive me, Kate. I meant you no disrespect. I am listening."

Her smile returned, I had turned the tables on my seductive admirer. I'd discovered her passion and her drive and her thing. I figured it out. It wasn't money or power or her God or her contribution to world fucking peace, like maybe for you and for me. No, it was another thing. That one singular primal thing that made her tick that gave her the strength to get up in the morning and had lowered her guard to me. Katherine Summers wanted me to finance her revenge and would give me anything for it. It is said that the enemy of my enemy is my friend and most of my enemies didn't look like me and neither did she. And yet this blonde child was trying to recruit me to finance her running ramshod up the heads of some white boys I knew nothing about.

> *"She shall undo her credit with the Moor..."*
> *"So will I turn her virtue into pitch..."*
> *"And out of her own goodness make the net,"*
>   -   Othello

"Or maybe out of my money make the net?" I thought.

Some time ago in my life I was forced to stop asking *"why me"* and instead began to concentrate on getting my shit together. As a rule, *"Rule #4"* actually, I try to remind myself whenever I come across these types of situations to *"mind my fucking business"*. Yet, unfortunately, I've found it hard as hell to see someone in distress and not extend a hand to help them. Fucked up don't know color. I learned this. See, I'd found GOD by the river, not too long ago, in a little tent, and oh, I cashed in on some reward money and now could do a shit load more than just finance. I could *succeed*. So, if her mission runs parallel to mine, then, hey, fuck it! Kate sipped on her Cosmo, which relaxed her, and then returned to twirling her hair. I said nothing as I had control, and not just because I was the money, but because it appeared I had survived and made it through her fire. Yay, Shadrac, Meshac and *A Bad Negro!* It was my turn to gaze, and I did so intensely.

Kate asked, "I get the feeling that you've got something to say and you're being neither truthful nor polite keeping it to yourself. So, what is it?"

"Kate, let's say we do this," I asked, "then what?"

"What do you mean, 'then what?'" she asked. "We'll make a lot of money and I'll be in your debt."

"I don't do debts," I responded. "My people got a long history of generational indentured servitude. The shit ain't cool... I want no part of it. In fact, I wouldn't wish that shit on the motherfuckers you hate."

"You don't know the motherfuckers I hate," she said.

"Maybe not, but I know motherfuckers, and I know hate. I also think I know enough to say that you being in that company, in my opinion, is a waste of a perfectly good piece of... *mind.*"

She blushed at my pearly whites and smiled at me still twirling her hair, and asked, "Ok, then what?" I watched as she moved in closer to the table, "What do you want from me, H?"

I peeped the turnaround as she now laid eyes on me. "*Watch your flank,*" I thought, "*... this is where them last nigs gave up the ghost!*" She chummed the water and wanted me to go swimming. And if I did, both me and all my money would be history, not to mention any credibility I might have just secured in this meeting.

> "*I saw it cummin' that's why I went solo!*"
> -   PMD

I realized that this might hurt me in the morning, but I answered, "Your trust," trying to live to tell the tale from it all. "Can I trust you?"

Her eyes squinted almost shut and then opened up again and the twirling stopped. I was riding a thin line between savior and next victim. Kate struck me as a very

116

volatile chick who masked it well beneath her overt sexuality. Right about now I needed to choose my words very wisely. I understood now what Mai saw in her and I agreed. Having her with me would be good for me. But first I needed to continue to gain her trust even if she wouldn't like how honest I needed *us* to be to do it.

"Well, I'm not going to steal your fucking money if that's what you're worried about!"

"I think I hit a nerve."

"Whoa… babe, hold on now. Chill. Do I seem worried?"

She snapped and replied, "Yes, you do!"

"Well, it is *my* fuckin' money and if I seem worried, it for damn sure ain't about it."

"Then, what are you worried about?"

"I'm worried about you, God!" I answered as I pointed to her. "You!"

I saw it in her eyes that she was pissed and struggling to keep it together.

"I don't need you to *worry* about me, I'm fine!" she said with disgust.

"Are you really? I mean, I ain't known you long and shit, but you seem kinda intense, especially around some trigger words. You invite me down here, you tell me you need my-"

"Want," she interjected. "I *want*… your help and what more do you want? You say you want my trust and what else? Say it! After all your money isn't coming for free, right? You wanna fuck me? You want me to be your bitch?"

She still thought she had me just like she'd had every other man that had copped a plea for a piece of ass.

"No, I want you to be trustworthy and whoever's bitch you decide you want to be, honestly that's *your* business- and good luck to that motherfucker! And another thing, since we on the subject, I despise that word... *bitch,* especially when its used to describe women. I don't care how fucked up. To me it's fundamentally and morally incorrect in its character description of women, don't you think? It's just a fucked-up stereotype. I've got two beautiful daughters and the fact that *that* word can be uttered so quickly towards them by *any* man for damn near *any* reason, is disgraceful to me. So, spare me your diatribe and your soapbox bullshit, will you please? I want to know, can I trust you, Kate? Put simply, is your 'yes' a yes and your 'no' a no? I want to know, will you run my money like your own and help me build my dream as you would want me to help you build yours? I want to know, will you have my back, fuck the money here or not? I want to know if I place my life in your hands will I fuckin' live to see tomorrow... Ms. Katherine Summers?"

She paused, then leaned back and laughed a deeply genuine laugh that beamed with gratification and satisfaction. I watched her and waited. She then settled in and reached over to me and placed her palms before me on the table for my hands, which I obediently gave her. Then she held them rubbing her fingers against the contours of each of my fingers, staring at them as she did it. I could tell she was reflecting on a memory. She seemed in a daydream momentarily, before she raised her eyes to meet mine and spoke.

"When I first heard about you, I saw a lucrative business opportunity and a payday, both wrapped up in a very attractive black man. But I must admit that some of the stories that followed you didn't quite bode well with your type."

"My *type?"*

"Your type," she qualified, *"New Money* rich. You see *most* guys in your position tend to flaunt what they've got… and then fuck everything that it attracts. Basic. They're easy."

"Hey? Don't judge me."

"If you control their dicks, then you control their money. This sort of works for old money too, but they're not as prone to falling for the basic tricks like you newbies."

"Are you tricking me now, Kate?"

She responded, "No, I'm not, though I had every intention of sleeping with you if I needed to, to get your money. Never to steal it mind you, I meant what I said. But, you're right," she said, with a twinkle in her eye, "I do have a few- *several* scores to settle and I want, no… I *need* your help." I chuckled and she added, "You're clearly not like the others, you know, the *motherfuckers?"*

I paused and took another sip of my orange juice and replied, "I accept your compliment graciously, Kate."

"You're welcome, H. You know the way I came on to you, any other man would have tried to pin my ass up against the wall in the bathroom by now."

I gestured towards it with my head and she smiled.

"I appreciate the courtesy," she said, twirling her hair again. "I never took you for a saint, H. A good man, yes," she winked, "but definitely not a saint."

I kind of got lost for a second in the thought of her thighs in my arms and that mole on her neck were both crosshairs and a bullseye for me. Once again she seemed to blush about the things I thought about her. Earlier, I had felt her French manicured middle finger trace the lifelines in my left hand and trace pass the ring on my ring finger and circle it. She touched it, looked up at me but asked no questions before slowly continuing down my ring finger to the tip and stopping. She then placed

119

each one of her fingers on the tips of mine and stroked them back and forth, at times barely touching.

Kate explained, "I make no apologies for who I am or what I do, H. These are the choices I've made to survive in the world that I live in with the fucks I *will* repay. I must admit, you are by far the first man I've come across good enough to play my *game.* You're smart, you don't judge and you're most attentive. I can really *use* a man like you."

"Is she gamin' me?"

"Really, for what exactly?"
She ignored my question as if I didn't even speak and continued, "Your willingness to share what you have with me and sacrifice it for me if you needed to, tells me that's not just your dick talking. That's your conscience." She paused and then added, "I doubt it's your *keen* business sense."

I laughed and I also thought of them thighs again. It was curious how I didn't get a response from her this time.

"Money doesn't move you anymore, does it, H?" she asked as I stared at her intently. She asked the question and wasn't looking up at me as she spoke. Instead she was looking intensely at my hands on the table like a child looks at a parents' hands. They were big and safe for protection, maybe her protection and guidance. She placed her right hand back in mine and whispered, "That's balls."

I'm not sure how Kate did it, but she managed to dull my senses to everyone in the room but us. The only sounds I heard were us and the only ones that mattered were us. She was bowing to me and I only just now caught on. When she realized that I did, she instinctively acquiesced and squeezed my hands and then lifted her gaze again to meet mine and spoke.

120

"Yes, H, you can trust me with your life as I will trust you with mine."

Kate had arrived at this decision of her own free will. She wasn't playing any more games or strategizing any advantages, I don't think, but she was taking one last leap of faith that she felt I had earned. Here, I had offered all that mattered to me as my dowry to her a stranger I had just met. I didn't hit it. She made me no promises to give it. All of this I did on the advice of a dear friend who was giving her an opportunity to ask for my help and I agreed. Exactly what help could I provide her, only she knew because I for damn sure didn't know and maybe I didn't want to know what this crazy ass chick was planning? Hiring hit men or waging holy war, I knew how much I had and how much I was willing to risk, and it wasn't going to be enough for Armageddon out this bitch, but then again for her it could be. This one wasn't wrapped too tight, so whatever she was planning I know she was going to make it exciting. Mai called it right. Kate is exactly what I need. I hope her and Becs hit it off if they don't just hit each other.

"Righteous," I responded as I gazed into her eyes and let go of her left hand while she watched me reach over to her and take a lock of her hair and wrap it around my finger. "Welcome to the family."

"I've told myself, time and time again, 'If you see a crazy bitch comin', get the fuck away!'"

Chapter Nine

Breakfast In Becs
"The Birth Of Rebecca Rubin"

Becs bought herself a beautiful co-op on the Upper East Side, which was so upper, the first time I visited her, I almost had to enter through the service entrance. It was still better than the main entrance of where she used to be. After a stern conversation exhibiting her legal poise with her board, management has been more than capitulating to my every request since and with the title of "Sir" too. All the same, I wasn't comfortable here and it's been a year now, but she was. It had the things she needed most, which was space, location, familiarity and safety because Becs could be a bit skittish at times. Certain situations made her nervous and it would make me aggressively ignorant around her like everybody's ass needed to be kicked without clearly understanding why. She didn't like being touched, I know that, and you had to announce your approach at times, or she'd be startled. I figured it was life in the projects. Uppity folks got issues too.

"You should've stayed your ass downtown," I told her sitting at the island counter in her kitchen.

Her stools were comfy, and they would need to be because she was still advancing in her new hobby of cooking and was making more of a mess than progress. I think it was to her more of a distraction in between fielding calls from me and realtors and investments that the guys were working on than a need for sustenance. We were amassing and collecting properties like tickets. P in particular was out of control, buying properties just because he could, and we were rehabbing them with a really good crew. He was making dough with Becs financing and cutting the checks.

"What's up? You cookin'? In a *skirt?*"

"Yes, why?"

"I don't think I've ever seen anybody cookin' in a skirt before except on TV. You ever see the white mom with the long formal dress with the pearls on and shit? Usually I see pants or jeans. I'm just sayin'."

"I don't like wearing jeans. I mean I have them, but I rarely wear them."

"Yeah?"

"Why? You want to see me in jeans?" she asked, flattered by his interest.

"No- no- no- no! I'm good, babe. What you wearin' is just fine. Just keep that hand," he pointed, "with the hot spoon, back!"

Rebecca laughed hysterically.

"I'm not going to hit you," she stated coyly and suspiciously. "In fact, I should never have. It was disrespectful and a mistake."

"Well, I shouldn't have tempted you. I deserved it."

She affirmed, "Yes, you did deserve it, but I should not have allowed my temper to get the best of me."

"You have a temper?"

"I'm a woman, of course I have a temper," she stated benignly while briefly pausing to look at me and then returned to stirring her caldron. "And, I'm a lawyer."

"Ite. Fair enough. What are you trying out today?"

Smiling at me cautiously and trying to determine what my punch line was going to be to avoid it, she replied, "Something different?"

"That sounds safe."

"Ah, shut up!"

We both laughed as it wouldn't have mattered anyway.

"I'm giving it my best, H. This shit is hard. Fuck!" she said, frustrated at her numerous and less than successful attempts at culinary palette-ability.

"Stick to simple, babe and you'll be fine."

123

She gave him the eye, so he continued to construct on his criticism in an attempt to appease her.

"Work the fundamentals. Take boiling for instance. Master the art of boiling water. Boil an egg, then work your way to rice. You know, basic shit. Get that and your cooking is half done."

"Ha ha. Funny! Yes... maybe." She sighed, "I know a couple of things my nanny taught us- taught me. I just want to be able to cook a big meal you know without hurting anyone, especially me?"

"Especially *me* you mean."

She smiled from feeling better that I was her taster.

"It's really not *bad,* Becs. I'm just fuckin' with you, for real. But cooking *is* an art and you can't approach it like a recreational drive by, you know what I'm sayin'? You fuckin' with lives here! You've gotta love it to put your foot in it." he said as he came over and touched her on her waist. She was conflicted again when she felt herself so close to him, so he apologized and stepped away. "Habit."

As he turned, she opened her mouth and almost called him back.

H continued, "... or at the very least the right proportion of ingredients?"

Rebecca threw a towel at him instead. It wasn't as sensual as her kiss, but it was softer than a slap.

"Thanks, that almost helped!" she said, looking at him while tending to her pots on the fire with their flame turned up as per the instructions of the well-fed woman on the screen, and commented, "You're doing better by the way."

"Huh?"

She looked at her chest and then back at him and continued, "Keeping your eyes on my eyes. I know it must be hard." Rebecca immediately caught herself and corrected her statement while laughing hysterically once again, "Difficult! I meant difficult! I know it must be *difficult* for you and I appreciate it! I'm sorry."

"It's cool. Laugh at my pain."

"I'm not, H," Rebecca stated affectionately.

He broke her gaze and said, "Becs listen, I ain't trying to cause no more pain and suffering in the world, and shit, but I still gotta get some pussy?"

She smiled, parking her eyes on him again and said, "I understand. Thank you."

H nodded looking only at her eyes and said, "You're welcome. Anyway, I'm happy to be eating again. I think I'm putting on some weight. See?" he said, tapping his belly.

"I'm so jealous of you. You can eat whatever you want and not gain a pound! Me, if I even look at food too long, I fear a higher dress size!"

"Well, as my boy would say, *'Rib cage ain't sexy'* and I happen to agree. I do."

"Becs, I'm scared as shit man... "I don't wanna fuck up my money, God, you know what I'm sayin'? Fuck this whole shit up and fall on my ass again?" he stated chuckling nervously but serious as hell.

Staring into his eyes and supporting the weight of him until it was all out, she wiped her kiss on his bruised cheek and smiled, *"Welcome to my world."*

"Am I smart enough to do this, babe? Can I guard this money and see shit comin'?"

"Yes, and you're not alone. You asked for my help remember?"

"Ask? More like I drafted your ass." He recalled, chuckling as he said it. *"Not much of a choice do you think, a payday versus a pay life? Do you consider it a choice to turn down the opportunity I threw at you?"* he said, laughing.

"He has this look. It was an expression on his face that from time to time he would have from looking straight through you like you weren't even there, like

125

straight beyond you, and when he did it, it was hard to recognize him if he spoke and further, what he was really speaking about. It was as if when he looked at you, he had to place the face because the person who he was at that moment, had no idea who you were. This is when I trusted him the least but obeyed him the most…"

"I got nearly a half a billion dollars and I'm fuckin' scared, God. I ain't never had this kind of money before, Becs. It's wild! It ain't like it came with superpowers and shit. The motherfucker hasn't made me bulletproof. I got so much shit I'm constantly giving away. Everybody is my friend. We were hangin' right, and nigs were just rollin' up on me, thirsty and shit, expecting me to look out. Motherfucker I don't even know you! I'm already playin' myself small. We get a table and the drinks keep comin' and shit, attracting women to each man his flavor, flavors, just having our fill of 'stupid.' I ain't lookin' for no problems, man. Fuck, I don't even drink. I'm the quiet one and don't even look like I got money."

"But they know," Rebecca summarized, *"the conversation, the attention and even instruction… they're all in your direction."*

"Yeah? Well, I'm chillin' and they all grateful and gon give up some ass. They just wanted a good time first and that's cool. They wanted alcohol, fine. VIP blah-blah bullshit, throw some money around, sure. Harder than that- dumber than that? You gotta take your ass on, baby. The nigs I was with, Griot and especially Black, they didn't play that shit. Not for me. They celebritized my ass," he said as she laughed, *"and kept me out of problems like a golden goose, but ignorance is a motherfucker. I can't fuck with that mentality. So many people are liars and cheaters and opportunists and traitors. I can't trust no one. I want to help so many but it's like whatever I give, ends up in one person's pocket. So, in order for me to actually help someone, I've got to personally deal with everyone. I heard so many fuckin' stories over some pussy… dayum?"*

H shook his head the more he thought about it and the more I thought about him I realized that what he needed was *me*, not his attorney, and not with my hang-ups over his attraction to me. He needed to *physically* be with *me,* and about anything and anyone at any time in any way. This was *his* definition of trust, and the only guarantee that I would have that the lines he insisted on blurring for him to completely trust me would not be blurred, would be for me to leave him.

"I had to get the fuck up outta there. The fuckin' world is crazy, Becs? Even these new guys I met, if they knew how I made this money, they wouldn't fuck wit' me. You know what I'm sayin'?"

"Wait," Rebecca said, touching his arm, *"you didn't tell them?"*

H replied, *"No."*

Rebecca was so relieved that he kept his wealth quiet. Though she had stressed it when they first met, she naturally assumed more of his friends and even family might have been brought in by now.

"Rebecca Rubin, the original list you have has not grown."

She couldn't hide her relief and he continued, *"You're my lawyer and you still look at me sideways. Imagine them?"*

"It's my job."

"To doubt me?"

"To protect you! Don't be concerned with how I look at you, H! Pay attention to who I am for you! I stand between everything and everyone and you," she stated and paused to appreciate his obedience to her instruction and then warned, *"and I don't give second chances."*

Rebecca was recalling the conversation she had with him the day she hit him, which was also the day she forgave him, for threatening the stability of her world with his comments by insinuating a plausible reality for her that she had fought long and hard to overcome and put behind her. She wasn't her family and she wasn't their history. The recent turmoil in her life had proven it and now she was rewriting it. H was her new life with a new story line as much to her as she was to him because he didn't miss as much as she made him think he did, and she couldn't allow him to hit more than he already had. Perhaps in her mind there was nothing to forgive as he was merely voicing a legitimate concern, but she did mean it. There would not be a second chance if he deliberately hurt her. On that she was firm. She had fought to be the lead dog and to stay one step ahead and to always be in charge and have the rest follow her and look at ass all day, and it served to her advantage that H was very fond of hers.

"Well, that's good to know seein' how I need you to help me stay up because there be some motherfuckers not happy I'm up, yet enjoyin' the benefits of it."

"You let me worry about that," Rebecca stated reasserting her role to him and instantly dispelling his fear leaving the funky t-shirt he wore as his well-tailored suit when he said, *"Behind every successful man..."*

Underestimating H was a mistake she would not make twice. He disguised an unimaginable heightened sense of perception and shrewdness behind a hoodie and skullcap and novelty t-shirts and a perennial search to fuck. He sulked and he pouted, and he brooded but he never stopped thinking and planning and remembering, as if guided by some unseen force. His conversations were very cryptic, and he made a lot of personal references and often versed himself in biblical analogies and references, but he wasn't religious. He turned his back on it and hasn't seen a day in church since *she* left. He had given Rebecca explicit instructions when they met regarding his remains, and in as much as she vigorously objected, she consented. He expects to be misjudged, he relishes being overlooked and he's *counting* on being abandoned. It fuels his obsession. The question is, *"What the fuck is his obsession?"* Rebecca wondered. H wanted to build but she didn't know what

128

exactly and why? He told her vaguely of his plans but there was still so much more. She knew everything about him since she reimaged his identity, yet there existed things that as close as she was *willing* to be to him, she would not be close enough for him to share with her. He was also keeping her busy. Nearly half a billion dollars required a lot of surveillance, oversight and maintenance. She found herself needing to seek others she knew and could trust but was unsure if she should approach them. H's money and his growing business occupied one half of her mind, which she dedicated entirely to him and her own life occupied the other. With no space left in her mind to occupy, H sought dominion over her heart, which she left unprotected and he was relentless in his pursuit. He respected her alright, platonically, just like she wanted and just like he promised, but he did it in a way and to the point where in his company or not, she was suffering from withdrawal. He was shrewdly making his lead dog chase her own tail.

"So, have I passed your test?"

H drifted briefly staring at her and replied, confidently, *"Yes."*

"You could have simply asked me, and I would have told you again what I told you then, H. You can trust me."

"Forgive me, God. I do."

I made my way back to my stool and as I sat, I caught her staring at me. I nodded my head as I held her gaze and repeated, "I do!"

Rebecca pursed her lips trying not to smile and to keep it hard for him to love her.

129

Chapter Ten

The Burbs And Katherine Summers
"The Birth Of Katherine Summers"

Kate was sitting up in bed with her tablet in her hand scrolling through the listings as I came in with breakfast in bed. She had spent the night with me, in the burbs as she called it and it was disturbing her delicate sensibilities. Kate was a city girl and didn't do LIC, although she was only a stone's throw away from uptown, she was still a hardship case.

"Ooh, my favorite!"

"Bagel and cream cheese and egg whites on wheat toast? Baby, explain that."

"I wasn't talking about breakfast, sweetie."

"Oh, my bad?"

"As for breakfast I've got to keep you watching my figure. Come sit. Look at this."

I crawled into bed with the plate on my stomach and peeked in on her tablet. She was viewing apartments in the city, for me.

"These caught my eye."

She handed me the tablet and grabbed the egg whites sandwich and kissed me. Then she threw the covers off of her and sashayed to the bathroom with nothing but my *Maggot Brain* by *FUNKADELIC* t-shirt on.

"Baby, I thought you were showing me something?"

"I am," she said as her ass cheeks made *me* a hardship case.

"Girl, you eat too much chicken. Ain't no way wheat toast giving a white girl an ass like that?"

"Road trip!" she yelled from inside the bathroom, placing my t-shirt on the sink and revealing more than just some corner thighs. "Wanna *cum* and join me?"

"Did she say, 'and join' or 'enjoy' me?"

It had been decided by Becs and now Kate, that I needed to be in closer proximity to them. Becs was uptown east and Kate was uptown west, so I needed to be where, Central motherfuckin' Park? I liked downtown. Folks down there were more embracing of my problem *complexion,* allowing for a more sublime integration of culture and tastes. Just because I had money didn't mean I was automatically accepted, nor was I trying to be. To them I was just a lucky nig coming up and I didn't need to take off my coat because they weren't expecting me to stay a while. Don't get me wrong, white folks aren't all bad. Just enough of them. Nonetheless, she was on my case, hard. I'm not sure who dispatched who, but Kate wasn't letting up. She was finding me an apartment eminently. Becs transferred into Kate's account the sum requested and my caveat of Mai being her partner on our contract was met with zero opposition. She was beaming and genuinely happy, so much so, that her sexuality took a back seat to her more emotionally creative side while we apartment shopped. Kate knew her market. She introduced me to many aspects of Manhattan wealthy living. These fuckers lived phat and high off the hog, but it wasn't me and she knew it, but I think she was feeling me out and testing my limits, as is Kate. As the day progressed with waning success in our search, leaving the only thing optimistic about our outing being the time we were spending together, and a sweaty quickie in one of the apartment's bathroom, she finally determined this leg of her research project inconclusive. So, we took a little break to refuel and walk, which she occasionally did. In her defense her dress shoes cost way too fuckin' much to be destroyed on concrete but today they were at home in her walk-in closet, so we hit the curb. It was interesting to me how she would go the gym on a regular, like a junkie high-maintenance, high-powered executive, but when she hit the streets in sneakers or flats and a baseball cap, she was just another cool white girl down for whatever. With the switch up, and with dough or not, you might could get that. We weren't sipping cosmos and orange juice today. We were having frozen yogurt from an obscenely expensive food boutique uptown. Don't ask? As we strolled down Second Avenue soaking in the uptight corded off natives, she continued her research.

"Hey, lover?"

"Sexy-Crazy-White Woman, what's goin' on?"

Kate, scooping her açaí berry secrets of the Aztecs yogurt while hugging the inside of the sidewalk, which by the way she never knew about and was flattered as all hell that I thought so highly of her, asked, "Why haven't you asked me what I'm doing with the money?"

I picked up on her body language immediately when she asked the question. She had a mouth full of yogurt already and was scooping up a second spoonful, while studiously focused on the spoon in her hand as it scraped against the rim of her Styrofoam cup. I didn't know Kate that long, but I knew she was highly intelligent and very perceptive and meticulously calculating in everything she did, much like Becs. She was still watching me closely, even though her focus seemed to be on the cup. I imagined she was skillfully analyzing my gait, my body language and verbal response for any sign of deception to guard against. Trauma is a bitch and she was presently walking by my side with her Masters in Psychiatry *and* she read minds.

"Was I supposed to?"

"No, not necessarily," she responded, "but I thought you would be interested."

She looked at him finally as if completing her determination of what his comfort level was with her. Since they met, H had given before Kate gave and she was continuing to give, and you could say he had substantially given enough to still be getting. Get it? Yet, he had since moved past it, as she discovered, but curiously not past her. The thought crossed her mind as he spoke.

"Money doesn't move you anymore, does it, H?"

"I *am* interested, baby," I asserted, "but more in you and your word and your safety, and most importantly your *sanity*. You can be a little intense when you wanna be... know what I'm sayin'?"

She looked at me as if I was about to embark on a lesson of some colloquial cultural instruction to explain my position. Honestly, she already had the money now, not me. My pop always told us, *"Never give anything you can't afford to lose",* so as far as I was concerned, our business been concluded. Nonetheless, Kate was still discovering on me, so I dug in to give her some additional insight.

"Check this out. I've found that anything done right, the byproduct is *always* money. Period. I don't give a fuck if it's a street corner or a boardroom, Jesus or genocide, nigs or crackers. If your shit is done right, you gon get paid. Now, I know *your* shit is done right, so at this point, I'm really only concerned in the highlights of your success. You dig?"

Her eyes fixed on me as I spoke. To tell the truth, it felt like it did when she drowned out all of the background noise in the restaurant where we first met. But this time on the street, we could have heard me whisper.

"Baby, as long as when I'm back strokin' in those pretty blue oceans you've got for eyes, the only trouble I see is the trouble I already know, then short of you requiring my help to do some heavy lifting, have at it momma."

133

When Kate heard that, a smile slowly lit up her gorgeous face into a crescendo of pearly whites and her eyes gave way to a promise that we would have to sweat some more before the day was through.

"Now see, that's why I don't talk to you, 'cause of *that* look right there," he said, pointing at her smile with his $2 plastic spoon. "You don't know how to act!"

Kate laughed, "Oh, trust me, I couldn't if I tried!" She stopped suddenly, "Oh, no. Not Ben!"

"… What?"

Kate fell into a trancelike state before his eyes.

"It was something you said when we spoke after your trip to Westchester and you gave her access. Do you remember that trip?"

"Yeah, I remember that."

"It got me-"

"Kate? Baby."

"Huh?"

"You ite?" he asked, touching her gently. "Where the fuck did you go?"

"What?"

"You said, *'Oh, no',* then zoned the fuck out?" he asked curiously, "What about… *Ben?"*

Kate looked like I just woke her up from the deepest of sleep. I don't think she even knew what day it was, and then she was lucid.

"Are you ok?" H held her and directed her to some steps, "Here come sit down."

"No, I'm ok. Just some work stuff, sweetie," she said, leaning into me and kissing me. "There's more where that came from."

So far, Kate was easy to me and direct than a motherfucker. If she respected me and I complimented her, she gave me some ass. If I pissed her off but she still

134

respected me, and I complimented her, she gave me some ass. Fuck it, just being me regardless of what I did, she gave me some ass. You dig? I really do believe, as Kate goes, she was in love with being in love with me. She told me so. It could've been the euphoria of the millions I poured into her account or the ecstasy of her orgasm and all that, but she did *tell* me, and I was free to do with it as I pleased. Her trust and now her heart, belonged to me and with no strings attached, which I interpreted to mean, "Don't fuck this up!"

It became abundantly clear to me that I wasn't going to live a productive life bitchin' over my past. The shit was done. I wasn't happy about it but what the fuck was I gon do? I heard all the clichés, man. "Think positive! Pick yourself up. If you don't let go, you can't move forward!" Yadda-yadda. I just hurt and I needed a good fuckin' reason for it, man. This is my life! I've only got one and I don't want to not enjoy it because a few fucks insist on their way at my expense. Fuck sacrifice and fuck heaven, that shit ain't doin' shit for me right here and right now? You mind your business and you do what the fuck you gotta do, why do you get fucked with? You ever feel like you just can't get ahead? That's me. Sex dulls the pain.

Chapter Eleven

Hegira
"The Birth Of Anastasia Movado"

"Hi, B," she greeted, hugging him as he leaned over to kiss her where she sat.

"What's up, little lady? How you doin?"

"I'm fine. I hope I didn't put you too much out of your way. I'm sorry? Thanks for meeting me."

"No problem. Like my man, I'm available anytime for you. Are we clear on that?"

"Yes, we are. Thank you. You look good… as usual." Anastasia said, complimenting his ensemble as Black didn't wear hoodies. He was *impeccably* tailored.

"Sir, can I get you anything?" The waitress asked.

"Yes. I'll have a coffee, please. Black, two sugars."

Anastasia smiled.

"Thank you. Lovin' the flattery," he said, placing his phone on the table and getting comfortable in his seat and his environment. "You wanted to talk?"

Anastasia was a bit hesitant talking to Black, which she didn't do often and never like this. He was a means to an end and an enforcer for anything grimy that needed doing when it came to his boy, who he has known since they were kids. Black was intelligent, well read and smart and physically disciplined and a hair trigger to fuck you up before you had time to react. And where money was concerned, his money, which meant H, Anastasia had an ally with muscle.

"You know, as much as I'm digging a kinesthetic appreciation for the conflict in the distinct postmodern pseudo retro ambiance, they got goin' on here," he said, gesturing with his hand and paying little attention to none other than his Latina beauty in front of him, "this hood ain't my style. What's on your mind?"

Anastasia carefully uttered, "B, I need you to tell me about one of H's girlfriends- well, ex-girlfriend."

"Girlfriend, hmm? That wasn't so hard, was it?" Black said, grinning. "Who you bitin' now?"

She answered, "I need you to tell me about M."

Black stopped smiling and not just because the waitress returned with his fresh brewed coffee with two sugars on the side. "Why you askin'?"

"She's back," Anastasia replied, "he met with her yesterday."

He raised an eyebrow and turned his head and looked out the window before tearing the two bags and pouring their contents into his coffee. He nodded and quoted, "It was the best of times... until it wasn't. That motherfucker ain't talk much, Ana."

Anastasia saw the concern on Black's face and continued, "I also want to know about Siren."

He shook his head while stirring his coffee and responded, "Never heard of her."

"You- what? Really?"

"I've never heard that name before in my life. Who's that?"

"No?" Anastasia persisted, leaning closer and confused by the certainty of her existence. "Maybe at the same time he went out with M?"

"Nah," Black affirmed, sipping on his coffee, "there was no one else. M was that man's sun, moon and stars and the fuckin' air he breathed. His whole fuckin' world. There was no *competition.* When she left him... that nig went dark. You do have her to thank he's still above ground, though."

"That's odd," Anastasia said, questioning the influence his statement implicated.

"What is?"

"I'm just thinking about how he is with his girls."

"Don't get me wrong, they kept him in the fight, but revenge," he chuckled, "has he told you how he hedges his bets?"

Anastasia replied, "Yes."

Black continued, "Ah... that boy kept breathing to get back at that ass."

137

"I know she hurt him."

"Hurt?" Black incensed, chuckled some more. "Hurt's a gunshot to the nuts, maybe two. What that bitch did was sinister. If she back, you gon need to bite harder."

"Did you like her?" Anastasia inquired.

"M was cool. She ain't bother me. A chick like e'rbody else, you know?"

"I heard she was pretty."

"No, what you heard was that she was *gorgeous.*" He said, pointing at Anastasia correcting her as he looked at her. "Homeboy tends to be very particular in his vernacular. She was more like," Black paused and thought as if picturing her face, "she was his *type.* She was in his DNA."

He stared at Anastasia as he did it and she asked, "I remind you of her, don't I?"

Black replied, "Like I said, the man got a type."

"What does she want?"

"I'm not gon presume to tell you I know what's going on in that woman's head or any woman's head for that matter, but it ain't gon be what you expect. Then again it might?" he said, enjoying his coffee. "But I do know this, you gon need the rules fuckin' with M. If she back, she got an agenda to put her first. M ain't second to *nobody."* he said, staring long and hard at Anastasia who sat obedient before him. "He also gon have an agenda, which is her, and she always been first. As of now, his brain ain't right and his decisions... you might need to check that shit. Along with his trust issues, now his dick and ego gon be fightin'. I hope he makes you proud."

Anastasia heard every word Black had to say and took a moment over her tea to soak it all in. It was all happening fast. One moment she was a distant albeit painful memory, then overnight she was a foreboding clear and present threat that she hadn't even had time to alert the troops. H couldn't have any more episodes or Rebecca would flip her fucking wig and she didn't need another confrontation either. Short of a cursory *"by the way did you happen to hear,"* conversation in passing with the four of them, with the resources she was given, she needed to do her job.

"B, can I ask you about something else?"

"Speak your mind."

"Ok. Did you know that H's GOD is a woman?"

Black chuckled, "Yeah, I know. I'm gathering with all of this questioning you've hit a wall with him, huh?"

"Yes!" She stated emphatically, "I have!"

"You just now putting that together?"

"No. I mean, yes? I don't know? I thought he was kidding or talking about his mom or some girl? You know how he talks, he confused me, and I just let the shit go."

"Yeah, that's his thing," Black said.

"Really?" Anastasia remained amazed at the thought.

Black acknowledged, "He presents a compelling argument."

"And I *love* that about him," Anastasia defended, "I do. He's always thinking outside the box and questioning and seeking and searching, but is he serious about this? Isn't this like... tempting? I mean, I don't know?" She sighed, "I'm confused."

Black sensed she was troubled and offered her some insight, "The motherfuckers who enslave you can't be the ones telling you who your God is, Ana. And as for tempting? You mean like the *real* God gon get him? Shit, the God they gave us is white. We been got! So, all that nig *can* do is tempt. Trust issues, remember? I wouldn't know the man if he didn't. *'Unlimit-hid'* thoughts, baby!"

Anastasia smiled coyly at Black's clever wordsmithing of the word *'Unlimited'* and settled in for her favorite part of the conversation with the adults in her life. The profoundly riveting explanation that followed.

"Ana, to dig him," Black sighed, "you gotta keep in *his* mind. H is about long shots. The most obscure, far-fetched and highly improbable shit is where he's throwing big money at." She acknowledged him as he stared at her as an example and continued, "That's that nig whole belief system, his mustard seed. That's where *his* God come in. As a rule, you know he don't ask. But if he does, he ain't askin' for anything he don't need or can't do or get himself, period. So, when he asks, *you* know your *whole* relationship with that nig is on the line 'cause that nig don't forget. You wit' me?"

Anastasia, replied, "Yes."

"God won't hear nothing from him regarding anything easy. That nig self-sufficient than a motherfucker. But heavy odds, impossible highly improbable shit, especially shit he's convinced is morally and consciously correct, that nig puts God smack in the middle of that motherfucker and *she* got to deliver. If she don't, he's built in a crushing blow to his... fuckin' psyche, his whole mental reasoning network that he *almost* cannot recover from. That nig brain frame is fucked! Having money now lessens the blow. As sick as it sounds, he's *got* faith. What he ain't got is *good* sense. H lays his life down for what he believes in whether she on board with it or not. And because he rarely wants something that isn't important, as far as he's concerned, when he wants what he wants," Black paused, staring deeply at her, "the world and God gotta stop. Now, I'm not sayin' I necessarily agree with the nig, but I have to admire the man's gumption."

Black stared at her sitting opposite him with her appetite lost and her mind in a spin, as he finished the last of his coffee and dabbed his lips dry.

"I didn't tell you all of this to worry you."

"Too late," she quipped. "He's mad at her, you know?"

"Yeah, well, show me a man on earth ain't got beef with a woman or vice versa. He'll get over it."

Anastasia understood but was still not at ease. Black's attempt at solace wasn't as comforting to her as he'd hoped. Clearly missing its mark at calming her fears, he offered her something more substantial.

"You should trust yourself more, little lady... like him and I trust you." Anastasia's eyes opened and Black continued, "Regarding M, you gon find more problems doin' things *Rebecca's* way rather than your own."

Anastasia stared at Black as he grabbed his phone to leave. He stood up and leaned over her and tapped the table with his finger.

"Don't get involved with them two, Ana, just pay attention and watch his back. I'll tell you this and you do with it what you want. I don't care what you see, what you hear or what you *think* you know, understand that under no circumstances will *that* man let anything or anyone least of all himself or his actions hurt you." He kissed her forehead and continued, "And, I ain't gon let nothin' hurt him."

"Well, this is an unexpected surprise," she said, peering out from under her dark sunglasses while taking refuge under an oak tree as Anastasia walked up to her.

"I called your office and Lena told me I would find you here. Is this your nature getaway?"

"Yes, it's an old habit I picked up and can't seem to shake. Come sit," she beckoned her and continued. "I've got a lot of memories here and they're not all bad. Fuck, nothing seems that bad anymore. Am I right?"

They both laughed while sitting on a bench in Chelsea Park, which was a far cry from the ultra-conservative sanctum she now occupies on the Upper East Side and the boisterous theater district Anastasia occupies in midtown.

"Mind you, it's a lot more reassuring to visit knowing I don't have to stay. But you didn't come all this way to join my impromptu *hegira,"* she said, reaching over and fixing Anastasia's hair behind her ear. "Let's have it."

"Rebecca, we need to talk about M."

Chapter Twelve

The Office
"The Birth Of Amanda Rosado"

My phone rang pretty early in the morning and it was Kate, as I figured, "Hello?"

"Hey, lover, are you up?"

"No."

"Good, I need you to meet me, like now. I'll text you the address."

"What's up, you ok?"

"Yes, I'm fine," she insisted. *"I'll explain it when you get here, like right now!"*

"Yeah, yeah, I'm coming!"

She replied, *"Without me?"*

I had to laugh. Kate was a very seriously crazy chick but crying wolf wasn't her thing.

"See you, lover," she said, flirting with me and hung up.

"Now, I got to go fuckin' fight with a cab in New York City."

After my shower and shave and shit, or vice versa, it turned out to be a less miserable cab ride than I anticipated. New cab, freshly cleaned, no game of 'identify the stain' or 'name that noxious smell'. Silence reigned supreme, the temperature was comfortable, and the driver drove as opposed to weaving in and out of potential accidents and close calls. And traffic seemed to be gratefully elsewhere. I gave Davide a nice tip and called Kate from the curb in front of the building. It was a cool spot downtown, in a sweet spot not too far down and not too far up, in a secret section in Midtown, but not.

143

"Where are you?" she asked.

I replied that I was in the lobby, and she instructed me to come up to the 11th floor, which I did hurriedly. She met me at the elevator and kissed me passionately, then quickly scurried me into the office like I was a secret.

"First," she asked, "tell me what you see?"

I looked around and then looked at her from the corner of my eye and in a sarcastic tone I replied, "I don't know, Kate, an office or rather what's left of one?"

"Nooo…" She dragged the word out and repeated her question to me, "What do you *see*?"

I took a deep breath and said, "Ok. Babe, I see furniture. I see phones, monitors…" I paused, "lots of monitors?" It started to dawn on me, "Wait a minute, did they use to trade here?"

"Exactly!" Her face lit up. She was the kind of woman that couldn't hide her excitement especially when she was the source of it.

"What happened?" I asked.

"They skipped out on the lease over the weekend."

"Oh shit, that's not good?" I said.

"It is for you! The building manager called me to find out if I might know of anyone that could get in here and assume the lease."

Her eyes sparkled as she looked directly at me. This was Kate at her brilliant best. This was the generous, thoughtful, selfless, caring, and the loving side of her that was determined to move heaven and earth to make me happy.

"You've always spoken about getting your trading business off the ground, right? Well," she opened her arms to reveal the big picture to me and compelled me to come, "here's your chance! You dig?"

Kate analyzed me as I walked around the floor and occasionally peering out the window.

144

"So, what do you think?" she asked, cornering me until I was trapped between her aqua blue eyes and the bright blue sky. "You wanna do this, *RH LLC,* here right now?" She ran up to me and turned my head and whispered in my ear, "Even the staff," then she licked my earlobe. It hadn't occurred to me but all the while we were talking, the employees were filing in. The commotion I was trying to concentrate over was the sound of unemployment hitting them. I could feel Kate's eyes on the side of my face as that reality sunk in for me.

"... The word is 'RIGHTEOUS!'"

"I dig, baby," I admitted, "but we need to call Becs."
Twirling her hair while looking at me, Kate said, "I already have."

Fury, anger, panic, worry, despair, in that order they were all there. They were on their cell, on their office phones, on their laptops and on any mode of outside communication searching for answers. Becs came in and spoke with Kate, and then they both spoke with Mark, the building manager. Then he left to do his rounds and while I was distracted, Becs came to me.

"Hey, are you ok?"
"Yeah," I replied as I leaned over and kissed her on the cheek.
She put her arm around me and rubbed my back and said, "They're not your problem you know?"
"Yeah, you're right, but I may be their solution."

In the ruckus, the same woman I was distracted with seemed to be the focus of a group's attention. I walked over to her and found she was sitting down and holding her head. There was another woman with her that was helping her. The two of them were concerned but not about their job.

"Hi, I don't mean to interrupt, but are you ok?"

She looked up at me and our eyes met, and she paused, then said, "I really don't have a choice but to be ok, don't you think?"

She sat up to reveal her plump little belly, which took up most of her sweet petite frame. She had jet black hair with flawless caramel skin. Her perfectly arched eyebrows and long eyelashes contrasted her big beautiful radiant light brown eyes that called to me as she spoke and were perfectly set on her high cheek bones.

"How far along are you," I asked and as she spoke, I watched her soft full lips grimace occasionally in discomfort.

"Seven months," she replied, and I noticed the title on her name plate on her desk: *Human Resources.*

"I'm H," and I offered her my hand.

She replied, "Pleased to meet you. I'm Amanda Rosado."

"Amanda, you were HR?"

"HR Assistant, yes," she said, correcting me while patting her hands on her thighs and reflecting on the company betrayal.

Maureen, the woman with her, rubbed her shoulders to ease her anxiety.

"Some HR I am, I didn't even see this coming!"

"Bet all the execs did," I said.

"Oh, yeah," she quipped, "they left us disposable employees out to dry. I can't even get that bitch on the phone!"

I had to give her that one because there wasn't much I could say. She could vent as much as she wanted to as long as she didn't go into labor.

"What am I going to do?" she asked, turning to Maureen. "Eddie ain't workin' and the baby is comin'."

Amanda broke down and cried. I lifted my head and felt Kate and Becs nearby looking at me. I turned to them as they approached me.

"The weight of the world isn't yours to carry," Becs softly whispered in my ear. "Sometimes it's easiest and best to just walk away."

Becs was right as always, counseling me professionally, I was paying her to advise me with *her* opinions and not mine and personally, she was only protecting me as any good friend would.

"Hmmm," I muttered as I instinctively turned to her gazing in her eyes and whispered my reply, "If either of you really believed that, babe, you wouldn't permit me to still be standing here." I returned my focus on Amanda and asked, "Amanda, what business were you guys in?"

She took a deep breath and answered, "We were a start-up, a "Boutique" brokerage firm. David over there was one of the top guys."

Maureen chimed, "He ain't top of shit right now. They left his ass!"

We all laughed and seemed to appreciate it.

"Boutique. So, *they* made the money?"

Looking into my eyes, Amanda replied, "Yes."

"And the rest of the staff?"

"They assisted by following current trends, watching the market and helping the process by finding the next big investment. Everything from properties in Indonesia right after the Tsunami to construction companies shoring up the walls around Chernobyl."

"Hmm, so the only thing fucked up here, pardon me, is that the *money* part of the business broke out?"

They both replied, "Yep, pretty much."

"David, you said?" as I pointed in his direction.

"Yes, and *that* guy in the blue shirt is Josh."

"Josh is the cool one." Maureen stated.

I felt Amanda's eyes and Maureen's on me as I left. Becs and I took a walk over to the trading area while Kate stayed behind and watched. I introduced myself to David who could give two shits about me.

"Hey, what's up, man. You guys traded here?"
"Yeah," he replied, "what's it to you?"

I introduced myself and I explained to them that I wanted to start my own company and maybe we could help each other. David practically ignored me, but I continued to speak to him anyway. Every now and again I would glance over at Becs to see how I was doing. Kate had the gaze of death in her eyes, which I could see from the office window that looked out over the floor, so either it wasn't looking good for me or she once dated David and his dick was small. The phone rang and David rudely interrupted me to take the call. It must have been good news because right afterward, he hung up and grabbed his jacket and bag and proceeded to leave with a group of motherfuckers in tow, except for one. This one who had to be the most important to him because he stopped and turned around to inquire, "Josh, what's up? Come on?"

"Hold on." Josh, *'the cool one in the blue shirt'*, looked me in the eye and asked, "Yo, can you deliver on what you said?"
I responded, "I can, with the *right* staff."

It would appear that while I was trying to reach David, my words may not have fallen on deaf ears after all. Josh inquiring on my proposal sparked a real interest in his peers.

He explained, "You say you want to start a trading company and for that you need traders, processors *and* money."

He paused, which I suppose was done for effect. If I was full of shit, then this would have been my LAST

EXIT BEFORE TOLL sign. I wasn't getting off, so he continued.

"Now, we've got traders and processors, have you got money?"

Becs, who was holding an electronic ledger replied from behind me, "How much do you need?"

"Damn, that's my girl! She knows exactly how to make a motherfucker feel good and look good too! Her fiancé fucked up, I'll tell you that shit!"

Josh looked around as several of the movers and shakers closed in, then looked at me and said, *"Twenty million...* to start."

The office went quiet and David, with a lot fewer minions, broke the silence with a small minded dickless rebuttal.

"Yeah, right, Josh, come on? You can't move that much volume!"

"True," he agreed, "not alone."

His head swiveled to his crew and silent nods came from three dudes.

"George, Javi, Cam and I have been following the selloff in Italy."

Green shirt added, "We noticed the buys going to Greece."

Yellow shirt said, "They're getting financed and changing it to Euros."

Grey shirt pulled out a tablet as he spoke, "We narrowed down three companies so far," he said, showing me. "Twenty minutes and I'll know where it's going, and the other big names involved."

The shirts took their stations and began working like they had a fuckin' job and I thought, *"Righteous."*

149

I looked at Kate who nodded from the doorway and Becs countered.

"*Ten million* up front with an additional *Ten* draw. Upon return of sixty percent principal liquidity an additional ten million draw in concurrent."

The rest of the office murmured and readied for work and I stood there like a pimp. A *good* one?

David said, "Bullshit! This guy is jerking your chain, Josh!"

Kate snapped, "Weren't you... fucking off, David?"

He replied, "Whatever, *sweetheart!*"

I don't know what he was thinking, but he piqued the interest of not just Kate, but Becs too with that 'sweetheart' comment. Kate smiled at him and *that* was also not good. Josh put his hand up to David to wait.

"How soon can I have it?"

Becs replied, "The money will be wired as soon as the accounts are set up."

Josh glanced at yellow shirt who responded, "On it," and asked, "I've got your word?"

Josh looked for confirmation of our arrangement. He saw an opportunity to go for his in an environment where *he* could grow and *he could* call the shots, and he wanted this shot.

"She speaks for me."

Josh looked at me and offered his hand and said, "I'm in!"

David shouted, "Unfuckingbelievable! You're a fucking dwik, Josh! Good luck with that!"

Josh said to the remaining traders standing, "If anyone else needs work, there's a job here for you."

"You've got to be fucking kidding me, man?" David continued to complain, "Whatever!" and stormed off leaving five of his traders behind including the one closest to him.

Becs walked up to me and said, "I'll take care of the lease too, but I'm sure *your* girl hooked it up," she turned and then stopped and looked at me, *"... boss."*

I grinned and watched her as she smiled and walked away, and I admired her elegant figure as she did. I also came to realize that I was one lucky motherfucker and my luck had nothing to do with my cash, but everything to do with these fine ass women that I had with me. Becs dropped thirty million dollars for my dream and Kate got me an entire office floor on the cheap. They were feeling what I was trying to build out here and were working to make it happen for me. For us.

"Thou hast given him his heart's desire, and hast not withholden the request of his lips."

After chatting it up with Kate for a while I asked, "Do you feel like a conference, baby?"

"Sure," she replied as she placed her finger on my lips. "You know how much I love the way you move your mouth. You have such *skill*... at discourse."

I smiled at her appreciation of my, shall we say, gift for giving and said, "First things first, baby, you got to focus or at the very least, don't distract me!"

She laughed and grabbed my hand as we headed back to Amanda and Maureen to continue working out some of the logistics of her gift to me. I'd seen that look from women recently as I approached them. Kate saw it too. I was delicious.

"Hey, Amanda," I asked, "do you have a list of all the personnel here, please?"

Amanda gazed at me and said, "Sure."

Her gaze lingered until she turned to her desk and pulled it up on her desk top and printed it.

"Mo," she asked, "grab that off the printer for me, please?"

Then it returned when she handed me the list.

"No," I said, "it's for you. Conference room?"

Amanda rose and led the way, aided by Maureen, and I caught her looking back at me from the corner of her eye. I also noticed the rock on her finger when she had covered her face in tears. My plan was simple. Determine all the troublemakers and get rid of them. Determine who was essential and secure them. The rest would be utilized as needed. Josh reviewed the list and tweaked it, getting rid of David loyalists and presented me with those who were to his satisfaction, and now I had my team. The *right* team. After sending him off to continue obtaining the info Becs requested, I continued my conference with Amanda and Maureen about their new role in our company.

"What was your salary, Maureen, if you don't mind me asking? I'm sorry, I hope I'm not like breaking protocol or etiquette or-"
"Nah, it's alright. Forty Thousand," she replied.
"Ite, for now hold sixty."
"Sixty what?"
"I'm giving you a raise. Is that good?"
"Oh? *Yes,* thank you!"
I was very amused with her reaction and replied, "You're welcome."

Amanda looked at me puzzled as if unsure how it was possible to make such bold stroked decisions in the midst of this chaos. Well, it was simple. Kate and Becs were my flank and were guiding me and had my back. Josh was my trigger and I had God money to cover me.

"Amanda," I looked at her belly and said, "baby? You went to Wharton, right?"
She smiled and responded, "Yes, how did you-?"

I lifted up my phone to show her and said, *"Google."*

Her gaze intensified.

"What was yours?"

She replied, "Fifty Thousand," and nodded as I shook my head.

"I don't like that number. We'll start you at eighty-four and revisit this for *both* of you once we get rollin'. My word"

Shock consumed her and both her hands covered her mouth, "Oh, my God, Mr.-"

I interrupted her abruptly, "Please, call me H. You've already met Kate Summers and the other lovely woman I am with is Rebecca Rubin. Yeah, my name is on the door, but you are the ones making me money. Please," he said, rubbing his hands together, *"own* that and run with it. Cool?"

They looked at him as if they'd just been scolded, because they were. They nodded their heads apologetically and submitted to his request, uncertain as to how all of this benefitted him, their new boss, more than them.

"Cool. Moving forward, Amanda, you are my Business Manager. Everything that's done here will go through you. You will *run* this house and Maureen will be your assistant. I need you to set up the structure for our operations and the image of our firm, RH LLC. Maureen, you will assist her accordingly and maintain the integrity of all of our partners. Oversimplified, Amanda, Josh will bring home *your* money and Maureen you'll see to it he's got no problems with that. Amanda, you'll pay the bills and then you'll pay us. Kate is my left hand and Rebecca is my right and like them, *you* now speak for me. Rebecca's word is final. Maureen, you and Josh will discuss all clients, office budgets, accounting, hires, fires, all that bullshit with Amanda. Amanda, you've got Kate and Rebecca if you have any issues. Work it out. Have I made myself clear?"

Still in shock they nodded and said, "Yes."

"Righteous, now I'ma go check on Josh."

When he left, the girls took the opportunity of some privacy and sequestered Kate for more questioning.

"Kate, I'm a little unsure about all of this as far as where all the money is coming from and what exactly he wants done?" said Amanda.

Maureen added, "I used the same Google as him on my phone and he ain't there."

"My Google must be busted too 'cause I can't find shit on him."

"That's because *his* Google has a last name… and wants to move to Canada," Kate quipped under her breath.

"What?" Amanda asked and Kate shook her head. "Who is this guy?"

Kate replied, "H is the guy giving *you* an opportunity to earn your receipt value. He has chosen you to set up and run the operation of managing his business as you see fit. This you will accomplish under the scrutiny of Rebecca Rubin, his attorney. This will be your office and will be run by *your* rules because quite honestly, H doesn't have a clue, which is why he's entrusting this to you. If you need any help for any reason at any time, Rebecca and I are always available to you to assist in any way that we can. But this is *yours.* You ladies did it for your last company and made them a shit ton of money, well now work that smart for H."

"When you say, *'manage his business',* do you mean this one he's making," Amanda asked, "or is there some *other* business he has?"

"This firm is and will be his *primary* business and it's going to be your *sole* responsibility to manage all of the assets it has, generates and receives."

"All?" Maureen squeaked.

Kate confirmed, "Yes, *all.*"

"How much are we talking about?" Amanda asked, shrewdly.

"H is worth well over *three hundred million.*"

"What? Oh, my God! *Him?*"

The girls freaked and Amanda needed cold water, which Maureen seemingly pulled from her back. This responsibility felt tremendous to her and she was uncertain if she was the right person for the job.

"Oh, my God, Kate, why me?"

"For that answer you'll need to ask him yourself, but as I know him it would be simply because he *feels* he can trust you- the *both* of you. The day he doesn't is the day you're gone. Also, everything that we are discussing here and will be discussing regarding H and *our* business, is to be kept *here,*" she pointed with her finger at the three of them, "and will be held in the *strictest* of confidence." Kate paused, "Have *I* made myself clear?"

For Kate, the girls instinctively knew that nodding would not be acceptable. Verbal acknowledgement of compliance was given.

"Yes," they replied.

"Good talk."

Kate got up to leave and saw that the girls were still immobilized by the shocking news, not to mention the trauma of the morning, and decided to assist them further.

"You both *still* look like you need a minute?"

"I do," Amanda responded.

"Ok. What's the first thing we need here?"

"Phones and communication," Amanda replied, "Josh will need that. Right now, they're utilizing their personal hotspots and secure Wi-Fi. Not a one of Josh's people believe in using public signals."

"Ok, how do we fix that?" asked Kate.

155

"I'll take care of it," Maureen said and left.

Kate sat back down with Amanda and consoled her saying, "Hey, you'll be fine. Wharton's no piece of cake and you accomplished it, didn't you?"

Amanda stared at Kate, which for most people, at the very least, would warrant an inquiry, but not Kate. She stares right back at you, assessing twice as much and twice as fast to maintain her upper hand.

"You know it's interesting that I've known you all of a couple of hours and you've mentioned my alma mater twice," as she held up the peace sign with her fingers to Kate. "I worked for these *bitches* for three and a half years and it never came up once. I was more qualified than the bitch I worked for. Hell, I trained her, and they looked out for her instead of me. And now by some *act* of God, you've come up in here giving me three hundred million and a firm to run and I don't know you from a hole in the wall."

"Yeah... that's about accurate," Kate remarked, "and I'm just guessing at the number. I haven't asked in a while." They laughed and Kate inquired, "You pray much?"

"Yes, I do."

"Well, I guess today you're cashing out."

They laughed again. It's very interesting to see Kate in a cordial setting. Her aggressive side recedes giving way to a gentler, normal disposition, like she's gone home to visit her past self. It's never permanent though. It's too weak for Kate and she will never allow herself to be dominated again.

"So, it's not the way you expected," she counseled Amanda, "it's actually easier. All the pomp and circumstance you imagined turned out to be just you, waddling into an office with a personnel sheet in your hand and your new boss, a rich black man with a heart of gold, following behind you."

"Why is that?" she asked. "Hard life?"

"I don't know, entirely," Kate responded. "I don't doubt he did. *'That little boy had no idea how real the world was. Then as a man, he was surprised at how comfortable was the lie,'* he once told me. But, where some grow up not having and horde when they got older, H grew up not having and for whatever reason, shares. It's the luck of the draw I guess."

"How did he make his money?"

"That is another *good* question," she confessed, "it was never important to me. In dealing with H, it's not one of the things that came *up*."

Amanda blushed at Kate's remark turning her head as she smiled.

"What I do know was that I wanted to be a part of something big and he was it."

Amanda blushed again and asked, "How did you two meet, if you don't mind me asking?"

Kate stared at her and then at her belly and responded, "God, girl? Over that, except without the proof!" They laughed hysterically some more, and Kate confessed, "I swear, I literally chased him down and offered him whatever he wanted."

"Ok, T-M-I," Amanda exclaimed.

"He turned me down flat!"

"Wait, what?" she asked in disbelief.

"Yep."

"You," Amanda motioned at Kate with her hand in a circular motion, "and *all* that?"

"Yep. Don't get me wrong I'm fucking him now but that's not what he wanted at first."

"Ok, so what did he want?"

"Trust. Amanda if he can trust you, he'll give you the world if it's in his power to give." Kate paused, "If you cannot be trusted, please do us the favor and leave now."

"Understood," Amanda replied. You need not worry about me. This is my opportunity of a lifetime, like you said, and if trust is all you require, then you have my absolute loyalty."

"Good! I can deal with just about anything. Hey, even if you want to fuck him, be my guest. Just please," she emphasized, "please do not fuck him *over*. I can be a *very* vengeful person."

"Thank you for the offer but I'm *very* happily married."

Kate gazed at her for a while and remarked, "Of course you are… congratulations. More for me!"

They continued to laugh.

"So, *chicka,* are you going to man up and show him what you've got, or what?"

"Yes, ma'am."

"Great! Welcome to the family."

They shook hands and Kate continued her gaze even after Amanda broke it off and said, "I should go cull the herd. It's kinda crowded out there. Lot of folks gon be happy."

Kate stated, "And a few *not* so… happy. She sighed and continued, "I'll leave you to your business. Enjoy your day."

Kate left Amanda in the conference room and to her administrative duties to find H, who saw her coming and interrupted his conversation to make sure she was ok. She assured him that they were good and returned her focus to him.

"Your office, lover!" She announced as she walked over to the left corner of the floor and he followed her. "New King and a new throne."

It was a nice size office at the opposite end of the space. She was very taken by it.

"Kate, shouldn't I offer this to Josh or Amanda? I don't need this. I could be in one of the middle ones."

Kate replied, adamantly, *"You're* the boss and *this* is where you should be!"

158

I pulled her aside and said, delicately, "Baby, I appreciate you more than life, but they're the ones working here making the money."

She stopped and humored me, then walked out and went into an office to her right and after a brief survey made her second choice.

"This one!" It was cozy and at the end of the center aisle with a couple of windows and a door directly in the middle of it with two side light panels. From my desk here and with the door open I could see everything and everyone coming through. It would be like a procession coming to see me. Dead ass. I agreed and she was satisfied. She modeled for me, then sat down and admired the view... of me. She put her feet up on the desk and folded her hands on her stomach and said, "Shitty throne. You'll need a better chair."

We cracked up.

"I'll have Amanda order you one. We'll also need to get rid of this shit," she said, pointing at some file cabinets that were along the wall, "and get you a small sofa." Staring at them and making the adjustments in her mind she continued, "I'll need a comfy place to get mine."

"GOD, she's hot!"

Rebecca and I spent the remainder of the day in the office coordinating our operations from personnel to phone lines to accounts. Becs worked out of the CEO's corner office, while I got used to mine. Kate ran errands and checked in with us periodically, and my new staff, grateful for their jobs, got down to their business of strategizing how to flip my money and grow my bank. Amanda informed me that they were all beat out of two weeks' pay by their former employer. So, based on the numbers she gave me, one of the errands Kate ran was to drop off $100,000 cash, which Amanda and Maureen distributed as advance pay to everyone, plus a little extra to make up the shortfall and an NDA. All in all, it was a good day. I put Amanda in a car until further notice from the car service her former firm used, and we started an account with them as well. We pretty much assumed the services and the vendors that were already in place, since Josh was familiar with them and he was our money. Maureen scheduled the field techs for tomorrow, so I called it a night and shared a cab home with Becs. I dropped her home first and then myself. The cabbie had no problem with that, as I gave him a nice tip.

"Thank you, Mr. H."

I looked up to see it was Davide.

"I'll see you first thing tomorrow. We'll do the same trip as now but in reverse."

"This motherfucker?"

"I'll see you at six."
"My brother, I don't get up before the sun."
"I love my wife, but I'll be here by six. Waiting."

"... I will bring her to you."

Chapter Thirteen

All Holes Are Not A Rabbit
"The Birth Of Amanda Rosado"

The next morning, I got ready to go to my new office, and shit. I liked the sound of that, *my new office.* We signed the lease yesterday, Amanda hired our essential personnel, and today Kate is going to sit with her to discuss the impressive portfolio she's been amassing for us, of which, I've only done a cursory review. Truth is, I have no idea what the fuck she's been buying, but she's in charge of all real property investments and infrastructure, meaning P had a new boss. Anything not that, will report directly to Amanda, and the details of my estate are handled solely by Becs. Amanda told me she would be at work by 8:30, so I aimed for 9. I managed to get out my tomb on time to iron horse it up there, when I stepped out the elevator into the lobby and I saw Davide parked at the curb waiting for me.

"What the fuck? That's one 'won't accept no for an answer' motherfucker, boy. Shit?"

"Davide, are you serious, man? Yo, you need *quantity* not quality to make money in the cab business, man."

When I got to the office, Amanda was there, and I reacquainted myself with my partners and helped everyone settle in as best I could. The field techs were already working on communications, so I stopped to get an update, then I left them to check on Josh, who I observed was lining up trades and positions on the monitors on the wall as they came online. I must have caught Maureen's eye, because she came over to me and appeared to already be comfortable around me. She was happy as fuck to see me this morning, commenting on

161

why I had my hoodie on in the office lookin' like the "Grim Reaper?"

She asked, "Do you mind?" and raised her hands. I lowered my head and her hands subtly caressed the sides of my face and went under my hood, and slowly pushed it off as she stared intently at it, as if amazed the whole time. "Much better," she quipped, making eye contact with me finally, only to tell me softly, "You walkin' 'round here scarin' people, *Grimmy*. Besides bein' the boss, that look is very intimidatin'. They been through enough. Stop that... please?"

I stood there staring at her, standing before me on *her* floor and before our audience, *her* subordinates and she was bold, confident and secure, unlike Amanda, and I complied, *"Grimmy,* huh? As you wish... Mo."

She smiled at me graciously. She needed that from me, and they needed to see her get that from me, respect and obedience. I left her and went and sat in Amanda's office and struck up a conversation to help her get over her issues, while she organized herself for her first day.

"What's the matter, the boss making you nervous? *She* makes me nervous too!"

She grinned and answered, "No, I'm ok, just preoccupied with getting things in order."

"Hmm. Not sure if you know this," he said as he folded his trademark skully and laid it on her desk, "but the second rule around here is, *'Never lie to me.'"*

She looked unsettled and vulnerable already being a prenatal mom and now an executive overnight. I could tell she was hungry, but this was new ground for her, and she wasn't yet comfortable trailblazing her way through it. But I was betting she would, if given enough time or the right incentive. I had already tried money, now I was thinkin' of something else.

Amanda recanted, "Ok, *maybe* just a little."

"You're overthinking this, babe. Relax and free your mind and you'll find that things kinda tend to wanna make sense."

I stood and she watched me walk over to the window behind her desk and after a thought or two, I asked her to join me.

"Amanda, momma, come here, please?"

Amanda rose and walked up next to me and we stood together soaking in the late summer morning sun in the naked city, waking up and putting its drawers on.

"Look down there at the street. Do you see all that down there?"
"Yes."
"Looks to me like confusion, how about you?"
"Yes, to me too."
"Yet even amidst that confusion, there's still order. You got folks going up. Folks coming down and some even crisscrossing. From up here, do you see that? Do you notice how order prevails?"

Amanda took a moment to observe it. She also observed in that moment that the office she was now in once belonged to her old boss.

"Yes."
"Now, look straight ahead," I asked, "what do you see?"

He had taken a page out of Kate's book to appreciate the value of a dear friend's instruction.

"I see the next building," she replied.
"Cool. Let's say that's a person in an office who has *made* it. Ok?"

Amanda nodded in agreement.

"So, you've got *this* person and *that* person and *another* person over there and so on. They've all got some distance between them and there's nowhere as many of them like the folks down there, right?"

"Yes," she agreed.

"See what I'm getting at?"

"I'm sorry. I don't understand, H."

"Babe, I think you feel that you are *competing* with all those people down there when you're really just standing your ground here. This building, this office is the *new* you and everyone outside that door are the same ones you see below running around in order *around* you," H said, pointing at Amanda to emphasize his point.

Amanda observed the orderly flow of pedestrians below her and allowed what H said to sink in and she saw it. He was right. She was above all of that now and orderly or not or by some strange miracle or by design, she had come and gone and crisscrossed her life into success. She had made it from down there, even though she had no clue how the fuck it happened.

"You balance your checkbook and pay your bills, right?"

"Yes."

"What do you think would be so different here?"

"Nothing, I-"

"Second rule, Amanda."

H interrupted her. Either due to impatience or for instruction, he stopped her and reminded her she was hiding from the truth and Amanda answered honestly.

"H, I need this job. I can't afford to lose it. I can't fuck this up and get fired. You have a lot of money and you seem forgiving and that might be the reason, but that's still a lot of pressure for me to deal with."

"So, you went to Wharton to avoid pressure?" he asked.

Amanda listened.

"What, you figured you'd rub elbows with the privileged so that you could get a good *job?* Maybe aim for the best *low* you could get? Is that what you're selling me right now, babe?"

Amanda stared at him and continued to listen. Another cool perk in having money is that people let you run your mouth without interrupting you, for the most part. My boy, Sly, once told me that *"If you're thinking about your answer 10 seconds into a conversation, then you've stopped listening."* She wanted all of that, just like he said, from thinking as most of us do that our true desire for *far and wide* and *a shot at the stars* or *a shot in the dark* couldn't actually happen. Yes, she wanted her resumé to stick out above the average one, but it wasn't her plan for it to compete with the best, even though she had earned her degree from one of the best and H considered her the best. Amanda feared success to the point of accepting the consequences for not taking it.

"I'm not gon argue with you about pressure, seein' how you're carryin' a new life in you and everything, but you might wanna try holdin' *$499,010,650* sometime. Gettin' past the sandy beaches and the crystal-clear waterfalls and you vacationin' in cabanas sippin' margaritas, and shit. And havin' all your bills paid and bein' able to afford whatever you want in the euphoria of the new life in which *'God has finally answered my prayers'* and 'blessed *I* art among women', *you* might wanna think. Stop and just think about wakin' up in the fuckin' mornin', every fuckin' mornin', and countin' the number of people in your life who you have to trust that if you lost it all today, would still wanna know you."

Amanda's stare was intense on him as he held up two fingers. She never interrupted because she kept listening.

165

"Amanda Nichole Johnson-Rosado, you'll shit prescription drugs knowing me if you don't toughen up, babe."

Amanda felt her baby move for H again, just like yesterday when they first met and she asked, "Is that how much you're worth?"

"According to Becs, this morning, yes."

"And you freely admit this to me, a complete stranger?"

H looked at her as if questioning if she was, and holding up those two fingers, he slowly raised a third.

Amanda took a beat, then asked, "I thought all rich people were secretive, greedy, conniving, pompous sons of bitches?"

"Probably are, but I'm *wealthy.*" H shook his head, "We *slightly* different folk." Amanda was tickled and H grinned with her and asked, "What is it you think I want you to do for me?"

She looked in his eyes and answered, "Set up, run and operate this office as my own."

"Perfect, but you ain't stoppin' there."

"I'm not?"

The look of panic took hold of her petite frame again.

"Nah. I want you to *control* all of my businesses, Amanda. Every last chicken I got and I'm hatching many." H grinned at the thought of his pursuits, which she would soon be made aware of and was content in himself, saying, "I've been farmin', and shit, and I want all my chickens to come home to you to roost. I want you to keep eyes on 'em and feed 'em and make sure they're layin' their eggs the way they're supposed to and keepin' you all tingly inside."

Amanda smiled.

"Now, the chickens that do this, I want you to feed them and nurture them and develop them. The ones that don't, put them on a plate."

Amanda caught his look from the edge of his hoodie unzipped and pulled over his head. He was in *her* office now, not gen pop, so Maureen's Law did not apply.

"Babe, everything I own and everyone with me including Rebecca and Kate fall under your purview to manage because in some way shape or form it's all business and makes me money. Do you understand?"

She replied, "Yes. But isn't what you're asking of me a little beyond *just* business, H? Nobody trusts anybody like that."

"I have to."

"Why?" Amanda asked.

H turned to her and answered, "The short of it is, I always hedge my bets. What *you* need to know is that you have a heart that makes me feel good when I look at you and makes me want to share what I have with you. It made me make you my family, Amanda, and deep down I feel that's where you want to be. Your problem is you won't let yourself *believe* it."

"Believe? After *one* day?" Amanda quipped. "Yesterday, I was broke livin' check to check and today I'm runnin' a half a billion-dollar business."

"You have no idea, babe." he thought.

H looked down at her belly and it made her look too and he responded, "Yep, it only takes *one* day." He then looked deep into Amanda's big beautiful radiant light brown eyes and fell under her spell and spoke, "And... I need you. Please?"

Amanda felt her baby move again and so did the earth, intimately for him and she confessed it, catching herself with an instant of guilt but surprisingly no shame.

"I'm here *for you.*"

H continued to be captivated by her. He was entranced in her eyes, her scent and her compassion.

"You will not fuck up because I will not *allow* you to."

She looked fondly at him and answered, "Thank you." Their intimate moment was interrupted when her phone chimed on her desk and she said trying not to sound disappointed, "That's probably Rebecca."

"Ga 'head, take care of that."

"Yeah, let me get my stuff."

H turned and asked, "Everyone's here, right?"

She looked around and replied, "Yes, *baby*- I mean yes, H!"

H was flattered and Amanda was embarrassed. He chuckled with her and nodded, *"Momma?"*

He picked up his skully and left Amanda, presumably moist, standing at her desk watching his silhouetted figure remove his hood as he walked out of her office. As he did, he noticed a trade on the monitor and something about it bugged him. He was also bugged by an employee who walked by and called him *"Sir"* when she greeted him, *"Good morning."*

"Hi. Excuse me, your name is?"

The slim, ebony beauty turned and replied, "Jasmine, sir."

"Hi, Jasmine. Beautiful name."

"Thank you."

"Jasmine, please do me a favor?"

"Sure," she replied.

"You work for me, but I would prefer if you worked *with* me. My office," he said, pointing, "everyone here is welcomed to come in and sit with me and talk and bullshit about anything or anyone at any time. Doin' that, will make us family. Call me H, and let everyone know that, please?"

"Oh- kay," Jasmine answered.

"We good?"

"Um, yes," she confirmed, nervously, "H?"

168

I offered her my hand and she shook it.

"Thanks, babe."

H peeped that trade again as Jasmine left him and it was bigger. Rebecca came in shortly afterwards and stopped in to see him to as she put it, "…break the Boss' balls for a minute," before leaving with Amanda, and he let her, probably because she had a wicked right cross. When she was ready to go, he walked her out to see her off safely and to peep a long hard look at her ass as she loved to let him, but when they stepped out onto the floor, he became distracted with that trade again and she became jealous.

"What's wrong, hun?"

Surprised as always by how sharp Rebecca is, H replied, "Nothin'."

"My ass it's nothin'." She shut her eyes and shook her head, saying, "You *know* what I meant."

"Uh huh."

Rebecca then looked in the direction that he was distracted and asked, "Is there something there you don't like?"

I admitted it because she wouldn't have given me peace until I did, "That trade is fuckin' with me, God. It's a bad position."

"Why?"

"They've loaded up on the wrong side."

Becs looked up at the monitor on the wall and then back at H as he stared motionless at the trade.

"It was as if when he looked at you, he had to place the face because the person who he was at that moment, had no idea who you were. This is when I trusted him the least but obeyed him the most."

She called out to Josh and her shout raised him to consciousness, and he said, "Nah, babe, it's cool."

169

Irritated by his passivity, she rebuffed, "Fuck *'it's cool!'*"

Josh came over and Rebecca interrogated him, pointing while making her way to the monitor on the wall, "Joseph, is this the trade that you were talking about yesterday?"

"Yes, ma'am."

"What's our exposure here?"

Josh replied, "700,000. We're fine."

Becs looked back at H and before she could voice her decision to Josh, he interrupted her and said, "Josh, I'm not feeling that."

Josh replied, "*Feeling'* what, that position? Do you even know what it is? I assure you I've got-"

"I know what you've got. I paid for it. I don't wanna pay more. Do this instead," H rudely and dismissively instructed, pointing at the screen. "This position here, buy it down to *here.* Javi... Javi, where are you?"

"Right here, H?" he replied, standing beside Josh. Rebecca looked at H and he caught her eye and continued, "Oh. Yeah, Javi, counter that 700 here and short *this* market," H directed him pointing at the adjacent monitor. "That's you *all* day. I want you to run with it 'til about the mid five's *here.* You shouldn't see six. *Secure what I need, then your greed.* Get our money and get the fuck out. Have I made myself clear?"

"Understood, H."

Javi nodded and H continued, "Getting back to *this* one, Josh, cap us at another 700 and not a penny over... and *now* 'we're fine.'"

Josh calculated, "Are you aware of the size of that draw?"

"Regrettably yes, and with heat. Dig, I ain't tryin' to be perfect... just right. If it doesn't correct by here," H said, drawing a line with his finger on the touch screen for the class to see, "start dumpin'. Otherwise hold, it'll go."

From the corner of his eye, he saw that Becs looked frightened, as did the rest of the traders and the office who were more confused than Josh.

"H, I have no idea what you're doing or where this is coming from and-" he sighed, "you're basing this on *what?*"

H looked through him and replied, "A lucky *guess*."

"A lucky *what?* H, that's not how it's done and please excuse my expression, but that right there is as fucked up a move if I ever saw one." Josh said, vehemently imploring him to listen to reason.

H looked at the monitors again reviewing in his mind his strategy, then leaned in and uttered, "Learn to make money, not noise."

He then turned and walked away and Becs recognized this and directed sternly at Josh, "And *you'll* make it work." Josh looked at Rebecca and backed off and she uttered, "Let's get those orders in people. Thank you." Maureen then shouted and got the quieted and stunned office back to work. "Joseph," Rebecca began as Amanda waddled up to her and he cut her off.

"Listen Rebecca, I'm sorry about-"

"You will keep me apprised, Joseph," Rebecca said, completely losing her train of thought with Amanda's approach and maybe that was Amanda's intent. Josh was attempting to apologize and explain his position but was again rudely interrupted. He could tell they were both annoyed with him and it didn't sit well.

"Thank you, Josh," Amanda said, ending their conversation.

Josh conceded and Amanda grabbed Rebecca and declared that she had to go pee from the stress that the order had placed on her.

"Ah, well, I done it now… drawing a crowd, and shit!" H thought. *I could imagine the sentiment. I was the rich guy that had just saved their jobs yesterday but was now talking shit about something I knew nothing about and certainly not more than they did, but they were following me even if it is under protest 'cause I signed their checks."*

171

The traders see my order as complete bullshit and a loss of some hard-earned commission coming to them, but at the end of the day, it's my money they are fuckin' with, so they'll humor my foolishness, hoping I will soon be taught a harsh lesson and fuck off. The techs murmured among themselves and resumed work once Becs left, intent on spending a good portion of the day wiring up the office. I want the state of the art everything, so they'll milk me for all they can get. After all, we are an investment firm and have to have everything just right for our business. One of the tech guys by the name of Glenn was cool though. I told him to give his number to Maureen for future work. Jasmine tried to avoid eye contact with me and so did everyone else, but I was just too fuckin' curious not to look at. I stayed in my office after a run to the fridge.

"One thing is for sure, they all know to call me by my fuckin' name now."

All was quiet until about 2:17 when I heard a commotion ensuing outside my door, prompting me to fold my skully off my eyes and rise to take a look see. The office had gotten busy as fuck all of a sudden, and through one of the door sidelights, I saw Becs standing in front of the monitors next to Josh, who was barking orders to the traders at their desks behind him. Amanda was outside her office as was Maureen, who was shouting at the processors to move their asses. I'm paraphrasing, maybe. I looked up at the account screen, which was like an overhead scoreboard the techs put up and we were green. My trade had finally corrected. Josh and his traders were scrambling feverishly on how to play it, being loaded up but capped as per my orders, imploring Becs to forgive them and open the purse strings so they could play. Becs gave in and Josh covered as they increased our positions and them boys ate it up on a run clearing us and when they were done, they closed out with a 2.4 million dollar gain on our first day in business off a fucked-up move as they had so forebodingly projected it. Javi countered with the position I had him run to cover the seven hundred-thousand-dollar hit we would have taken on their original position, if I hadn't intervened. Josh's original signature trade was now in a better position to pay out, as we were now less exposed at a better price. I caught Becs' stare as well as Maureen's and my nervous manager, Amanda's, and Jasmine's as the floor celebrated. Becs stood in front of the monitor soaking it all in as did Amanda, a little ways off, who turned her attention to Josh, who was all smiles. Maureen got busy reconciling our accounts and Jasmine never took her eyes off me. I returned to my office to continue fuckin' off.

"Josh," Amanda asked, "can I have a word with you in your office, please?"

Josh, celebrating and excited over the money they just made, turned and headed to his office with Amanda following.

"Can you believe it? Holy shit, Amanda, I had no idea this guy knew how to trade!" he said, amazed at the accuracy of H's predictions. "Can you be-"

Amanda shut the door and furiously interrupted, "You will not ever, *ever* contradict H in public or disrespect him the way that you did and certainly not within earshot of Rebecca ever again or your ass is on the street, am I clear!" she said, attacking him.

"Amanda, I'm sorry I had no idea? I didn't think this guy knew shit. It's unbelievable how he-"

"I don't give a damn what you thought! I swear to God I should fire your ass right now! I went to bat for you and you go and mouth off to him on the floor and in front of *her* of all people? Are you out your goddamn mind? That woman will crucify you for him! What the hell are you doing?"

"Amanda, I'm sorry," he said, realizing how serious Amanda was, Josh abandoned his excitement for an urgent apology in hopes of appeasing her.

173

"Sorry?" Amanda asked, "You would have never done that to-"

"It won't happen again! I promise! I swear, please! I thought I was doing the right thing. I was looking out for him."

"You were looking out for *your* ego, Josh! You can't wait to stick it to David, and you had this trade lined up to do it. But when H came in threatening your payday, you embarrassed him. I bet you're *really* happy now, aren't you? He schooled your ass!"

Josh said nothing while she reamed him.

"Yeah, I know. Now you can go brag about your million-dollar payday out your new house and shove it down your boy's throat."

"The chickens that do this, feed them and nurture them and develop them. The ones that do not, put them on a plate."

"But, you're not."

"What?" Josh exclaimed, resisting her request.

Amanda snapped and grabbed him by his arm and pulled him against the door and said, "What the *fuck* did I just say! Josh, I swear to God, if you make me have this baby here, I'll kick your motherfu-"

"Ok? Ok!" Josh pleaded.

Looking up at him, she ordered, "You will tell *no one* about him calling this trade and make sure your minions keep their fuckin' mouths shut too. You will collect your check and take the credit for it, and if I even hear so much as a peep involving H anywhere around this win, you're *gone!* Boy, you've got a good thing here and you'd better *not* screw it up! H is slick. Don't let that skully wearing motherfucker fool you. And Rebecca, you better watch your ass. She is *most* unforgiving and not one to make your enemy. That woman has got way too much money for too little conscience. This position you've put me in today, don't you ever do that shit to me again, Josh! You hear me?"

174

"Yes, Amanda, loud and clear."

"I hope so. Next time it won't be me."

Amanda stared at him and was grateful it was her this time. Rebecca hadn't said anything to her regarding the incident, but that didn't mean she wasn't observing it. Josh was clearly insubordinate to H and undermined not just his authority but Rebecca's and hers as well, which was grounds for immediate termination and her responsibility. She chose instead to reprimand him and chalk it up to youthful assness, keeping in mind the potential she believes he has, given the opportunity to develop here, and that was her decision to make in this, *her* office.

"I expect to hear about your monumental ass kissing first chance you get!"

"Thank you, Amanda."

"Move!" Amanda said, "Just move!" and angrily opened the door and walked out.

Becs came into my office and locked the door behind her. She stood over me as I had my feet up on my desk and said, "I'm listening?"

"You sure you want to know?"

Becs thought about it. Her first instinct with me was always responsibility or plausible deniability. But that was getting tired now. She struggled being both responsible as my lawyer and denying me as my partner too. She had one foot on solid ground and the other on that slippery slope of my mojo on which I accelerated on every day.

Curiously, she asked, "Was it real or *ethereal?*" She saw his face as he appeared stymied over the safest answer to give her and caressing the top of his head, she indicated her acceptance and understanding of his position and sighed, "You need to protect me, and I need you sane."

175

"Becs, I don't know how far this rabbit hole goes."

"We just made 2.4 million on a trade you called!"

"I called?" he asked, confirming she really didn't want the truth.

"Whoever called!" she asserted.

"You say it like I'm supposed to be surprised, Becs?"

"I believe you now," Rebecca declared exuberantly, squatting before him in her designer dress. "H, I believe *everything!*"

Her eyes sparkled so full of life and he stared.

"God, H, do you have any idea what this means? What we can do?"

"We? Say word, you with me now?"

"I've always been with you-"

"No, Becs, you haven't! You've stayed just out of reach that if *crazy* prevailed, your ass wouldn't get carted away too, and I can't say I blame you. That shit out there that 'we' as you say just did, wasn't me? I just walked on water and you here tryin' to convince yourself I knew where the rocks were. You say you finally believe me, now? Well, it's about fuckin' time, you think!" He said, firmly, "There are no fuckin' rocks, Rebecca! Get it?"

H was angry when he spoke and stared at her but couldn't see through her for the first time since they'd met, and he was very curious.

"Hun," she asked as his stare hurt her, "why are you mad? Please, don't be mad at me? Please?"

"Please, don't be mad at me?" H mocked, frustrated the more he looked at her and said, "Fuck it. I don't win arguments with chicks."

Feeling the justification for his anger, she responded, "I deserve that, but I still can't-"

"Won't!" He insisted, and she softened her voice to appease him. H is a different person when he's angry.

176

"I *won't* join you on that side, a fact which I'm sure you already realize? Baby, if I lose touch with these devils out here, you and I and everyone we love and everything we're striving to build will be fucked. I will not allow that to happen nor will I allow you to go through it alone, but I must remain here on earth, H, for all our sakes."

H tried to be serious but laughed and she laughed with him, but her words made every bit of sense why she was given to him. He would fly and she'd hold the kite string, never allowing him to get so high he couldn't return down to earth to her.

"Can you imagine what we can do?"

"Again, you keep sayin' it like I'm supposed to be amazed. You really haven't grasped what I've done so far, have you? Woman when my head is on fire, and shit, and when I can't eat, and I can't sleep and you all insulted 'cause of how I'm *lookin'* at you-"

"H, my pussy will *not* heal your ills!"

"This is what I mean! This is what I…" H seemed to lose his thought thinking for a second and then chuckled softly and said, "Oh, *ye* of little faith?"

Rebecca blushed, hiding her face in his arm where he sat as he gave her a curious look again though smiling with her and it frightened her and she asked, "What is it?"

"I don't know. I've started somethin' I can't stop, and I must get through."

"Ok. Now you're scarin' me!"

"Sorry about that." He quipped, "I really should work on my *paranormal* sense of humor."

Rebecca waited and while she did the noise on the floor outside their private moment grew noticeable and distracting and when it had become too distracting, she cautiously asked, "H, what exactly just happened? I saw you zone out and speak in a way and about things I had no idea you knew anything about." He caught her stare and she asked, "Tell the truth, am I really the person you're mad at?"

177

H stared at her again and again and answered, "No."

H began to speak, and what he had to say riveted Rebecca to his side as she marveled at him in astonishment, finding it unbelievable the things she heard. He made light of some things, perhaps trying it on for size to make her laugh, but other things he was so deadly serious and looked the part, that it made her think long and hard about what she had gotten herself into. Imagine a million in a day, every day, 5 days a week, 4 weeks a month, 12 month's a year. She had only begun to scratch the surface of her gift goose who trusted only her with his eggs. He had given her so much and could give her so much more and more importantly, he wanted to.

When he was done, she asked, "We're going to have more days like this, aren't we?"

Again, he answered truthfully, pointing at the monitor in front of him, "I already know tomorrow's trade.

Rebecca looked at his screen, "Oh, my God? Are you-?" The reality of it hit home again for her as she stood as if pacing, "Oh, my God! H? Alright, you will speak only with *me* regarding your... *lucky guesses.* Am I clear?"

H continued to just stare at her.

"What?" she asked.

Cautiously, he answered, "Nothin.' I'm just-" he hesitated, "Our secret, right? So, are you *flattered?"*

Confused, she responded, "Huh? What do you mean?"

He smiled, shaking his head, "Lucky guesses. Hmm... got it."

H sunk into his shitty throne, still with his feet up and scrolled through markets and charts on his desktop and deliberately ignored Rebecca, standing beside him and presumably wrestling with her obvious feelings for him. Today he had given her even more truth and it wasn't enough. It *still* wasn't enough, and she wondered, as she presumed he also wondered, when *would* it be enough? He wasn't mad at Rebecca. He was mad at himself. It fucked with him the thought of what he would give for her to have been someone else right now. Someone else he could have made so happy that wouldn't have a care in the world, but Rebecca didn't deserve for him to sour hers with his regrets. Neither did M, who soured him. He had dreams with her too. None of which came true and would ever come true. *"Everything just came so fuckin' late,"* he bitched, saying that he never asked for an upgrade, only the means by which he could keep that which he was grateful to already have. "I just needed everything to fall into place, instead everything just fell apart." Now, it was making others happy, and fulfilling their dreams, when it was supposed to be just for the two of them, making Rebecca his unwitting, voluptuous consolation prize, and this made him angry. They say that God knows best? Well, Rebecca deserved better. Why did God think that this was the best way to make him happy? So, the plan was, know a man's heart, anticipate his fuck ups, then compensate for said fuck ups by upsetting his presently perfect apple cart, rather than, what does it say in Job, again? *"...made a hedge about him, and about his house, and about all that he hath on every side? Blessed the work of his hands, and his substance is increased in the land."* Well, who can argue there? That's a whole lot more aggravating and *so* much more work. It's easier to just fuck with a man's peace. Great fucking *Job!* My girl is gone, my dreams for us are shot to shit, but no matter, *"Look at who's standing beside you now, son,"* said the Lord.

"Shit, Becs, I guess GOD is your pimp?"

But time is money and her money needed her time, and Becs knew what he wanted and what she also wanted and given everything at stake and everything to gain, when would it be enough, and was there enough to
179

be had? She bent down and hugged him where he sat and caressed his head where she held it to her stomach, and he refused to accept her as their consolation prize. He simply accepted her, and she wasn't conflicted.

And their moment was no longer private.

"What you lookin' at, Kate?" Amanda asked, looking up from the paperwork in front of her as Kate had just arrived and was standing in the doorway fixating across the aisle through the sidelight into H's office.

Kate answered, "I'm not sure yet. What did I miss?"

Chapter Fourteen

French Kissing In The PTA
"The Birth Of Anastasia Movado"

For the first PTA meeting of the new semester it was decided by my little one that I should attend. She had an angle, I didn't know what it was, but I went anyway. It could never be a bad thing for a father to show up for these things. It was a cool night in October, so I didn't complain. I showed up and found a seat stashed near the back of the crowd in the lunchroom where we gathered and did my due diligence as a doting father for my beloved yellow child. I've got two daughters. One yellow and one eggnog, and I'm chocolate. We went through the usual 'who we are, what we want to do and how you can help' speeches and then it came to my favorite part of the evening, raising capital. Their ideas were tried and true and 'hey, if it ain't broke,' but I happened to really dig my daughter's principal. I respected and admired her efforts and made myself only available to assist in the one way I can. That attendance thing, however, nah… that ain't gon happen. I raised my hand, the one and only time I did, to ask a very specific question.

"Principal Reilly, do you have an idea of the budget required to accomplish our goals for this year?"

"I do, Mr.?"

"H, I'm Hashei's father."

"Oh, hi?" she responded, "How are you? I'm happy to see you made it!"

"I'm devoted."

The cafeteria of parents laughed, and Laurel Riley said, "It's a lot. I figure the best way to approach it is to plan our events and then see what the board can contribute."

"Can you tell us the number please?" I asked." It's not my intent to put you on the spot, but maybe I can assist?"

"Woo, great," she said, with a hint of sarcasm and an unenthusiastic wave of jazz hands. "That figure is around $3,400."

"Ok, thank you."

When the meeting was over, I made myself available for the 'help us help your child' literature and bent her ear for her schedule for tomorrow.

"I'll be in my office any time after 9:30 am."

"Great, I might have an idea for you that could generate the numbers you need."

What I really meant was 'I'll have a check for you', but I was trying not to be vain in the presence of *so* many women. It's a fine line between being charming and being a whole ass, as I've been called, and I just wanted to get home and chill the fuck out in peace. However, staying at the house, while still working through my emotional pangs for just being in the neighborhood again, was grueling. And though *Majorska* would've helped a lot, I wasn't sick. Some things you really ought to let go, you know? Surviving the rough night, the next morning I got up and got myself ready to see Laurel Reilly. I walked in, showed ID, signed my name, got wanded like I was visiting a maximum-security prison, and was directed to the office by security, where I requested that my envelope be given to her since she was on the phone and I didn't feel like waiting. A beautiful Guyanese sister capitulated to my request and assured me my correspondence would be given promptly, for which I bade her farewell and good tidings for an outstanding day and tipped to break the fuck out. On my way, I got bagged.

"Mr. H?" I heard from down the hall that would put the kibosh on my speedy getaway. "Hi," I said, drawing a blank and waiting for a clue, Ms....?"

"Howard," she replied.

"Howard," I repeated and confirmed that it was on the tip of my tongue. "My apologies."

"Parent-teacher Coordinator," she continued, shaking my hand vigorously, "and you are *exactly* the man I wanted to see."

"He would've made it... he was just a little too slow."
- Decisive

No sooner she postured to explain to me the reason behind her enthusiastic salutation, when Laurel Reilly came out of her office and looked down the hall and eyeballed me, "Mr. H, a word please?"

"What a nig got to do to get the fuck out of high school?"

"Principal Reilly," Ms. Howard retorted as we both looked at her. Then she returned her gaze to me and said, "Mr. H, I desperately need to speak with you today. Can you *please* see me before you go?" Ms. Howard asked in a very serious tone. "I'll be in my office down the hall to your right, room 117."

It is customary to wait for a motherfucker to answer before you give him the digits, but I guess like she said, she was desperate, so I consented, "You have my word," and she left me with her smile.

As I made my way back to Laurel Reilly, I saw my envelope in her hand with my check on the outside of it.

"Can we talk?" she asked.

I was a grown ass man, yet I was in school and going to the principal's office. She asked me to be seated and instructed Sonora, my Guyanese beauty, to hold her calls as she closed the door, and I thought to myself, *"Just cash the fuckin' check?"*

She started, "This is quite an assistance you're giving us? Don't get me wrong, it's very much appreciated, but may I ask why?"

183

I looked in her eyes and responded, "Because I like you, Laurel Reilly. May I speak freely?"

Her eyes widened and she said, "Please?"

"For the past year that my daughter has been here, I've seen you or heard of you hustling and busting your ass for all the kids in here and you've got the faculty drinking that Kool-Aid too, and that is one hell of an accomplishment. To me, also finding ways to keep the lights on for your side projects, shouldn't be an added burden to your workload. I've chosen to help you there and perhaps ease that burden in exchange for some consideration for my abysmal PTA attendance record." She laughed heartily agreeing with me while I continued, "Seriously, Laurel, if a check is all you need to keep your hustle tight, then just call me."

She looked amazed and at the same time very flattered by the offer. I wasn't bathing her in platitudes, and she knew it. I was just trying to be an instrument she could use and have at her disposal to achieve her admirable goals for the kids.

"Wow," she said, "thank you, Mr. H-"

"Please, Laurel," I interjected, "just H."

"Thank you, H. I really appreciate your kind words, but you know it could be misconstrued under scrutiny that a quid pro quo interest may be in development here."

"Shei?"

She replied, flatly, "Yes."

"Fuck 'em." I said, and I swear she got moist when she heard it.

Holding back a grin, she cautioned, "It may not be that simple, H."

"Why not? 'Cause brown children got all day to deal with Broken Ed's bureaucracy?"

"No, but-"

"But, figure out how you need it to work and I'll get it done. Charitable donations, receipts, found money in a brown paper bag, shit, bake your cookies, and I'll buy 'em, at a premium."

Again, she was very surprised at my candor but appreciated my support, with a smile.

Laurel eyeballed me and after a minute said, "I will see to it that your assistance is put to good use."
"Thank you. Keep up the good work."

I rose and shook her hand and saw myself out. Senora made sure to get my attention, but I was late for my date with Ms. Howard, who was waiting for me around the corner when I made the right. She must have known to look out for me to make sure I did not escape, and I didn't.

"So, how may I help you, Ms. Howard?"
"I would like for you to speak at the Career Day we're having at the rec center I work at, this Saturday, please?"
"This Saturday?"

As she spoke, I couldn't help but be distracted by a plate in her office that looked very familiar to me. When she was done, I agreed to be there and offered to take my plate if she didn't mind. She grinned.

"You've got a shrewd little soldier there, Ms. Howard. Please let her know I took it home."

That Saturday, I debuted my early Christmas gift from Becs in time for Halloween, which was a brand-new *Lamborghini Aventador* in matte grey with black leather interior, red piping, black gunmetal rims and a smoke tint. Mo will have *fun* with this. I arrived at the center in Cambria Heights and pulled into the parking lot catching the eye of every young soul and then some in there. My beloved daughter couldn't make the occasion with me, after all, her services were no longer required. She got what she wanted, so I showed up solo. I parked and walked inside and was immediately greeted by Ms. Howard, through the buzz of on lookers of
185

course, and introduced to her colleagues and noted guests, of which I was he. Everyone there had come to hear me and what I had to say, including two young adults that would influence me significantly. How much are you willing to bet my beloved daughter knew about this, and was instrumental in bestowing upon me the honor? Not one for suits, I wore an ensemble that Emily, our personal fashionista, put together to captivate my audience. And at the appropriate moment, I was invited on stage by Ms. Howard and given the opportunity to go captivate.

"Good morning all. My name is H, and I'm honored to be here..."

I was given a very warm reception as I spoke of myself and a few of my accomplishments, which weren't much more than me sitting on a bag of dough, which essentially was all I was doing. What *we* were doing. We were building infrastructure according to our plan, but it wasn't bubbling yet. My impatient kid, however, thought it was time for a run, a bull run, and so I opened the floor to questions, queries and comments, which began very superficial at first.

"Mr. H, sir, your car outside, the Lambo?"
"Yes?"
"That car is *sick,* yo!"

The audience laughed with me at his enthusiasm.

"Thank you. I'm guessing it got your attention?"
"Yeah."
"Good! Now maybe I," as I pointed to myself, "can keep it? That car outside is one of four at my disposal, which could not be possible without what I've got up here," I said, tapping my temple, "and in here." I held my hand over my heart.

All in the room murmured loudly except for Ms. Howard. It was not known the extent of my wealth since

I had kept myself to a low profile as per the Rebecca Rubin's *'Rags To Eventual Riches'* back story, but she knew Shei, and at half a million dollars a pop, I had just confessed to owning two million dollars in sports transportation alone and my young minds were impressed. Now I needed to impress upon them.

"My colleagues and I at this center are here to inspire you to develop your mind so that you too may fill your pockets if you so desire."

The kids loved that. One student in particular that bent my ear, sat next to a peculiar girl he kept speaking with. She was peculiar in that it seemed the whole time I spoke, she was disinterested and exhausted my talk on her tablet. After the presentation, he came up to me and introduced himself and her.

"Mr. H? Pleased to meet you, sir," he said, offering his hand to me. "I'm Raphael Johnson and this is my sister, Anastasia Movado."

"Pleased to meet you both," I replied, and shook his hand as Anastasia just looked at me.

"In a sea of water, find me THEE... drop."

"I was wondering if I could ask you some more questions, if you don't mind."

"Sure," I replied, still observing the disinterest in Anastasia as he spoke. He unloaded a fusillade of questions on me and I answered each one. He informed me that they were both economic majors at the same high school and he wanted to know if I had any time in my schedule for workshops, which struck a nerve with me as an incredible idea. "Do you think you could fill a room, Raphael?"

He responded, "I don't see why not. I know *we* would be there."

Anastasia didn't seem to share his enthusiasm, but she didn't disagree with him either. I gave him my number and instructed him to coordinate his efforts and get back to me on its progress. Depending on the interest he received, we would speak further. I shook his hand and then offered mine to her and she looked at me and hesitated before she shook it. It was that hesitation, looking in her eyes that triggered it, and it remained with me while I made myself available a while longer as a courtesy to Ms. Howard. She stood beside me proud as all hell, advancing her platform off the attention I brought her. When I felt she had received her notoriety's worth in pastry bribe I exited very ceremoniously through the parade of onlookers I garnered. Raphael got back to me within the week with ten people committed to making it worth my time to meet with them, so I did. Make that eleven, with Anastasia.

Ms. Howard had a small room with a view to the alley that was adjacent to the hall space that we could utilize for our workshop. I brought with me my laptop and Glenn, my freelance IT guy, to make sure everything was groovy the following Saturday, when I stood before the group and captivated them yet again, teaching my young students the basics of Day Trading. The next build, we drew in such a crowd that the workshop in the hall had to cancel, because our small room overflowed into it. Yet throughout the buzz and still showing little interest, Anastasia was in attendance with Raphael and his boys, Jakeem and Rishon. She did not participate but she did pay attention. I know this because on many occasions she seemed disgusted, with a roll of her eyes or a shaking of her head, with students who answered incorrectly. Raphael was sharp though and approached me with his idea to form a trading club, which isn't new, but it was new to him. He wanted to know how I felt it should be done. I offered my suggestion, to which he was very receptive and agreed to assist him *when* he was ready. Anastasia continued to show little interest in my class but was in attendance every time.

"I want your mind and not your money…"
- Chaka Kahn

Chapter Fifteen

Child Of Kate
"The Birth Of Anastasia Movado"

For the past several workshops, I've observed her constantly writing and texting. Her head would be down, and she'd be into her tablet. She doodled a lot on her notebooks and seemed to care less about what I had to say. She intrigued me though, I won't front. Something about this girl was calling to me but every attempt I made to get her involved just fell short. She didn't care much about money, which is to say that she wasn't interested in me, and I didn't see her messing with dudes too tough, other than Pha, Rish and Jah. Anastasia Movado just seemed pissed all the fuckin' time. She and Raphael were a package deal though. Anastasia was unrelated enough to him that he considered her his sister and close enough to him that he wasn't rising without her. He got her attending my Saturday classes regularly, which were going well. I was reaching the kids and I had their respect, which in all honesty is easy, when you're rich like me. They liked the things I possessed but those things didn't define me. You dig? They only got me in the door with them and then I had to do the rest. During one of my workshops one Saturday, I saw that she was tuning me out more than usual. Raphael wasn't there that day, so I figured that was the reason for her distraction. I let it slide. It was clear she was smart, but I just didn't know how to reach her. My classes were voluntary, and she showed up and she did her work. She just could care less to give me the satisfaction of her attention. I could stand up here all day and speculate daddy issues and probably hit the nail on the head. Raphael had confirmed it, plus some issues at home with her mom that didn't help much. I love my daughters more than my life itself and I couldn't understand any daughter with a living father living a reality other than that. I walked up to her and saw she was blogging, so I inquired about it.

"Hey, that's pretty cool. You did that?"

She was doing an online visual promotion thing, and it caught my attention. She looked up with her eyes but never moved her head.

"Obviously."

"It's pretty good," I said. "It reminds me of some of my daughter's art through college."

"You have a daughter?" she asked as if the thought couldn't make sense.

"I have two beautiful girls and they're my sole purpose for living, "S-O-U-L," I spelled, and smiled.

She returned to blogging and as I stepped away, I heard her say, *"Lucky* girls."

I asked Raphael about it later and he confirmed that she did have a blog and he gave me her site info, so that night I went on it and read her stuff. This girl was amazingly creative. Her ideas were bright and her perspective and knack for presentation was slick. The following Saturday, we were helping with decorations at the center for the holiday food pantry, which again Raphael wasn't there for, but she was. The money part was licked. I was going to write a check to the center on behalf of the kids for this worthwhile endeavor so that it turned out very profitable. Face it, you ain't paying for a dance, baking fuckin' cookies, unless they're made of hash. And there won't be a whole lot of yuletide glee if you can't pay the bills. We finished quickly and again, I saw her doing her thing and aside from eye contact, I let it go. Kate was with me today and as usual, she aroused a lot of attention from the kids attending to the staff at the center. We were doing volunteer work on a Saturday in the hood. A sort of give back to the community from me, but Kate wouldn't do dress down. In her fuckin' pajamas and bunny slippers you were still ejaculating. Bad analogy. Point is, no matter what she wore, there was a fetish for it. She was in a beige body con dress with dark shades and matching Louboutin pumps. I'd just seen her naked and it was a brick outside and I'm telling you, she still was under that dress and was unconcerned to deny it.

I leaned into Kate, lowering my eyes to her breasts and she responded, "The chill gave it away," and I agreed, nodding fiendishly. "Would you like to warm me up?" she purred.

Astonished, I responded, "Fuck?"

"Yes, lover, that's what I'm offering," she teased, laughing as I walked away.

In her defense she had a last-minute engagement for the holidays and wanted to spend time with me prior to it. Truthfully, I think she was punishing me for not playing hooky with her, so, Bo Peep decided to follow her sheep to work today, especially since I was giving gifts. Since we met, I've become her favorite hobby with most of her free time spent consuming my mind, which has made me exceedingly grateful to her. And, this is the most my class has been attentive in a while. I noticed a little eye volley thing going on between Anastasia and Kate. I wasn't sure what it was nor was I looking to get in the middle of it.

"Sound like famous last words," I thought.

I was walking around the room in discussion with the class and again I saw her tablet and the imagery on it blew my mind.

"You did this?" I interrupted her asking, "May I?"

The look I received as she handed me her tablet was that of *distrust,* not dislike, which was good because it meant I could be allowed to earn it.

"I could really use your talents promoting some of our activities and for PR for my company, Anastasia. Do you think you might be interested?"

"I've done it now."

192

She lifted her head and looked at me and said, "Not interested."

"How come, if you don't mind me asking?" as I slid her tablet back into her outstretched hand.

"I'm busy," which she said like she really was busy.

"How busy?"

"What's it to you?" she asked as she was very annoyed.

"I don't imagine it taking too much more of your free time," I answered. "I would love to hire you as a consultant."

At this point not only did I have the attention of all the class but Queen Bitch II herself tilted her shades down to reveal her aqua blue eyes.

"I believe you've got very marketable skills, Anastasia, and this could be an opportunity for development of those skills and not to mention a paycheck."

She stated emphatically, "You can't afford me."

The class laughed and so did Kate. In her zeal to hand me my ass she might have also handed me some leverage.

Her friend next to her said, "You should try it, Ana. Shit, he payin' you."

Anastasia repeated, staring right at me, "Like I said, *you* can't afford me."

"Can't afford you or you won't *allow* me to afford you?"

I must have really hit a nerve because she glared at me with those *'go-kill-yourself'* eyes that all teen girls seem to have perfected, but interestingly enough she did not disrespect me. Kate was on the phone and stopped talking to observe over her shades. Anastasia saw her and I sensed some fear, but I couldn't tell you why. I mean, I know Kate's a crazy bitch, yeah, but what about her unnerved this girl? I offered her an out and a way to

193

save face to the class as it was my intention to reach her and to offer support, not to embarrass her.

"OK, that's a fair assumption on your part," I conceded, "but considering what you know of the work that may be involved will you at least name your price?"

Her eyes went back and forth between her tablet, Kate and I and I started to think maybe I should fight another day and another way, but I hated to back off feeling on the verge of a breakthrough, so I pressed.

"What will it take to get you to work for me, Anastasia?"

Her friends urged her, "Come on, Ana."

"You want me to work for you?" she questioned.

"Yes, I do."

She tilted her head up at me as I stood in front of her at her desk and said, "I want $50 an hour."

I backed up, "$50?"

This wasn't about money, but fuck if I knew what it was about as I heard Kate say, "I'll call you back."

"Wow, that's an awful lot of money for your services, I think."

Her anger returned and she glared at me. Whatever nerve I just hit again, this time made her oblivious to Kate, indicating to me that her issues were deeply distracting, and I had become the personification of whatever grievance she couldn't resolve. I had to figure this shit out, and so I countered with $10.

She said, "Please, I can make that working at McDonald's!"

The class erupted in laughter and she regained momentum in her favor.

"Ok, my low ball didn't work," so I went up.

"$15."

194

She inquired, "Are you deaf? *Debes ser sordo.*"

That was an interesting choice in adjectives. Kate sat still and sophisticated with her legs crossed and her shades on. I was on my own to break this kid.

"$18," I said, fighting my sensorial challenges.

Staring at her tablet and faking looking busy, she added, "Wow, not just deaf..."

Ooh, the class loved that! She was handing me my ass and making me look really bad, but here's the curious development that I kept my focus on. Anastasia and I were managing to get past our pretensions with each other. It was true that her insults cut deeper the higher my numbers got to hers but after so many Saturdays she was finally talking to me.

"Why should I pay you your price, Anastasia?"

"You're the one that wants me to work for you right?" she barked.

"Yes, I do," I replied, "but are you worth it?"

The look in her eyes changed and she hesitated. She didn't seem to know how to answer me. Anything smart would be inaccurate and she seemed lost. So, I pressed.

"Are you?"

She answered, "You seem to think so."

"Perhaps, but maybe she'd do it for $18," as I pointed to her friend next to her. She looked at her friend and then right back at me as I continued and turned around and pointed, "And maybe him for $15. *Te prometo que no soy,*" I replied and tapped my ear.

Anastasia's eyes widened and she froze and looked at me just at that moment a kid said, "Shit, man, I'll do it for ten. Fuck McDonald's!"

"Shut up, Rishon!" she shouted.

The class blew up and she seemed uncertain. I had pointed to members of Raphael's trading group who

195

were willing to undercut her value. My comparisons to her threatened her worth and she confirmed my suspicions. Raphael had informed me that her parents divorced when she was young and that her father pretty much abandoned her for his new family. I offered $18. She looked at her friend who would work for $18, and then across from her to Jakeem who would accept $15, and then to Rishon who would beat them all out for ten, and her anger returned. I turned to look at Kate, who raised an eyebrow at me, which was short for, "I hope you've got a plan?" and suddenly I did.

I petitioned, "Class, let's stop right here and discuss this, please."

Anastasia seemed interrupted when I looked at her. I wasn't sure what I had just prevented, but the look on her face made me feel better.

"Here you have what we call an *impasse* between parties. The party of Anastasia wants $50 an hour and the party of H is only offering eighteen. How much of a difference is that?"

The class answered, "$32!"

"Righteous, $32. Now, this does not mean that her request is outrageous or mine absurd, it only means that we need to sit and further discuss what the product or the service that's needed or being arbitrated over is worth."

My class listened attentively as I spoke, especially Anastasia.

"I would like Anastasia to consult for me to help me grow my business presence and PR, Public Relations. I can afford anyone I want, but I want her. Are we clear on that?"

My class nodded their understanding as I made sure to make eye contact with all my budding adults in the room.

"As a result of this, I'm compelled to stay at the table and negotiate. Now, I'm going to make some presumptions on behalf of you, Anastasia, and say that you want to work for me because, hell, I'm *swell* and I'm easy to work for." I said, grinning. "What you say, you agree?"

She stared at me as if she needed more coaxing to play, but finally submitted to my charms, all the while fighting back her desire to smile and responded, "Yes, I heard you're a *swell* guy to work for."

The class blew up from the way she mimicked me and when they had settled down, I continued.

"So, we want to negotiate in what we call *good faith*. Does anyone know what that means?"

Rishon responded, "It's when two parties each compromise their position in the favor of the opposing party in an attempt to reduce the distance of the impasse."

We all took a beat and I was shocked as fuck as to the accuracy of his explanation because he couldn't have looked it up that quickly and he simply didn't. Kate stared at him.

"Wow? Rishon, that is absolutely correct?"

"I know," he retorted, and went back to being a comedian. I made a note to pay attention to him since Kate already had.

"So, Anastasia, we began with you at $50 and me at $10, right?"

She nodded, "Right."

"Since then, I've offered $15 and $18 and you've remained at $50. Would you like to make an offer now in good faith to meet me?"

She stared at me and answered, "$40."

I stared back and offered, "$20," to which she countered with $35.

"Ok. Here is where I want to take some time out to discuss fiscal responsibility for a business," I said.

"Every employer has a built-in cap that he can't afford to exceed in salaries, like a salary cap for let's say a sports team. I have a salary cap in mind for Anastasia that she is still exceeding. Now this does not mean that she isn't worth her price. It just means taking into consideration my bottom line, which is," I turned to Rishon for an answer.

"Profit after expenses," he responded.

"Correct... *again*," I thought. "Class, my bottom line is my maximum amount I can afford to pay an employee, proportional to the income he or she generates. The more income an employee generates is the more that employee is worth to a company and their income commensurate with it. Y'all get that?" I looked around and murmuring nods were all I saw, so I followed, "Not every employee is a franchise player, but they all want franchise money. We good?"

That analogy got more of the response I was looking for.

"Ite, cool. Cool. So, Anastasia, since I have made every attempt to make you happy and sought to the best of my ability to meet your expectations in salary, is it possible that you can accept a figure that is within my bottom line, please?"

She took her time and gave it some thought, occasionally making eye contact with me as she did, and when she was ready, she said, "Ok, $25," and then stared me down and declared, "take it or leave it!"

I admired her tactic as I pondered her number. Since I had met her, I had been giving her my full attention and I haven't let up. She liked it, but she couldn't trust it, so she's been pushing me away to see if I would quit. What is it with women and testing me, GOD? If I chose to quit, then I didn't really care about her, and if I didn't meet her price, then she really didn't matter to me. I wasn't her father.

"Congratulations! I suppose you've found your worth, Miss Movado," I said, peeking the faintest smile as she took my hand. "Now, will you please lose the attitude?"

"Sure," she said, "since you're such a swell guy."

I walked away and the class celebrated Anastasia's victory for standing her ground and getting paid. I hoped her win meant more to her than just that and that maybe I had gained her confidence to some degree. During their celebrations, I discerned that she was visibly shaken. She avoided eye contact with Kate, who had been staring at her the entire time and during her phone call for a car. When Kate was done, she stood up and came over to me and slowly placed her right hand on my lower abdomen. With her head next to mine, she whispered in my ear that she was leaving and that we'd talk later, to which I agreed. Then she leaned in even closer and kissed me on my cheek and paused. This got the class quiet. Kate's subtle yet obvious public display of affection for me was not only her foreplay but her assertion of her place at my side. With Anastasia now to be around, she was simply marking her territory. Kate's possessive ways were entirely for my benefit, I've discovered, to protect me from people and circumstances that she feels could do me harm. The only other woman she'd allowed close to me was Rebecca and that was probably because she was already here. I don't think she's quite warmed up to Amanda, just yet, and Amanda is married. Maureen seems to be of no concern to her. We aren't exclusive Kate and I. She is *done* with being anyone's property. Our bond had set her free and she was enjoying spreading her wings, very much like Rebecca. I think she saw sex as her spoils that I had earned the right to with the friendship we had made, and since most of the time it was her initiating it, I believed she was at long last enjoying it and enjoying the power it presented to her. She turned and was walking to the door and I began to get back to my instructions when I saw her stop. She acknowledged no consequence for her continued interruption of my class and headed down the aisle. Row by row, Kate passed with the slowing rhythmic clicking of her $5,000 pumps on the hardened terrazzo floor, growing more and more ominous the further away she got from me until she stood silently in front of her.

"Anastasia, right?"

Anastasia reluctantly raised her head and replied, "Yes."

Still peering at her through her shades, she introduced herself, "Hi, I'm Kate Summers," holding out her hand and lowering her shades with her other hand to reveal her deep sensual blue eyes, and while leaning forward wearing her sinister grin declared, "your *other* boss. Welcome to the family."

The look on Anastasia's face was priceless. Her mouth opened, yet she remained speechless as she watched Kate turn and look at me, then walk straight out the door. All that remained was the fading rhythm of her heels down the hallway and the scent of her perfume.

Rishon sang, "Ooh, Ana...you done fucked up now!"

The class fell out and I watched Anastasia put her head down on the desk probably fearing for her ass.

"Your *other* boss ain't *having* your shit, Ana!" Jakeem suggested, "You better get right!"

After airing their hysteria, I called for everyone to settle down and the questioning began.

"Yo, Mr. H."

"Yeah, man, what's up?"

Rishon asked, "Kate, that's your girl?"

I responded, "Kate's nobody's *girl,* brother."

"But you are hittin' that though, right?"

They all fell out again and they would receive no answer from me as I regained order and continued with

200

the lesson. When class was over, everyone said their goodbyes and filed out with their gifts I had given them, except for Anastasia who remained in her seat. Her friend had also left her, so it was just the two of us. I stood at my desk collecting my stuff when she decided at last to approach me.

"What would you like me to do?"

She was timid and uncertain and nothing like the furious opponent that had challenged me a short time ago, when I responded, "I would imagine you can hold your head up for starters? You sound awfully down for someone who just went first pick in the draft."

Anastasia barely moved.

"Is something wrong?"

She didn't answer and continued to avoid eye contact.

I exhaled, "I'm hungry. Can I interest you in a bite to eat? You can sit and talk, or you can watch or blog over a meal or ice cream or iced coffee or anything that'll put a smile on your face."

Still there was no response.

"Please?"

She looked at me, finally. I could see in her big beautiful brown eyes that she had no idea what to do with her new-found winnings. I imagined she had aimed so high assuring herself she'd be disappointed that she had no contingency for winning. She beat me and still felt like a loser, it seemed, and something needed to be done about that.

"Fine."

I looked at her all bundled up in her jacket and confirmed, "Ok, fine."

We walked out of class and out of the center to my truck parked outside in the brisk December afternoon, and she remained quiet. When I held the door for her, she looked at me as if the act surprised her.

"Bad habit," I said, "you know, respect?"

Anastasia got in and sat still clutching her knapsack and settled in. I closed her door and went around the front and climbed up into the driver's seat.

"You wanna let you mom know you're with me, in case she has any concerns?"
"No."
"Would you mind if I did?"
"I can find my own way home if you want."
"What I want, Anastasia, is for you, a teenager, *a minor,* to alert your parent that you are with a man she does not know should she have any concerns. It's what I would expect from my daughters and it's what I expect from you."

She gave me that look again and took her phone out and texted her mom as I requested. When her mother replied she showed me the text. It read '*Ok.*'

"Thank you, Anastasia."

It occurred to me that she might have only been cooperating because she was working for me now and not because she wanted to, and I was cool with that. We drove to a nearby diner and when the waitress came over, I told Anastasia she could order whatever she wanted.

"I'm not hungry."
"Really? Oh, yeah, that's right," I said, sarcastically, "you ate yesterday."

She glared at me when the waitress laughed.

"Well, are you thirsty?"

She eyeballed me and ordered a shake.

The waitress asked. "Would you like whip cream with that, hun?"
"Yes, please," she replied.

'Yes, please' we were getting somewhere. She had manners. *This* was good. I ordered the same and an order of fries.

"What exactly do you want me to do for your business?"
"I'm not exactly sure. I was hoping you might have some ideas," I responded after sitting silently, waiting for her to break the ice. "Here's the deal."

I ran down everything about us and what we were doing, being new and private and all that, and she listened attentively.

"A thought that occurred to me was to view my company through the eyes of a young innovative mind. I'm thinking that mind is yours."
"Me?"
"Yes."
"I don't understand?"
"I want you to see what we do and tell me what you think we can do better."
"I don't know anything about investing. How am I supposed to do that?"
I looked at her and said, "By learning. Learn what I do," as I pointed at myself, "and learn how my business works and help me grow it yet keep me under the radar. I don't know everything, Anastasia, and I don't want to? But all too often, I think I'm expected to. Often times I fuck up."

"You do realize I'm a *teenager,* right? A *minor?"* she said, looking at me closely and adding the quotations with her fingers.

I laughed and surrendered, "Give me *that* right there, about *everything* you see around me, and I'll be satisfied."

She giggled like she was about to hand me my ass.

"What?"

"You want me to give you *my* opinion about *everything* I see around *you?"* she questioned. "And if I don't like it?"

"What you see or the job?"

"Both," she answered, curiously.

"Change it or quit."

My response surprised her and the waitress returning with our order. Anastasia questioned and deliberated internally why would he go through all of this trouble to hire her only to allow her the freedom to quit whenever she felt like it?

"Why me?"

"That answer is simple," he said, arranging the items in front of them. "You are the only person I've met, that's not impressed with my money."

"I'm not," she said, confirming.

"I just said that," he said, reconfirming. "That's why you will be honest with me, and *honesty* I trust!"

She paused, still deliberating and took a sip of her shake, then looked at me and swallowed.

"I think you're a dick."

I paused. Was she testing it out already? I hoped not. Maybe she changed her mind and wanted me to fire her? I had to come up with something quick because she was waiting.

"I'll do better than *swell.*"

Anastasia furrowed her brow as that answer was nowhere near the answer that she expected, then she blushed.

I picked up the basket in front of me and asked, "Some fries to go with that shake?"

Reluctantly she laughed and I looked into her eyes and saw I had made a breakthrough and that she might finally be warming up to me. I was grateful for my daughters. I've had a lot of experience fuckin' up and reconciling with them and I was fortunate to be able to put some of that learning into practice with her. I hoped I had made my point that I was not backing down and that I wanted to be someone she could possibly depend on one day. Raphael believed in her and I believe in him, but he would never allow himself to grow constantly worrying about her. He needed to make sure she was safe for both their sakes and I needed to make sure she was mine for me.

"Sure," she said, and I had some too.

When we finished our first business meeting, I dropped her home. We pulled up in front of her house and there was a car in the driveway, so I guessed her mom was home. She didn't seem thrilled to be home, which was reassuring that this teenager that I was just warring with might actually have enjoyed my company. I left it alone and this time didn't press. I told her to wait as I got out of the truck and got her door.

"Hey, *Nana,* you have my number and here's another gift for you."

She hesitated when she took it.

"It's the address of a company apartment if you ever need a place to just get away for any reason, no matter what time of day, it's available to you. I will give the doorman your name. He has the spare key. The day you use that key, you hold on to it."

I'm not sure what that look was for that she gave me. I realized I fucked up her name or it might have been my unsolicited act of kindness, but she accepted both when she took the paper from me and said, "Thank you," and walked to her front door.

I called to her, "Hey, Nana?"

"Hey?"

"You still think I'm a dick?"

She looked at me and then turned her back and replied, "Don't ruin it... *boss!*"

I smiled and watched her go inside her house before I got in my truck and drove away.

"Hi, honey."

"Hi, mom."

"I saw you in the window, who was that?"

"He's the man I texted you about."

"Is he that rich guy that Ralphy is learning to invest with?"

"How did you-? Yes, he hired me today to be a consultant for his company."

"Oh, honey, that's great!" putting her hands on her daughter's shoulders. "This could be so great for you, learning how to invest! You'll make some money and make new friends," she said, with encouragement, "and maybe get you out of your shell?"

She paused, "He's cute too!"

Anastasia glared at her mother with loathing and walked away.

"Ana? Ana, come on!" she pleaded, *"Mi hija,* I meant nothing by it. Ana!"

Anastasia went upstairs to her room and shut the door and put her bag down. She sat on her bed and looked at the paper H gave her, still clutched in her hand. She opened it and put the address in her phone and saw where in the city it was and the directions to get there. She saved it under H's name and took the paper to her desk. There was a new unopened letter from her father there. She used a key from around her neck and took out her diary from one of the drawers and leafed through the pages and found another letter from her father and placed it with that one. She then leafed through the pages again and found another letter and removed that one as well. This she continued to do until all the pages were turned and all the letters were removed. Anastasia then placed the paper H gave her in today's entry date and closed her diary and put it back in the drawer and locked it. She then gathered up all her father's letters and threw them in the wastepaper basket.

"At the end of all of this, the narrative is going to read that God did me a fuckin' favor. Unfortunately, that's not how it feels right now."

Chapter Sixteen

No Banging My Teacher
"The Birth Of Anastasia Movado"

"You're late!" she bitched. "You live down the block!"

"Technically not, but I'll get you there don't worry about it. Let's go! Let's go! Let's go! Come on, get in! Sit down! Shut up and enjoy the ride!"

"Ughhhhhhhhh! Oh, my *God,* you're annoying!"

We raced through the neighborhood avoiding the buses, the school buses and Sanitation and pulled up to the front of her school in enough time, just as I predicted.

"You've got me out here like a celebrity."

"You are now. It's your job, babe. Attract attention and look good, so I don't have to."

She tried not to move her head at all towards the eyes that were peering in at her and said, "I could use a friggin' Camry right about now."

We laughed together as there was still a little time to spare as we looked out the windows.

"You good, right?"
Anastasia replied, "Yeah, I'm good."
"Got money?"

Anastasia chuckled.

"What?" he asked. "It's a habit, I know. My bad."

"You must drive your daughters crazy," she wondered.

"Yeah, they probably think I suck too. If I don't say the right shit, I get an attitude. If I don't say the right shit fast enough, I get more of an attitude, so?"

Anastasia paused and looked me in my eyes and said, "I don't think you suck, boss, well... at least not today... right now," and laughed.

"Funny," I said as I couldn't help but stare at her and it caught her attention.

"What?"

"You're happy, Nana."

"Ok? Why do you say that?"

"It shows on your face and in your smile. Far cry from the *grumpy puss* I met a short time ago."

"I was not a grumpy- whatever the heck you just said. Grumpy-"

"Puss!" I exclaimed.

"Was not."

"Was to"

"Was not!" she emphasized with her chin turning up at me.

I chuckled and said, "Keep smiling. It suits you."

Nana blushed looking at me and I took the pressure off of her by changing the subject, "Where the guys at?"

"Ah, *they* inside already."

"Ok. Ready for your grand entrance, mami?"

She stared at me and slowly nodded, and I opened my door and got out to open hers. She stepped out with her hand in mine like the celebrity she was and put her bag on her shoulder.

"Oh, there's Ms. Velez!" she said, waving to her. "Boss, I want you to meet her!"

"Yeah, sure," I replied as I was distracted by the paparazzi.

"Hi, Ms. Velez."

"Hi, Ana. How are you?"

"I'm good!"

I turned around to see *another* beautiful Latina standing before me.

"Oh, I gotta hit that!"

209

"Ms. Velez, I'd like you to meet H. H, this is Ms. Velez."

I extended my hand to her and she said, "Elaine. Nice to meet you."

"Same here, Elaine."

"Ms. Velez is my Economics teacher, my *favorite* teacher," Anastasia said, proudly.

"That is quite a distinction, Elaine. I've concluded that Nana can be very particular in her designations."

Nana smacked me.

"See my point?"

"I just started interning for his company as a PR Consultant," Anastasia said, proud of her designation.

"Oh, wow, that's *great,* Ana. *Congratulations!* What line of work are you in, H?

"I'm in *private asset management*, Elaine."

"I see. Ana, that's perfect for you! She is extremely smart and perceptive in my class. I'm sure she'll be a fine addition to your firm."

"She already is."

"Well, if you'll excuse me. It was very nice meeting you, H."

"It was a pleasure meeting you, Elaine."

She turned to Anastasia, "See you later, *Nana."*

Anastasia blushed some more and waited for Elaine to leave and then interrogated me.

"Were you checking out my teacher?"

"Come again?" Returning my attention to her, I asked, "What are you talkin' about?"

"You were, weren't you?"

I confessed, "Elaine is very pretty."

"Ughhhhhhhhh, no banging my teacher! What is with you? I have to live here and *her* I like!" she stated agitated and annoyed.

"Seriously? No. Nana, seriously? Nana!"

Anastasia smiled and walked away into the crowd, "Maybe!"

"Nana! Well, ok, which ones *don't* you like?"

"I'm not listening to you!"

"Text me if you need a lift!"

"Yep!" she yelled.

"Oh, you heard *that* though," I said as I closed her door.

"Hey, Denise," Elaine said, reaching the top of the steps at the entrance to the school building.

"Elaine, who was that?"

"Who?" she asked, curious as to what she may have missed.

"Girl, don't play with me! You know who I'm talking about. That guy right *there* you was just talking to."

Elaine started laughing, "That was H, Ana's boss. She's interning with his firm."

"What firm? What does he do?"

"He's a Trader."

"A what?"

"Wall Street, girl," she responded to Denise's economic ignorance.

"What? How'd that child get that job? He is cute!"

Elaine laughed, "Get your eyes out his pockets!"

"Hi, Ms. Velez," a group of students greet as they're making their way up the stairs. "Hi, Ms. Reynolds."

"Hey, baby girl. Good morning." She continued with Elaine, "And my eyes are *way* beyond his pockets, and do you see that car he's driving?"

"It's hard to miss."

"How can you be so *calm,* Elaine?"

"So, he's rich, and?"

"And? Girl, you play your cards right, you might get yourself a *piece* and get the hell up outta here from these damn kids! He was checking you out too!"

Elaine was flattered but retorted, "No offense, but guys like him have women just like you, throwing their drawers at them all day long and I'm not trying to be no man's flavor of the month."

"Shit, it'll be the best tasting month of his life!"

211

They laughed.

"Denise, it's *too* early, and too cold out here. I don't have time for this. I gotta tend to these *damn kids*."

"Ooh, look! Look, he's wavin'… Hi!" Denise frantically exaggerated a wave at him.

Elaine looked over her shoulder and returned his smile.

"We all serve a purpose to somebody and that purpose makes us important to them. The day that purpose stops being served is the day they forget your name."

Chapter Seventeen

The Hit
"The Birth Of Yvette Williams"

"I need someone over there to ensure that we're covered. Our volume has picked up and I need a buffer between you and our principal. Amanda, you need a stop at that office. It must be done!"

"You're right," Amanda agreed.

Rebecca paused, understandably frustrated as they heard her sigh through the speaker, *"I'll call you when I have something."*

"Ite, talk soon, Becs."

"Bye, Rebecca." Amanda and Josh responded.

"Ok, cool. So, Amanda, Josh, we'll wait to hear from her."

"Josh, limit our exposure today, in fact, until Rebecca is happy, please," Amanda ordered.

"Yes, ma'am," Josh agreed and excused himself.

"Thanks, Josh."

"So... Grimmy, when she gon be happy?" Amanda asked.

"She's just carrying a lot of responsibility and something slipped past or more like fell short, that's all. We will get someone in here and make up the hit." I said as I caught a view of the floor through Amanda's window. "Look at them," I pointed, "everybody out there is nervous as shit and I've seen that look before."

Amanda asked, "What are you going to do?"

I picked up the phone to call Amy in and answered, "Right now, order lunch for everyone. It's harder to worry when your belly is full."

"No, you know what I mean," Amanda said, urging a serious response from me.

"Yes, I do know what you mean. We are going to wait-to-hear-from-Becs." I continued, "Run, tell that."

Amanda did not like my reply and it probably sounded harsher than I had intended it, but on this issue,

which is the other basis for *all* employment with me, I
needed it clear that Rebecca's word is *final. Do not* fuck
with that.

She paused, then got up and said, "Yessir... *Mr.
H!*"

"*Fuck!*"

Nana was in class when her phone vibrated with a
message from Kate. *Call me ASAP!* Once the class was
over, she called Kate.

"Hey, Kate, what's up?"
"*Hey, sweetie, have you spoken to H?*"
"No, why?"
"*We took a pretty big hit today.*"
"What do you mean?"
"*They were way over exposed on a position. Josh
couldn't cover and they had to dump it. He lost two
million. It's a mess!*"
"Oh shit, for real? Who did that?"
"*One of the new traders. Rebecca is ballistic-*"
"And H?"
"*I think he's just trying to calm things down. Hey,
you win some you lose some you know?*"
"Shit?"
"*So, avoid the office today, ok. Text him. If he needs
you he will let you know.*"
"What about you?"
"*I gotta cover my ass and close some deals. FYI.
I'm going to draw from his personal account.*"
"How much?"
"*About half a mill-ish?*"
"Shit Kate, that will make a 2.5 million-dollar
hole," Anastasia said in disbelief.
"*Wow? Smart girl. You are learning! And yes, I
know, more pain. Anyway, sweetie I gotta go. Talk
later.*"

Anastasia made her way to class obviously disturbed by the news frantically texting Raphael to tell him.

RAPHAEL: *Damn Ana, that's a lot of fucking money! Is he ok?*
ANASTASIA: *Dunno. Crazy over there. Can't get a straight answer. Ttyl."*

Anastasia walked into her economics class with Elaine Velez, who noticed something was wrong and asked her about it.

She replied, "Bad day at the office."

"With H?" Anastasia nodded her reply and Elaine offered her sympathy, "Oh, I'm sorry to hear that Anastasia," she said. "Is he ok?"

"I'm not sure," Anastasia replied, dejected. "He hasn't reached out to me and he's not answering my texts."

Elaine responded, "Maybe because he knows you're in class or he could be busy," but none of her explanations seemed to comfort Anastasia who appeared unusually worried about a situation she had no control over. Elaine whispered, "Tell you what, when he does answer you can excuse yourself from class and take the call, ok."

Anastasia was very surprised by the gesture and graciously accepted, "Thank you!"

Elaine shushed her, "Just between us," and smiled.

Anastasia took her seat and impatiently texted Amy. *Any news?*

AMY: *Not yet, but Rebecca is here.*
ANASTASIA: *That's not good.*
AMY: *Nope. I think he might get fired. They're not trading right now. Rebecca suspended trading."*

"Shit!" Anastasia said to herself and texted Kate. *Anything new?*

KATE: *Meeting. Talk later.*

Anastasia worried because she hadn't heard from H and it wasn't like him to not be in touch. She also worried that the happiness she had been enjoying lately might be in jeopardy having grown very fond of her new bosses and her job and being included in something special where she had a voice and a feeling of self-worth. She raised her hand and asked for the bathroom pass.

Elaine asked as Anastasia walked up to her, "Anything?"

She answered, "Someone might get fired."

"Aye, no!" Realizing Anastasia was deeply upset by the situation, Elaine gave her class a break and followed her into the hallway to talk to her, *"Mija,* I know you can't give me the details of the problem you're having but I'm sure it will work out."

"He lost a lot of money," Ana looked at her and stated confiding in her. "Two million on a bad trade not including draws, which it looks like he'll need to cover out of his personal account."

"Oh, my God, that's a lot of money!" cried Elaine.

"His attorney is at the office and he's not texting me back."

"Shit," Elaine agreed, "I can see why?"

"Everyone I reach out to keep telling me that they'll 'talk to me later.' Nobody is telling me anything other than that, so I don't know *what's* going on. What if he goes out of business and I lose my job?"

Elaine assured her, "Ana, relax or you're going to worry yourself sick? I'm sure everything will be fine. I would imagine that his office is probably very *crazy* right now and it has *nothing* to do with you."

Anastasia insisted, "He can at least text me 'I'm ok?'"

Elaine reasoned with her, *"Mija,* would you feel like talking if you lost that kind of money?"

Anastasia thought about it, "I guess not."

"And you would probably be trying really hard to get that money back right now, wouldn't you?"

Anastasia answered, "Yeah."

"So, it's very likely that's why he hasn't called you!"

"You think he's broke?"

"Aw, baby, *no sé qué pasa con su dinero,* but I hope not?" Adjusting her tactic Elaine said, "Listen, they say *'no news is good news'.* Let's just wait to find out before we jump to conclusions, ok?"

"Fine," Anastasia retorted.

"Ok, *mija, vete al baño…* hurry back." Elaine ordered, directing her to the bathroom to get back to her class.

"No, I'm good." Elaine stood there confused and Anastasia told her, *"Esto es lo que quería. Gracias."*

Flattered by her influence on her, Elaine hugged Anastasia full of encouragement and they walked back into the classroom together. After school, Anastasia met up with Raphael to go to his house. He too was worried and worried about her, knowing how much H really meant to her. She felt safe and secure with him and the thought of losing him terrified her.

"You should eat something, Ana," he urged as she lay curled up on his bed. "It'll make you feel better."

"I'm not hungry. Why hasn't he called me?"

"He's busy, Ana. Just be cool. It'll be ite," is what he told her, but his mom he texted differently.

Anastasia's phone rang but her excitement faded quickly.

"Hey, baby girl."

"Hi, Ms. Johnson."

"Ralphy told me what happened. How are you doin'?"

"What if he doesn't need me anymore? What if he goes away too?"

"Oh, baby, you can't think like that."

She does her best to console her on the phone, but Anastasia breaks down, so Raphael leaves his room to

217

give her some privacy. Lynette doesn't know H and has never met him, but she has heard the many things her son has mentioned about him, which she hasn't paid much mind. Whoever he is, it was clear the impact he had made on Anastasia in the short time she's known him, and that is what she was most concerned about.

"Baby girl, you've got to be strong and pull yourself together. Just give him some time. I'm sure he will be ok. But, listen, I've still got some stuff to get done before I make my way home. You gon be there?"

"Yes, I'll wait for you," Anastasia promised.
"Ok, then, I'll see you soon."

Raphael tried to make her smile, even acting the fool, but it wasn't working.

"He's not your father, Ana," he stated, then thought about it afterwards and prayed she took it the right way. After a moment of silence, she did.

"Ralphy, if he's not around anymore, this too wasn't my fucking fault!"

"You can't think like that," he advised.

"Come on! If I have no job, what other fucking reason would he have to still be around?"

Raphael had no answer for that one as her phone rang again and she sat up urgently, wiping the tears from her eyes.

"Kate?"
"Hey, sweetie, what's up?"
"Is he ok?"
"Yeah, he'll be fine." Kate, hearing her sniffling and the sound of her voice asked, *"Are you- are you crying?"*

"I don't want him to go away, Kate," she cried. I didn't do this!"
"Do what, Ana? What's wrong?"
"I don't want him to leave!"

218

Raphael stayed with her this time second guessing that his decision to leave the first time might have been insensitive.

"Leave? H?"

"He lost a lot of money and if he's broke, I won't have a job and he won't need- me."

Kate paused to understand her concern, then said adoringly, *"Oh, sweetheart, you've got it all wrong. H isn't going anywhere? I can assure you of that... and you're definitely staying in my life!"*

Anastasia chuckled somewhat.

"Aw, you poor thing! Listen, stay by the phone and I'll call you back."

"Ok."

Raphael asked, "What did she say?"

"She said that 'I got it all wrong. H is fine and he's not leaving me,'" she said, wiping her tears, "and neither is she.'"

"See? I told you to just chill," Raphael said, feeling much better himself too.

Kate called H at the office and interrupted his meeting with Rebecca.

"Hey, babe, what are you doing now?"

"Hey, just reviewing some stuff with Becs. Why?"

"I need you to stop that and call Anastasia, right now. She's freaking out!"

"What happened?"

"For some reason, she thinks that you're broke and that you're going to fire her and leave her."

"What?" he asked, chuckling. "Where the fuck did she get that shit from?"

"I don't know? You didn't take her calls?"

"Oh."

"And that's not what I told her when I spoke to her this morning, but that's where she went with it. Can you please call her now?"

"Ok."

Kate repeated her request firmly, *"Now!"*

"Yeah! Ok, bye."

Anastasia's phone rang again and this time her face lit up.

"Boss?"

"Hey, Nana, what's goin on?"

"Hey?"

"What's up, babe?"

"Nothing. Everything?"

"Yeah? Listen, I'm sorry I haven't been in touch with you today. I didn't mean to worry you."

"Are you ok?"

"Yes, I'm- I'm fine. It's been hectic here but I'm fine, and you're fine and we, you and me, we're fine. You dig?"

She laughed as he seemed to know how to find stupid yet cute things to say to get her to.

"Yes," she said, finally comforted for the first time today.

"You and I will need to talk about this soon. Please, just give me a moment to take care of some things and we will, I promise. I'm not broke and I'm not firing you and I'm not leaving you. Ok?"

"Ok."

"Now- you did your homework?"

"Ughhhhhhhhh!"

"See," he said, laughing, *"You over there messin' around worrying about me when you should be worrying about yourself. You need to take care of that. Plus, it'll distract you."*

"Fine."

"Fine. And no more crying, ok? Babe?"

"Ok."

220

"Good. Listen, I've got to go. Remember what I said."

"I will."

"Ok, bye."

"Feel better now," Raphael asked, seemingly reassuring himself.

"Yes," she replied, seemingly beaming with joy.

Raphael asked, grudgingly, "Wanna eat?"

Anastasia looked at him and answered coyly, "Yes?"

"Thank you, God! I'm fucking starving, yo? Damn!"

Finally, *he* got her to laugh and hysterically too as she jumped out of bed and followed him downstairs, texting while listening to him complain about his stomach. Her phone beeped: *You're welcome, sweetie.*

She was at the Starbucks counter waiting on her Venti Caramel Macchiato, her usual order, the next morning when Rebecca walked in and stood near the door in her usual designer dress and matching pumps. She used her app on her phone and took the foamy overpriced concoction with one hand and her outdated Gucci bag in the other and turned to leave.

"Rebecca Abigail Rubin," she stated walking up to her.

"This bitch is carrying a fuckin' Birkin bag... compared to my shit," she thought, envious of the handbag on her left arm. *"She on the list? And red bottom pumps and some expensive ass dress? How this bitch get this shit! What the fuck... is that on her finger?"*

Yvette was about money to the average eye but standing next to Rebecca, she was a little short.

Putting her guilt aside, Rebecca replied, "Yvette."

Yvette's gaze finally met Rebecca's eyes and she responded, "I see life is treating *you* well. Excuse me."

She pushed past Rebecca to the door and headed outside.

"Yvette, wait!"

"I don't have time for *this,* this morning, Becca," she said as she hurried down the sidewalk, "I'm running late."

"Please listen to what I have to say."

"Becca, I'm not interested in whatever it is you have to say."

"I know I left you in a bind-"

"A bind, Becca? Is that what you're calling it?" Yvette asked, enraged by the subdued intensity of the event. "How about *'fucked,'* Becca! That would be a far more accurate description of how you left me! I was ass fucked, with no lube, for you! Going out on a limb for you! Sticking my neck out... for you! And you left me and *never* looked back!"

"Essie I'm-"

"Don't you fuckin' call me that, you-" Yvette's emotions overwhelmed her, and she closed her eyes and took a deep breath to calm herself. "I trusted you and you betrayed me."

"I didn't betray you," Rebecca pleaded. "I would *never* betray you. I panicked. I was weak, scared and I'm sorry."

"Sorry? Do you have any idea what he did to me Becca? They stopped just short of disbarring me maybe out of sheer mercy. They probably figured they'd throw a nig a bone, so I wouldn't show up with my own goddamn lawyer! With a suspension on my record I would be lucky to work as a fuckin' notary in a UPS Store!"

"Yvette, please? I can make it up to you! Give me a chance!"

Yvette turned to snap at her or more like hit her, but their powerful bond won over her rage.

"Shalom, Becca," she bade, then walked away leaving Rebecca standing lonely on the busy rush hour sidewalk in midtown.

Later that evening, Rebecca went to a familiar place in Brooklyn. She rang the bell and the door opened.

"Hi, Ma."

"Rebecca? Rebecca is that you?" she asked.

"It's me, Ma."

"Oh, my lord," she shrieked as she embraced Rebecca tight until tears ran down her face.

"I'm sorry, Ma," Rebecca pleaded. "I'm *so* sorry. Please forgive me?"

"Now, now baby girl, you ain't got to be sorry about nothin'," she said, comforting her in her arms.

Yvette came down the stairs to see who was at the door and asked, "Momma, who is it? No!" she yelled. "You got some nerve!"

Yvette lunged to attack Rebecca.

"Essie Vette!" Ma Jolie screamed, and her tone stopped Yvette dead in her tracks. "Now, I don't know where your manners done gone… but you needs best find 'em and find 'em quick!"

"Huh, manners? Momma, do you-"

Rebecca argued, "Ma, she won't-"

"Enough! *Goddammit!* Both of you… like fuckin' kids!" Ma Jolie ordered. The agitation in her voice took them both back to their childhood when she raised them as Rebecca's nanny. When they both found their manners, Ma Jolie continued. "What is it you want, Rebecca?"

"Ma, I need to speak to *her* for just a few minutes," she said, pointing. "I need *her* to hear what I have to say, please?"

223

Ma Jolie looked her in the eye and invited her in and Rebecca thanked her. They sat in the parlor living room and it was just as Rebecca remembered. The house had been in their family for over 70 years with history and photos and traditions on display all around them.

"You don't shut the door on nobody come to speak peace," Ma Jolie grumbled and reminded them.

Rebecca spoke with them both of her version of the circumstances that caused her to abandon her best friend that came to her aid. She spoke of her fear and her panic and her trauma no more and no less than what Yvette went through setting her free from her husband.

Rebecca looked at Ma Jolie and said, "Ma, I wanna make good." She turned to Yvette, "I wanna offer you a job."

"What is it *this* time, Becca?" she asked, snapping at her.

"I need a shark for a trading house."

Yvette's gaze changed.

"It's a *thirty million-dollar* account right now, and you will answer to me and our client *only.*"

Rebecca took an envelope out of her bag and placed it on the table in front of Yvette, then pushed it towards her. Ma Jolie watched as Yvette picked up the envelope and opened it and stared at it and then looked at Rebecca.

"Can I tell you more… *Ess,* please?"

Yvette handed the envelope over to Ma Jolie and replied, "I'm listening."

The next morning Becs called me and wanted to see me. Her tone was a bit off, so I offered to stop by her place, but she had a few errands to run and said she would be by me later. I knew it wouldn't be too late because she asked me what I wanted for breakfast. In other words, she wanted to feed me when she knew I would be hungry and most amenable to whatever she had to tell me.

"You gave her how much?"
Rebecca replied, "$250,000."
"Cause she that good or 'cause she your friend?"
"H, come on!" she petitioned.
"Ite, I'm sorry. I didn't mean that… *it,* like *that."*

"Fuck? Straight face. Straight face."

Rebecca was with him in the morning and with breakfast and in *jeans.* She was bothered about something and wasn't feeling H's displeasure or his attempts at humor and it had nothing to do with the loss they took. He sincerely doubted it had anything to do with money at all. As well as she had gotten to know him this past year, He'd also picked up a few things and had gotten to know her pretty well too. She would talk when she was ready.

"H, she's worth every penny and when she moves there's no one better at what she does."
"Ite baby, you don't have to sell me on her. If you say she's good, then *we* good."
"She's exactly what we need there to keep those guys in line." Rebecca looked at me and turned away saying, "I also would like to break up the company and add a layer of insulation for us."
H responded, "Really?"
"Trading is a very volatile pivot to our operations and with one wrong trade we could take a hit and regrettably end up just like the company we took over. So, to insulate us, Yvette will be named CFO of RH and I will manage her."
H cautioned, "You know this only works if she takes the job."
Rebecca, knowing what he meant, responded, "She will. It's in her *blood.* Once she gets a taste of it, she

won't be able to let it go, and Amanda will head the new company as COO and oversee both companies."

I watched her as she walked over to my window facing Williamsburg behind me. She leaned against the window wall and with her left hand moved the sheer curtain to get a clearer view. She was deep in thought about something and was negotiating the terms of its surrender to me. I knew it was personal because the last time she put herself through all these trepidations I proposed a merger and she accepted. She was my *Ivy League Queen* with a heart of gold and a voluptuous body to match.

"Ite. What about Josh?"

"Yes," she replied as she walked over to where I was seated. "I support you in keeping Joseph at his position." She moved my feet off the ottoman and sat down curiously enough in front of me. Then she indicated to me with her hands to put my feet back up on her thighs saying, "I've learned how much a person can be motivated to improve after a supreme fuck up."

"You have?"

She then leaned in very close to me taking hold of my hands and continued, "After all, we *all* make mistakes."

"Hmmm." Now I wasn't sure where Becs was going with this but with her twins sitting up in my face, she wasn't exactly softening me up for the news the way she looked at it, but she was making me amenable as hell. So, I acknowledged her and agreed with her and then responded, "Ite, baby, whatever you feel is best."

She gazed into my eyes and said, "Thank you. Now, there's one more thing we need to discuss. It's about me."

Becs told me some things, some additional even *more* things. which I could understand didn't need to be discussed at the time. I understood her apprehension not to mention embarrassment telling someone you just met that you were physically abused by your husband, a surgeon, during your marriage and that you had a bitter divorce, in which you lost everything including your very best friend. Maybe I didn't need to know all of that when at the end it didn't hurt me, it only hurt her. Still, I wish I knew. I love Becs like oxygen.

"I don't want you keeping anything else from me as I make it a point not to keep *anything* from you. You keeping things from me questions the trust we have in each other. *That,* I can't afford."

She explained, "At the time, it didn't seem important, and truthfully, I didn't see it coming up."

"But it did come up, now, didn't it, and because of her? Would you have told me if it wasn't for her?"

Rebecca tried to stand, and I wouldn't let her. I couldn't let her. I refused to let her put any more distance between us when she had come all this way to try and reach me. Sometimes we become so myopic in our view of things that we lose the distinction to adjust our angles to see the bigger picture, which I needed to do here. This wasn't just about Becs it was about me too. About whether it was possible to be as open and honest with another human being as you are with yourself, rendering us vulnerable to the harshest of criticism? She was doing this and I needed to see it.

"My God, baby, forgive me please?" I held her close rubbing her face next to mine and baring my soul in a gentle whisper in her ear and consoling her with my devotion to her and what she meant to me. "I was making this all about me and I shouldn't have, but I am scared that as close as I want to be with you, I may never be close enough. I'm scared of losing you and if you won't let me in completely, will that eventually happen? That's not a reality I want to experience ag-"

"You won't lose me," she said, with her cheeks next to mine and when she said it, I froze and she saw it in my eyes when she spoke, "but sometimes your words, yours, hurt me just as much as his fists and the pain I feel is *no* different."

227

She gave me a moment to think about it and I did too, then I asked, "Is this why you wouldn't let me close to you when we met?"

"Physically, yes. It hampered me from having... *meaningful* new relationships until you came along," she stated holding my hands again. "You think you've got trust issues?" she asked, chuckling and wiping away a tiny tear from her eye. "I kept everyone I could away including my parents whom I haven't spoken to in forever, my very best friend whom I alienated and Ma... and as for those meaningful new relationships, well forget that. The men I met concluded something was *wrong* with me because I *did* want to have sex but didn't or rather wouldn't, and the more they pressed is the more I couldn't. And then the one man I did meet who told me flat out that he didn't want to get in my skirt and had all this tremendous insight into me and said all the right words and immediately broke through all my defenses offering to save me and not only supported my selfishness, but also justified it. That same guy, from the moment we met even went as far as offering to share with me all that he had and was willing to lay down his life for me, the *Princess,* asking for nothing in return," she paused, "initially, but my trust and is the only one that should get in my skirt," she added, chuckling, "happens to be *black.* "

"I *should?* "

She looked at me with that *'thanks-to-you-I've-gone-past-the-half-way-point-so-I-might-as-well-see-this-through-with-you-till-the-end-fuck you'* look and said, "You, H, may have had a dream, but I certainly got a fuckin' reality check."

H laughed and rubbing his cheek said, "Hmmm, shit becomes what it comes because of what it *is,* baby."

"What?" she asked, laughing and seemingly relieved she had conceivably assuaged her guilt. "What does that even *mean?* " She shook her head, "You crazy fuck! You know what's even *crazier*, now I'm talking like you, is that I might even understand what the fuck you're saying? My God! Really? Is *that* what you got out of *everything* I said?"

H replied, "It was an earful. I took the highlights."

Rebecca stared deeply into his eyes.

"You know, once you go-"

She interrupted, "Don't say it! Don't you dare fuckin' say it!" pursing her lips, then laughing hysterically as he tickled her and still continuing to protest him finishing it.

"Choc-o-"

Rebecca interrupted him staring at him, "You gon stop being an asshole, H?"

"Wait. So, just to be clear, you *don't* want me to be an asshole?"

Rebecca replied candidly, "No motherfucker, I don't!"

H thought about that and inquired, "Ok. Can I be a dick?"

Rebecca laughed as he set her up once again.

"Yours?"

She pursed her lips some more and blushed.

"Thought so. I like it when you cuss too," he said as he kissed her neck. "You had a nice little cussin' roll thing goin' on there. Rolls of cussin' like that baby fat on your neck, right there." He kissed her some more as she laughed and he asked, "So, you done purgin', Rubinequa? Becshauna?"

Rebecca fell on him and commented, "You just love talkin' shit, don't you? Runnin' your mouth. You know what?"

"Ah, there you go... fuckin' up that Harvard grammar again, Ms. Princess."

Rebecca admitted to the pain of her trauma to H, who represented the revelation of a higher purpose with him beyond ethnic dogma. She started therapy soon after they met feeling the need for it the moment they touched.

She whispered in my ear, "I'm sorry. Would you prefer for me to fuck up something else?"

It didn't seem fair but when her gaze caught mine *it* just came out. She wasn't timid about being touched when she responded with her hands. The way she looked at it, she didn't like me wearing jeans either.

When he got to the office for the meeting that Becs called for later that *build,* half of his team were already in the conference room. He saw heads glued to their monitors as he made his way to his office to wait for Becs who was but a moment behind him. H hadn't even gotten to his seat when she came around the corner at the beginning of the aisle in a smoking blue Sheath dress by *Dior,* in a classic hourglass silhouette that flattered every inch of her figure. Accented with a string of pearls and earrings set from Emily's Boutique, she was looking drop dead gorgeous at him as she closed in. Next to her was a fine chocolate brown sister, slightly taller with *firm* tits, in a green Tea length dress by *Prada* that hugged her form and draped over an ass that he caught a glimpse of from where he was standing and presumed screamed momma's Sunday dinner too? Her hair was long and every detail of her was appointed, which meant she had spent some of his dough getting nipped and tucked for him. When he saw Rebecca, he couldn't control his smile, which was inescapable, and neither could she. They arrived at his door and entered. H rose both ways to the occasion, and Rebecca introduced them.

"Yvette, I'd like you to meet our employer, H. H this is *Yvette Williams*, our new CFO of RH LLC."

Yvette shook my hand and I saw on her face ebony pupils on bright white eyes that created that familiar stare that penetrated me. She was a Harvard Law Graduate too, also at the top of her class, so that what came out of her sculptured lips intimidated you. She wasn't taller than me in her pumps, but she looked down at me. And where most would've considered that a slight, I graciously took it as a bow. Yvette would be my shark after Rebecca.

"A pleasure!" she said. "Rebecca has told me many good things about you. I look forward to this tremendous opportunity. Thank you."

I held her hand and it happened again, like before, and as I suspected it would. Becs has become more in tune with me, being the first and being with me the longest. And just like Kate at the restaurant, and Amanda at her desk, and *M* with me that morning when I woke up, I had found number four. It had also happened with Nana at the center, but she was young, and I seriously still questioned it. The trouble is, Nana fit perfectly.

"... and fuck if hers wasn't the strongest."

"Can I trust you, Yvette?" he asked, as her gaze never let up on him where she stood desperately hoping to prove that she was eager, sincere, committed and yes, loyal. Her accomplishment of this teetered on the precipice of the next few words he would speak, regardless of what Rebecca wanted.

"Yes, you can, H."

"Quid pro quo," he thought, looking at Rebecca.

"Righteous... Vetty," he nodded and smiled, fully content in his decision. "Welcome to the family."

Rebecca looked at me with sincere gratitude and appreciation, and relief and asked, "Baby, are you ready?"

I replied, "Yes."

I made sure to keep Becs, followed by Vetty ahead of me. The office was a murmur with even the traders whispering as we made our way to the conference room down the hall. God, Becs was on fire and feared by all and she loved it. When we entered the conference room,

231

I saw my team of Amanda, Kate, Maureen and Josh waiting patiently for the news of changes that had come.

"It's a pleasure to meet you, Yvette. Welcome to the family," Amanda said as introductions were made, and we sat at the table while Rebecca stood and addressed us.

"Everyone, Yvette will be assuming management over all investment and legal operations of RH LLC. She will be in house counsel for RH and our newly formed firm and parent company, *RG INC,* and will answer to me. Amanda you will move up as COO of RG INC and will oversee the operational management of both firms, which includes all business concerns. HR responsibilities, hiring, termination, payroll and promotions, income, accounts receivable and payable. RG INC is now the parent company for all of H's businesses and business interests moving forward. Amanda," Rebecca asked, still shell shocked from being named Chief Operating Officer of not one but both firms now, "it is our belief that Maureen can continue to be of assistance to you in handling the additional accountabilities now diverted to RG and that her title and pay should be commensurate with these responsibilities. Do you agree?"

Amanda replied, "Yes. Absolutely."

We all laughed at Amanda's genuine love and expressiveness, especially Maureen whose eyes said to me, "Thank you."

"Good. Katherine, you will now consult for RG INC as our Portfolio Executive."

Kate uttered, "Yay!"

"A new contract will be drawn up for your continued disregard," Rebecca quipped over the laughter.

"Ugh, Becca, you're so good to me!"

When Rebecca got to Josh, she was a bit hesitant. She followed through as per her decision with me, but she was firm in her appointment.

"Joseph, you still have my confidence and the confidence of the entire office and will retain your position as trading manager, but you will now answer to Yvette. Please understand that those traders out there are *your* traders and therefore your responsibility and your liability accordingly. I am expecting you to improve in managing their activities. Yvette will monitor your trades, positions, executions and our exposure and her calls regarding the aforementioned supersede all, including mine."

That last part tapped even my head when she said it, and all eyes refocused on her, so that she needed to clarify.

"Joseph," she said as she moved closer to him pointing at the trading area, "that is *your* floor and you've earned it, and we want you here to continue to grow and be successful, but your floor is now in *her* house," pointing at Yvette making sure to convey the urgency of a correction.

Rebecca made a deal with Yvette that made her accountable only to her and me. This regrettably put Josh in the crosshairs of being a liability if he didn't perform and heat came down on her. I wasn't thrilled with it and I wasn't going to hang Josh out to dry either, because I understood why he did what he did. But my top priority is always Becs to protect us, all of us.

"Have I made myself clear, Joseph?"
Josh didn't look at me because he knew that would be disrespectful to Rebecca, who always spoke for me. He also knew that he was still here because of me, so he kept his focus on Rebecca and answered, "Yes, ma'am."
She smiled and winked at him, "Thank you, Joseph."

Now that the new pecking order had been established, we continued with the matter of the mitosis of my dream company into a parent and child. My shit was official. Kate determined that additional rental space was needed to comply with Rebecca's legal mandate for two companies and secured some space on the 14th floor pending my review, which was a formality, really. My girls had autonomy in my company, according to the edicts of my vision and Rebecca's execution of it. I was now CEO of two companies with Rebecca as my partner, my *power*. Kate as my lieutenant, my *body*. Amanda as my Warden, my *heart* and Yvette as my battle axe, my *vanity*. But I still thought myself short one though she had already come. Kate had already made the difficult decision easy for me, seeing how hard I had worked to earn her. Anastasia would be my *soul*.

"... Everything I have to say, everything I have to do, everything I have to put in place, I've done. It's up to you."

"Boss. H," she said, shaking his hand as he sat at his desk with his feet up, which was typical for him. "I've been standing here for a while, where have you been?"

He shook his head disregarding her question.

"Are you alright?" Anastasia asked.

"Yeah, I'm cool. What's up?"

"Are you sure?" she asked with Yvette.

"Sorry, someplace else."

"You do that a lot, you know?"

"What can I tell you, Na, the search for peace?"

Yvette asked, "Where the fuck is you searchin'?"

"Nowhere close. Success-" he looked at her and muttered, "it gets me through this haunting. 'Sup?"

"Nothin'. We just came to bother you. Well, I did," Anastasia clarified pointing at herself, "I don't know about her."

"Same." Changing the subject, Yvette shouted, "H!" and proceeded to get to the point of her visit. "I want your opinion on something," Yvette cooed as she came around his desk in front of Anastasia and leaned over, fine as hell, and took control of his keyboard and mouse.

Anastasia stretched out on the couch with one leg on the floor and began working on her phone. H paid her no attention, but he always had hers. She laid there observing how carefully Yvette machinated through her curt explanations to him on various positions she thought were potentially profitable, and his reaction to them. These "zone outs" of his intrigued Anastasia, and she wondered, as she looked at Yvette who was flirting with him, why he searched so much for someone who, from what she could tell, had everything a man would want.

"Well, that all depends. I think it'll swing to here," Yvette replied, "so a couple a mill? That shit's been depressed for a minute and due for a run."

"True, but I don't think it's ready. That minute gon be a while," H said, disqualifying her first choice.

"For real? How? H, look at these numbers?"

"Babe, you asked for *my* opinion," he remarked.

"Yeah, but-"

"But I don't see it," he stated clearly to her while looking up at her as she stood by his side.

He was talking about the "Carnival," and I'm not sure why she gave it that name. When boss called trades, no matter what we were trading, stocks, forex or futures, he was *"looking for the highest probability of success. I gotta see it,"* was his explanation to her and effortless bullshit to me, but she sweated that knowledge, bad. She is constantly on him to teach her the accuracy to his calls, but the explanations he would give her to accomplish them were always missing something crucial, yet simple, that if I'm right, was right in her face the whole time. Her vain ass just couldn't see it.

235

Chapter Eighteen

Congratulations On Your Promotion
"The Birth Of Anastasia Movado"

"Hey, H, what's up?"

"Nothing much, Godfadda. Chillin'."

"Well, that's good."

"What's goin' on?"

"I'm cool. Just calling to check up on you. I haven't spoken to you in a while? What you been up to? How's LA?"

"Nah, I got back Tuesday. I'm home."

"Tuesday?"

It was Friday.

"And you ain't call nobody?"

"Fadda, I was just hiding out a minute. I was going to call you today. I swear. I know it's your day off!"

"Have you spoken to Laney?"

"No, not yet, but I will call her."

"Well, make sure you do?"

"I will."

"She's got some shit goin' on over at the house she had mentioned to me. I had to take care of some things while you were away."

Godfather ran down a brief wrap up getting me up to speed on a dear friend in Brooklyn. I was indeed hiding out. You'll be surprised how much more my phone will ring the closer I get to Queens. He was looking out for me as usual because if she found out I was here and didn't tell her, oh God, it would be my ass. When I saw Mo this morning, she giggled as she approached me.

"You didn't have to do that, Grimmy."

"Habit."

"How you feel?" she asked, feeling my forehead. "That LA sunshine fucked you up, huh?"

"Nah, babe, it's my return to this arctic blast."

"Where's your skully?"

"On my desk."

"Here," she said as she put my hood back on. "Cover your head. I don't need you catching your death of cold on my account." She smiled as she adjusted it to her liking, even pulling on the drawstring and whispered, "See, because *I* couldn't give you the attention you would want... maybe even need?"

"Funny."

She gazed at me alluringly and smiled, continuing her way and said, "Don't lose your balance," as she naturally shook her ass and knew I would look.

"Definitely 'Need.'"

I remember Mo and I spoke once, outside the office after work. We were leaving together, and she had a car waiting and was offering me a ride, and I asked, "Mo, question."

"Yeah, what's up?"

"No disrespect-"

"From you?" she remarked, sarcastically and smiling as she always did. "I'll try."

"Yeah, well... whatever. We close. Babe, why you hardly wear pants?"

She laughed at me and asked, "Oh, my God? No disrespect, huh?"

"No! I mean- The reason I ask is because it's pouring out here and it seems to me it might be easier if...? Warmer maybe? I dunno, I'm just askin'?"

She kept looking at me and smiling, I guess waiting for me to make sense of my question.

"When we first met," I said as her smile became contagious, "you were and you did, and I can count the times I've seen you in one since, on my pinky."

237

Mo gazed at me, woefully losing every ability to control herself and keep from blushing, even briefly turning her head, smiling as she held her umbrella over both of us.

"You've noticed?"

"Yes."

"Grimmy, you pay me to look good," she began. "My mom's sittin' at home right now in her shows 'cause you see to it that I live good. Nig, I feel good, like in *so* many ways, I could *thrill* you to know. I'ma wear my dress and my skirt, and I'ma turn heads showin' off my legs and my thighs up to this fine ass of mine 'cause I feel good, 'cause of you. I can wear pants for any nickel and dime motherfucker out here, of which you are not." She moved in closer to me and said, "We *are* close. Thank you for the compliment, baby," and placed her hand on my chest and leaned in and kissed me on my cheek, pausing before she finished. "Get home safe."

I watched her walk to her driver as he opened the door and the Goddess got in and I stared as they drove off into the uptown traffic. I fixed my hood and realized, I gotta get an umbrella?

"You want me to do what, now?" I asked her as she sat in my apartment.

She'd taken a car here straight after school to hang out and I believe to stay in the city. She was starting to spread her wings a little bit. Amanda told me her expenses were increasing.

"Parents-Teachers conference," she said as she got up and walked over to me and knelt before me pleading her case. I had seen *this* before. "You're concerned for my wellbeing, aren't you?"

"Of course, I am, babe."

"So, then *that* qualifies *you* as my *guardian,"* she said, batting her eyes and grinning from ear to ear."

"Brat!"

My phone rang and it was the doorman notifying me of a visitor. Nana rose and unlocked the front door, as she went to the bathroom. She could talk shit with the best of them. The more secured she felt with me, is the more confident she became. The more confident she became, is the more she trusted me. The more she trusted me, is the more she loved me. And the more she loved me, is the more she wanted to be with me. Sophia was available, but she didn't want her. She wanted me and wanted to show me off, and I was flattered. But as I thought more about it, it occurred to me that her father had never done one of these with her. She had never had the opportunity to express her pride in a father figure, I guess, so this was a privilege that I was being granted. I felt deeply honored and made sure I was going to be there.

"What's up, man?"

"My nig, what's good?" he asked, as he walked over to me where I sat, and we shook hands. Spotting her jacket, he inquired, "Where your pit bull at? Oh, there she is!"

"Hi, B," Anastasia greeted as she walked up to him, hugging him affectionately as he wrapped his arms around her.

"What's up, little lady? How you doin'?"

"I'm fine," she replied as she released him.

"How are things coming along? Knockin' shit out?"

"Yes, I am."

"Good. Good... very good."

Anastasia hadn't known Black very long, but H trusted him completely and that was enough for her. And much like with H, she knew what was up when she had heard one *'good'* or one *'cool'* too many.

She said, "I know he keeps you informed."

"Yes, he does, but I like to hear things for myself when I can... sort of like first generation bullshit, if you catch my meanin'?"

Anastasia blushed and hugged him again and affirmed, "I *am* taking care of it." Changing the subject, she asked, "What y'all getting into?"

Black replied, "Just gon hang out and talk some business over here with my man. You stayin'?"

"Who me? No. I can't testify," she responded, putting on her jacket as they chuckled."

"You hear that? She can't *testify*. Sounds like you. You rubbin' off on her."

Anastasia smiled and said, "So, I'ma leave y'all alone. Save the world but don't get into any problems. *¿Claro mis amores?"*

"Ah... yes, ma'am? I'm not sure what you said, but it sounded like some deep shit," Black said as Anastasia laughed. "I'm gon just nod my head in agreement, assuming I'm correct. You got some sharp teeth there."

Anastasia bit at him and then kissed H and said, *"Sé bueno, boss,"* then grabbed her bag to leave.

H and Black watched as she left and the door closed, then Black commented, "That's that Spanish that be fuckin' you up, huh?" pointing at his heart.

"Yeah, man," H replied.

"I see," he said as he shook his head taking off his jacket and headed to the fridge for a brew. "At least you understand the shit. Want one?"

H, still in thought and smiling, shook his head, "I'm good."

"It shows, you know," Black said, returning from the kitchen to counsel his old friend.

"Na? Yeah... I'm noticing," he responded.

"What you gon do about it?"

H wrapped up his thought and replied, "Hopefully nothin' stupid, I'll tell you that! Yo, enough about that, man. He signed it?"

Black took a swig and replied, "We 'bout to eat."

Nana deserved a jacket or at the very least a dress shirt for her efforts, so on the day of the conference, a visit to *Emily's* kept me on the cutting edge of style and *nouveau riche* swagger with both. Nana and I walked in and she took my hand and kept me by her side the entire evening as she gave me the tour of her school. She had become even more popular lately, but everyone that saw her, saw me and assumed accordingly. I was tangible, having made a slight name for myself with *Mist,* and she finally felt vindicated. Usually at these things, you see mostly moms with a sprinkle of dads and we, the dads, stick out. Just to show up to one of these things requires from us a whole lot of effort on our part and or threats on their part. But regardless, we were such good dads in the eyes of every woman that saw us, and Nana enjoyed them seeing us. In our travels we met a teacher who asked Nana who I was. She must have been aware of her household and probably knew Sophia. I know Nana thought about it when she asked me to the conference, but I don't think she really thought it through or rather it hadn't been real enough to be thought through until this moment. I sensed her hesitation and answered, "Hi, I'm H, a friend of the family. Pleased to meet you."

"Oh? Um... hi? Jocelyn, likewise."

"I've recently moved back here from out of town and wanted to see what my girl was up to and catch up on my quality time."

"Aw, wow, that is so encouraging of you! Ana, aren't you special to have such a loving support system around you?"

Nana stared at me very proud and said, "Yes, I am, Ms. Gibbs."

I took over this conversation and each successive conversation and by the time we were done with the evening, Nana had barely spoken at all, which was her intent. I enjoyed the responsibility she requested of me. One encounter after the next, Nana led the way and I played the role even when we got to Elaine, who was very surprised to see me again by the way she greeted me. She stood marveling at me and asked, "Are you playing employer or parent tonight?"

"Friend of a parent," I replied, correcting her, "from out of town."

"Congratulations on your promotion," she flirted.

I felt Nana's eyes on me as I pondered my response, so I let my eyes do the talking and Elaine understood.

"Please be rest assured that Ana is my dream come true as a student."

"Oh, really, Elaine? Do tell."

"Well, H, Ana is a *very* smart and dedicated student who's receptive of my curriculum no matter how boring it may get."

"Maybe that's because she doesn't value money like most, but rather how money is made and its influences around us," I said.

Nana replied with a smile, "Maybe."

"She grasps the work really well and does the homework. I'm told you have a firm influence in that?" she asked, and I nodded.

"Thank you?" Elaine said.

"You're welcome. I believe in reward for discipline and determination."

Nana corrected me, "You mean torture."

H responded, cynically, "That's my little girl."

"But really she's great," Elaine said, continuing her praise. "I'm blessed to have her in my class."

"That's a glowing recommendation if I ever heard one, but you know she already has the job, right?"

We laughed and I caught Nana looking at me with her stern 'no banging my teacher eyes,' so I broke it off.

"Elaine, I thank you so much for your efforts with her. Please keep in touch with me on her continued progress, if that's alright with you?"

"I don't see why not."

I gave her my card, "Great. Have a good night."

She replied, "Thank you. You too."

242

But what I really heard was, *"The two of us could have a good night."* I tend to transmute shit in my head occasionally... often, all the time. It occurs most where tits and ass are concerned. I think Nana must have heard it too because I felt I was gon get my ass reamed when we got outside her classroom and sure enough, she smacked my arm first and then she grilled me.

"What was that?"
"What was what?"
"You were flirting. You really like her, don't you?"
"I told you she was cool."
"What's so cool about her besides the obvious *tits* and *ass?"*
"I don't know. Is there something else? Nana glared at me while I chuckled, "Na, I'm just messin' with you, God. Uh, and I don't know if I feel comfortable talking to you about this, babe?"
"What, Sex? I'm a woman."

It was a curious thing to me because wasn't it not too long ago she was all shy and timid and shit, at least around me?

"Yes, you are, and a *fine* one too, but a *young* one, nonetheless. In fact, *a just starting out* to be one. One that I can't help but feel overprotective of and super embarrassed to be talking to about asking your teacher out, especially your favorite teacher. It's a little uncomfortable for me. You dig?"
"Why? Even if I had a problem with it you would anyway, so."
"No," I stated.
"What?"
"I said no, I wouldn't. Is that how you see me?"
"Seriously?" she stopped walking to look at me.
"Yeah, seriously," H replied, shrugging his shoulders. "Don't get me wrong, Nana, I mean, I dig Elaine- no doubt, but you've got my heart. I wouldn't want to do anything to jeopardize that."

243

I saw it in her eyes, and she smiled when I said it. I guess she must have been thinking about it because she got really quiet as we walked. Suddenly she tugged on my hand and made me stop again and then said, "As long as I remain in your heart, I don't care who you date, unless of course she's *bad* for you and Elaine isn't bad for you. She might be bad for Kate though?"

We laughed and her gaze never left me even after I agreed, "Yes- *woman.* Who's your next victim?"

"Global history, Ms. Andrews. I need her to bump up my grade, so pull out all the stops. Can you mind-fuck her too? I'll turn my head."

"What? You Funny! When the- How did I become a piece of meat?"

Nana took me by my arm hurrying me down the hall to Ms. Andrews saying, "I don't know but work it out. I need an A," and in I went to take one for the team.

"I may not accomplish what I'm setting out to do out this motherfucker. I may fail miserably at it, but I can't give up. I can't go the other way. I can't shove my head up my ass and convince myself the air is fresh, man. You know what I'm sayin'. I get tired of failing, I do. That shit kills my soul, but I can't quit. This bitch got to give at some point. The value system that they have taught us demands it and if it don't, I'm not going to make it. A part of me is cool with it already. If you really do give a shit, then fix this bullshit. Stop giving excuses. My bitchin' is an excuse too. I know it. I knowingly admit mine. Y'all can't? I got a fuckin' manual that reads crap and I can't call it that? Sin? That was mankind's' lynchpin? You get mad at your kids and kick them out the house and set them loose on the world. Is that what you call being a responsible parent? I've got a sin for you. Y'all fucked up creating man. As fuckups go, I think that one was pretty goddamn catastrophic. I want to do good. It feels good to do good. You can't leave me in jeopardy when I seek to do good! Stop making it hard for me and others like me to do good. It's a simple ass concept."

244

Chapter Nineteen

How's That For A Trade?
"The Birth Of Anastasia Movado"

She came home from work and after announcing her arrival, went upstairs to visit her son, and found Anastasia there as well.

"Hi, Ana."

"Hi, Ms. Johnson."

"How you doin', baby?" she greeted, hugging her and kissing her head.

"I'm fine."

"You look fine. You look different."

Anastasia blushed, "Thank you!"

"You smilin', what's up?" Lynette asked, with that maternal curiosity.

"Nothing," Anastasia replied.

Ralphy, y'all eat," she asked, while looking around. Lynette looked around some more and asked, "Ralphy, where's all your stuff?"

Lynette Johnson was a fine chocolate brown sister with dark brown eyes and an old royal soul that compelled the truth out of you and repelled any bullshit you suggested her way especially those with no effort. Her body was sweet and curvy and where you looked at her ass as an ass to set your drink on she looked at her ass as what you could kiss approaching her with that ignorant shit. She had her jet-black hair cut to style, short and sophisticated, and a small scar on her left cheek that looked a decade or so old. Over the years it had evolved into a beauty mark that distracted you while she picked your mind for a hidden agenda. Raphael was her second and only remaining child and was taller than his mom. Hell, he was taller than me and I was taller than his mom too. She had no fear and would break her foot off in his ass if he ever got any imaginations or conceived to jeopardize the life she felt he deserved. They both got quiet.

"Ralphy?"

"Ma, I got this."

"What you got, baby? I hope it's your stuff because I see some shit missin' up in here."

"I sold it."

"You did what???"

"I sold it to raise money."

Scared to death, he doesn't finish his thought and his mother does. Lynette's eyes widen and she locked in on Anastasia.

"Girl, are you *pregnant?* You knocked her up? Boy I will fuck-"

"No," Anastasia screamed. "Oh GOD, no! We're *friends!"*

"What that mean?" Lynette snapped.

"No, Ma," Raphael exclaimed, "Anastasia is not pregnant! I'm raising the money to trade."

"Trade what?"

"Day Trade, Ma. I want to play the market."

"What?"

"Ok, you know the classes I've been going to on Saturdays at the center?" he asked.

"Yeah?"

"Remember I told you about a man over there that volunteers every so often? A rich guy?"

"Yeah?"

"Well, I want to invest with him."

"You wanna do what? Boy, have you lost your *damn* mind!" With that said, Anastasia turned to leave, and Lynette asked, "And where do *you* think *you're* going? I know you a part of this!"

Anastasia froze and didn't even answer.

"Raphael, what are you doin'?"

"Ma, please just calm down."

"Don't tell me to calm down! I am calm!" she screamed.

Raphael and Anastasia both looked at each other and he pleaded, "Ma, please?"

Lynette realized he had to explain himself and he couldn't do that with her inciting a riot in his room, so she calmed down.

"What's goin' on here, baby?"

Raphael looked at Anastasia and then at his mom and answered, "Ma, I've got a plan to make some money and I need you to hear me out, ok, *please?"*

Lynette took a seat on the bed and Raphael with Anastasia standing guard next to him explained A to Z to her the chronicles of Mr. H. Raphael explained that not only were his X box and games gone but also his comic book collection and a couple of his Jordan's as well. She was also surprised to hear that Anastasia had contributed five thousand dollars of her own money she had saved up, which included mostly pay from H since she started interning with him. Anastasia sat with her and explained that he was the reason for her smile and also all the good things he had done for her even after what she had done to him. Raphael took his mom through everything he'd been doing with the club he started and the plan he was putting together and how they'd raised eight thousand dollars to trade.

"Ma?"

Lynette just stared at him.

"Ma, you're too quiet."

She took her gaze off of her son and turned to Anastasia sitting next to her on the bed. Anastasia was like a daughter to her and would confide in her where she couldn't with her mother.

247

"How are you doin', baby," she asked Anastasia.

"I'm good," she asserted, "I am, I promise."

"Yeah, you look it. And this guy's done all this for you, huh?"

"Yes, Ms. Johnson."

Lynette's gaze resumed on her son.

"Boy, you know that's your college money you fuckin' wit?"

"Yes, Ma, I know."

"You *better* know 'cause if this shit don't work, you screwed!"

"Yes, Ma."

"I'll cover it, Ms. Johnson," Anastasia affirmed. "I can give it to you as I make it."

"No, baby, that ain't necessary," she said, patting her on the thigh, "I'll take you at your word. The two of you been joined at the hip since grade school. He *'shit'* and you *'talk.'"*

Anastasia and Raphael both fought back their smiles in front of his mom.

"Ma, I really could use your support on this, please?"

There was a long pause for them for what seemed an instant for her where she seemed to drift away. She replied, "Ok, Fine."

"Yes!" Raphael exclaimed and gave Anastasia some dap.

"Boy, you gotta be smart, ok?"

"I will, Ma. Thank you!"

"Hmmm, fuckin' with you two I need me a drink!"

She left Raphael's room and Anastasia exhaled, "Your mom is a *nut,* yo?"

They both laughed hysterically keeping their voices down. Lynette respected the bond between Raphael and Anastasia, which grew stronger after the death of his sister, her only daughter. Raphael would always seem to

248

get into "shit" as a child and Anastasia would "talk" or abuse her cute to get them out of it. That bond would never break, so fighting one was like fighting both and Lynette had a different strategy to take.

"Thanks for that, Ana, for helping me out and shit."

"I got you," she said and gave him more dap. "You just gotta make sure this works that's all. You'll be fine."

"Yes. Hello, Lynette? This is H, returning your call. How are you?"

"Mr. H, I'm fine, thank you!"

"Good. Please Lynette, call me H."

"H," she repeated.

"How may I help you, Lynette?"

"I would prefer not to discuss it over the phone. Can we meet today? Is that possible, please?"

"Sure. Are you in the city?"

"Yes, I am."

"Perfect! Maybe after work then?"

"Sure," she asserted.

"Good. Let me give you my address."

"Lynette?" I asked, as I opened the door. "Hi, please come in?"

"Thank you." She gracefully walked it and said, "I won't stay long."

"It's no inconvenience I assure you. Please, make yourself comfortable," I said as I watched her eyes wander around my apartment, assessing. There was a lot to see and assess.

"H, I just wanted to speak to you briefly about my son, Ralphy?"

"Raphael is a fine young man," I continued, "you should be proud!"

"Oh, yes, I am!"

"I'm not sure if you're aware of it but he wants to invest with you and has raised eight thousand dollars, some of which is his college money to do so?"

"Yes, I am aware of it. He mentioned his conversation with you regarding it."

Surprised, she asked, "He did?"

"Yes, he did."

"Well, then you know that I do not agree with what he's doing," she confirmed.

"I do."

I paused to see how she would take it and she took it the right way.

"Unlike you," she said, perusing with her eyes around my apartment, "we ain't got it like that and he can't afford to lose this money. What guarantee do you have for me that this won't happen?"

"None," I said, bluntly, "I'm sorry. That's not the way investments work."

"So, what happens if my son loses his money?"

"He must start again and do a better job in his trading decisions until he overcomes and perseveres to profit. That's the game," I said, staring her in her eyes.

"Game?" she asked, indignantly. "My child is *gamblin'* away his college money tryin' to get rich because of *you* and you're callin' it a *'game'?"*

"Yes, Lynette, I am."

"Well, you got some set of balls-"

"Yeah, about that…"

"Lynette, please have a seat," I gently suggested, smiling and trying to hold my composure as I pointed towards the living room, "I have a story you might be interested in hearing."

"I don't wanna hear no fuckin' stories!"

"Ah, well… then you came to the wrong fuckin' house!"

She got heated. It was hard to not look her in those pretty brown eyes of hers, but it was even harder not to laugh.

250

"H, I want you to convince my child to get his head out of his ass and stop chasin' this *pipe dream* of his and focus on a *guaranteed* future in his education!"

"Do you think he's not gon go to college if he loses his money?"

"Well, how the hell is he supposed to pay for it?"

"Lynette, I really don't want you to whip my ass up in my tomb... not this one anyway, so I'm going to ask you to please, as one parent to another, sit with me so that we can discuss this issue to your satisfaction. Please?"

She took off her bag and coat and placed it on the armchair in front of her. She was wearing an armless silk top and contrasting pants with matching pumps that punctuated her hourglass figure perfectly. Her accessories were ethnocentric, yet subtle enough, so that their juju did not disturb the office sensibilities. I loved her earrings as they caught my attention when she sat in the adjacent armchair near the window with both arms along its shoulder high frame and side eyed me.

"Would you like something to drink?"
"No, thank you!" she replied.

When I came around to sit in the sofa opposite her, I couldn't help but feel the awe of her majesty seated before me. Through my windows to the left of her, New York City's setting sun showered her with golden rays that made her look absolutely divine and I was instinctively humbled in her presence.

"I'm going to lead with the highlights first because you look just the *tiniest* bit agitated."

She glared at me with disapproval. I might not make it.

"That envelope on the table, Lynette," as I nodded, "is for you."

"What is it?"

"Please, see for yourself."

251

She opened it and stared at me. I can't explain it, but I'm going to try. We all catch hell when we're short of money, to each his brain chain. But *one* curious thing occurs for all of us when we get some. That hell that we were so absorbed in, and so desperate in, and had us so defeated, suddenly evaporates and heaven's door, for lack of a better term, opens up. I call it '*Illumination.*' It's like bustin' a metaphysical nut.

"What's this for?"

"*Who,*" I corrected as I compelled her undivided attention and explained, "is this for? That is $10,000 for you, Lynette. $8,000 is for you to hold for Raphael in case he loses his investment and $2,000 is for your time and your carfare home. Now, can we please talk?"

She must've stared at me for what seemed like a whole minute, motionless and speechless, probably still cummin', and then she smiled reluctantly, avoiding eye contact with me and said, "I'll take that drink now."

While we spoke, my phone, which was also on the table in plain sight, rang, and we both saw that it was Anastasia. I interrupted Lynette, "Forgive me, but I must take this."

"Please, don't mention that I'm here." she asked, with urgency in her voice.

I indicated that I wouldn't and picked it up, "Hey, Nana, what's up?"

She was checking in with me as part of her routine, as per Kate, becoming more involved in my day to day activities. I assured her that I was fine and that I was in for the evening.

"*Nothing, just checking in on you. How are you?*"

"I'm fine, babe. What's goin' on?"

"*I finished the mockup for Kate and the numbers for Griot. Have you got a minute?*"

"Cool! Yeah, let's hear it."

"*The production is still within budget, so that's good. I spoke with Griot and everything is going smoothly down there.*"

"Righteous!"

"Yes, Amanda will be happy."

"Yes, she will."

"He will be asking for another installment soon though. FYI."

"Gotcha. What about the mockup?"

"It's still kinda rough but I think it's a strong start? It's what she wanted, and I think you'll like it too? I'll send that over to you as well."

"Good work, babe!"

Anastasia's mother stood in her bedroom doorway holding a glass and it wasn't water and it wasn't soda and saw her on her bed with her legs folded and her books all around her, which was her favorite mode to multitask. Anastasia's phone was plugged in and she had H on speaker.

"So, whatcha doin'?"

"Chillin', staying home out of trouble."

"Right," she remarked, insulted by the lack of effort in my persuasion. *"What's her name?"*

Lynette put her finger to her mouth to remind me.

"Nana, I know nothing of which you speak. I assure you I will be spending a quiet evening at home watching some athletic competition on TV."

She cracked up laughing and said, *"Oh GOD, you're so lying! You are the worst liar in the world! You need to give it up,"* she exclaimed, *"for real!"*

Lynette laughed silently.

"I'm the boss. It don't matter. But enough about me, have you finished your homework?"

"Ughhhhhhhhh! You're so annoying, too!

Lynette enjoyed herself when she heard Anastasia sigh loudly over the phone. It made me laugh too.

Anastasia asked, *"What is it with you and homework, anyway?"*

H reflected while she waited for his response and answered, "My pop was a very intelligent, well-educated man, and very strict with it."

"Oh, I didn't know."

"Plus, I know how much it really *fucks* with you, so..." he said, laughing and they all cracked up. "I'm having fun at your expense."

"Bossssssssss!"

"I'm paying you to do it. Quit complainin'."

Anastasia continued to moan over the phone.

"You're on the clock."
"I am- wait! I am?"

She got quiet and began to follow.

"Ah, you didn't think of it *that* way, did you?"

Then she started to run it down to him over the phone.

"This is a business call, so it's billable to you."
"Yes, it is."

"So, let's say, if I finish my homework within the hour of this call, then technically you're right, you are paying me to do it?"

"I know I'm right. Again, I'm the boss."

Lynette laughed and Anastasia sighed, again.

"I need a raise."

"And I need my momma."

Anastasia laughed and threw in the towel and said, *"Fine."*

"Text me when it's done!"

"Yes, boss! Oh, but that might be a while" she said, alarmingly. *"I see that I too will be spending a quiet*

evening at home, putting in some serious overtime… studying?"

Sophia entered Anastasia's bedroom when she got off the phone inspired to finish her homework and commented, "He's sounds like fun," and Anastasia ignored her. "You guys are getting along well, I see."

"It's my job."

"Just your job?" Sophia asked. Anastasia knew where her mom was heading with this as Sophia moved in closer to her and stated, "He likes you, I can tell."

Anastasia left it alone.

"Nana', huh? He's got a pet name for you now?" she asked, questioning her daughter because she had heard it a number of times now. "What's that about?"

"Nothing, it's just a nickname," Anastasia replied, trying to discount it.

"Just a *nickname?"* Sophia asked and nodded.

Anastasia remained quiet as her mother moved a book out of the way and sat next to her on her bed.

"Well, I seem to recall a little girl being very particular about the names she was called. A little girl who insisted on being called by her *full* name 'Anastasia' and maybe 'Ana' for short." She inquired, "So, a nickname, *dime, ¿cómo hizo esto?* How did he accomplish this incredible feat?"

"He called me that, maybe by accident one time, and I guess it must have stuck."

"Must have stuck'," Sophia wondered, thinking about the plausibility of the statement as she admired her little girl. "I see, and you never corrected him?"

Anastasia glared at her mom and asserted, "I'm not a little girl anymore."

"Hmmm, no you most certainly aren't," she said, fixing her daughter's beautiful hair behind her ear and looking upon her lovingly as Anastasia tried her best to ignore her. "Everything wrong in your life isn't my fault,

255

mi hija," Sophia stated as she finished playing with her hair.

Anastasia turned to her and remarked, "Maybe not *everything* mom, but certainly the ones that count."

"She's right you know," Lynette quipped at Anastasia's cleverness, "you are a *terrible* liar."

"The truth ain't fared me no better, GOD," he stated, sparking Lynette's interest. "I'm sorry about that, but I gave her my word I'd answer whenever she called."

"Really, may I ask why?"

"Well, for starters, she's my assistant and she can't very well *assist* me if she can't reach me. And second, I would like to be someone she can depend on, so I'm starting her off on good habits. Plus, I get the impression she's a bit rudderless and I've got two daughters of my own and that kind of shit doesn't really fly with me."

"Are these them?" Lynette asked, pointing to my left as she rose with her drink and walked over to the table to see the photos. She picked up the frames and admired them. "They're lovely!" she said, beaming with pride. "How old?"

"Sarai, my oldest is 22 and my youngest, Hashei is 15."

She remarked, "22? Shit! Nig, *you* don't look like you got a 22-year-old!"

I grinned.

"Thank you, again, and you don't look like you too mad at me anymore."

"Oh, I'm still mad," Lynette said, glaring at me and then returning to a smile, "but I'm presently appreciating an alternative perspective to my difficulties." I laughed and she joined me and then asked, "Same mom?"

I nodded.

"How'd that work out?"

"You don't drop off milk for one kid in the house and not *all* the kids in the house."

She tilted her head and looking at me curiously, remarked, "Sounds personal."

H stared at her appreciating the warmth in her eyes and replied, *"Suffer little children, and forbid them not...* I didn't bring her home from the hospital, but I did *borrow* her. I kept her too."

Lynette Johnson stared back at me and then slowly placed the photos back down exactly the way she found them and returned to where she was seated, then unexpectedly instead of sitting, she slowly walked around the arm chair and sat on the sofa next to me. She then crossed her legs towards me and while sipping on her drink with her left arm on the back of the sofa holding her head up asked, "Do you always keep your word, H?"

Her gaze felt hot on the right side of my face or maybe it was simply her proximity to me, but I thought I might need to turn down the heat, open a window or take off an article of clothing or two. Now she was assessing me. I kept my cool and turned my head to her to make eye contact and that's when I really noticed her scar and replied, "I do, as much as I am able to.

"You say it like its hard?" she inquired.

H snickered, "I try not to say shit I don't mean. I try not to waste my breath. For this I get knocked for being too quiet, like I'm better than somebody." His stare penetrated her, "Rich or poor, a man is only as good as his *word* and his word is his only true currency. You dig?"

Lynette nodded.

"But fuck if sometimes, life ain't got its own fuckin' plans though."

Lynette gazed into my eyes and took a sip of her drink, making it a point to wet her lips. I returned my gaze to my glass of orange juice on the coffee table in

257

front of me. Her thighs were just eyeballing me in the dress pants she had on and her right foot was within inches of my calf.

"She's really taken a liking to you, you know," she paused and then continued, saying it with a grin and making it a point to enunciate the syllables, *"Na-na."*

"She has?"

"Oh, yes," she said, assuring me. "She speaks *very* highly of you. You've managed to reach that girl in a way that neither I nor her mother have been able to and for damn sure not her father."

"Lucky me?"

Lynette put her glass to her lips and corrected me, "Oh? No, baby, lucky her."

When she was ready to leave, Lynette leaned over and placed her drink on the table next to mine so that she was almost kissing me when she did it. I made eye contact with her and felt her breath that was still cold from her drink and warmth from her eyes diligently investigating my lips.

"I'm gon let you handle your business, H. Ana trusts you and my son trusts you and I trust them." She clasped her hands together and rubbed them methodically and declared, "You may be exactly what they need in their life right now, a strong, successful and honest black man. There is after all but so much a woman can teach a child." I reflected as Lynette uncrossed her legs and reached for the envelope I had given her, still on the table. I watched her as she pulled out a hundred-dollar bill and placed the closed envelope back down in front of me. I also listened very closely when she commanded, "You handle your business, and take care of my kids," and then stood with her snatch right in my face as I looked up and she gazed into my eyes and ran her finger along the left side of my chin and finished, "and I'll handle mine."

Lynette held that position just long enough that when I did nothing, she didn't just whip my ass in my own tomb, but the Goddess punk'd me as well. The truth is, I believe deep down that Lynette didn't want me to act on her divine and overtly sexual proposition now, and knew I wasn't the kind of man who would. This made it *really* easy for her to be so bold and aggressive knowing she'd be safe. Nah. The real purpose behind her proposition was to merely incentivize me to produce a very favorable outcome in my business dealings with Anastasia *and* her son, because as she confirmed, they are a package deal. Put simply, she would be mine if her kids made money.

"Talk about putting your money where your... well, *my* mouth is?"

She replied, "How's *that* for a trade?"

I accepted her proposal even though it was absolutely unnecessary to guarantee success for Raphael. I had no intention of pimpin' his mom so he could be successful, but I appreciated a grown woman and a grown woman's perspective. And if I did move on that, it would be mutually beneficial, believe me. At the same time, I also needed the kids to experience real life. It's easy to make money following the *rich guy,* but I wanted them to accomplish success on their own merit as well, which is why I had them practicing with simulated accounts and monitoring their progress. They are going to make it regardless of momma puttin' out, but damn if that offer wasn't good money! Lynette stepped back allowing me to stand up for real this time, because there was no way I could've before without a mouth full of pussy and an overnight stay. She walked over to her bag and coat and I followed. The view behind her challenged the future ahead of her.

"I trust this arrangement and my visit will remain between us?"

"Have you given me any messages for anyone, Lynette?"

"No. No, I haven't," she said, smiling as I got the door.

259

"I could call you a car."

"Or you could just call *me*," she replied, flaunting a beautiful smile. "I'll be fine. Maybe next time."

"Can I hold you… to that?"

Lynette stepped closer to me and placed her finger on my lips, then took a mental photograph of my face and walked out. I stood in the doorway until her elevator arrived and she wished me a good night. It was Spring on the calendar but still too cold tonight for *"next time"*. I had a car waiting for her when she got downstairs, the perks of *God money* and Priority Executive Status, and she could bitch at me from the warmth of the backseat of an SUV. She offered me a text instead. *Thank you.*

When she arrived at her Queens home a few blocks from Anastasia's house and walked up her walkway to her front door, the lights were on, meaning Raphael was home, and he had better be. She thought about the position she put herself in and reaffirmed that she had done the right thing passing on the money. She knew H wasn't bluffing and it was hers if she chose it, but she also knew she had to stand her ground and couldn't allow herself to get played like that, well-intentioned or not. H had everything going for him. He had looks, charm, money and that aura of deliverance, if you were blessed enough to be in his good graces. She thought about the money he had lost and how panicked Anastasia had been, and then literally overnight, it was like nothing had happened. This man ate two million dollars in one day and didn't flinch and had the undivided attention of the two most precious people in her life that believed in him like he walked on water. She had presented her case to him and wondered if she had gone too far but consoled herself in Anastasia's faith that he was a man of his word.

"Ralphy!" Lynette called out, coming in the front door.

"Yeah, Ma," she heard him bellow from upstairs in his room.

"I'm home."

"Cool, Ma."

"Ralphy, what you doin?"

"Trading, Ma!"

Lynette whispered, "Lord, I hope I did the right thing."

She went upstairs to his room and found him on his laptop on a video conference with his boys, looking at charts.

"How's it going, baby?"

He muted the call and answered, "I'm up $162.50 and Jah and Rish are up $150 for $312.50."

"What do you mean 'up'?"

"Our income for tonight, Ma."

"Tonight?" Lynette reacted.

"Yeah, Ma. I told you we got a plan."

"You put your money in already?" Lynette asked, panicking.

Lynette hurried over to Raphael's laptop to understand exactly what he was talking about. As much time as she had spent complaining about the risks involved in his 'gambling' as she called it, she never did take the time to know exactly what he was doing.

"Yes, Ma."

He got up and let her sit down and then he went through in detail every step of the way what he had done to earn $300 so far tonight. Lynette looked at her son kneeling down next to her explaining what he had been taught by H, including the signals to look for and how to execute his trades. From his set up, she made more in 30 minutes than she had made all day. It blew her mind to discover that Raphael had been trading live for the past two weeks after depositing their money into trading accounts that H helped them open, and that Anastasia had bank rolled their new company with her own money. She didn't want him to risk his college savings. Lynette was told that this was already in place even before the hit that he took and that he was looking out for them way before her proposition. Satisfied, she kissed her son and gave him her blessings and left him to his work. She then went into her bedroom and sat on her bed and immediately texted H. *You knew all along, didn't you?*

H: *Hi, about what?*

LYNETTE: *I'm not playing with you! Ralphy trading live!*

H: *Yes.*

LYNETTE: *And you said nothing to me, the whole time I was there! Why?*

H: *Nana didn't want to upset you if it didn't work out and Raphael didn't want you to lose faith in his dream.*

LYNETTE: *They formed a company?*

H: *Yes. Raphael, Rishon, Jakeem and Anastasia are the principals.*

LYNETTE: *Did you know it's her money they're trading?*

H: *Yes.*

LYNETTE: *And you let her do it?"*

H: *Yes.*

LYNETTE: *Nig, what's with the one-word answers! Why?*

H: *I arm kids so that they can make informed decisions in their lives, Lynette. Your kids want to succeed and got a passion for it, so they need to accomplish in something they believe in and what they believe in first and foremost is each other and that's powerful. When I finally told them they were ready, Nana told me she was taking her bonus money to fund the account. She worked for it and she earned it. I had to support her decision.*

LYNETTE: *So, you're really not helping them?*

H: *No, but I am keeping an eye on them and what you see is all THEM. You gon whip my ass now?*

She thought about it for a while and replied. *No.* She thought about it some more and added. *But I may be owing you some!*

262

H: *Lol! You owe me nothing, except maybe some cough medicine for that cold ass shower I had to take after you left me?*

LYNETTE: *Well, if you get sick please let me know and I'll come over and rub you… up and down, so you can feel better. You can hold me… to that.*

After a pause she saw his reply. *Ehem, Cough-Cough, hachew!*

"I fucked with the shit all day. Nothing. The shit was broke before I went to bed. In my sleep I had a dream that I fixed it. I woke up and now the bitch works fine."

Chapter Twenty

Meet My Mom
"The Birth Of Anastasia Movado"

"Hello?" she answered, groggy from sleep from hanging out the night before.

"Nana, what's goin' on? You up?"

"Does it sound like I'm up?"

"Come on, rise and shine. I need you to take a run with me."

"Where?"

"To P's house."

"Who's P?"

"My boy. A business partner."

"Ah, you and your friggin' gang!"

"No gang? A small social club."

"Whatever. Your *revolution*. What *time* is it?"

"8:00. What time will you be ready?"

She thought about it and sighed heavily, "An hour."

"Cool, I'll pick you up at 9."

Then she thought about his response, but he hung up, "Wait! Ah, this fucking man, yo! Ughhhhhhhhh!"

An hour blazed past and again she is awakened groggy from sleep.

"Ana? Ana, honey wake up."

"What! *Aye Dios mío, ¿qué es ahora, mom?"* she barked.

Sophia, curtailing her reaction to her daughter's disrespectful tone, informed her, "H is downstairs waiting for you."

Reality hit and Anastasia asked, "Oh, shit! Mom? What time is it?"

"9:10, mi hija."

"Oh, my GOD, H?" Anastasia screeched and ran to the stairs in her sweats calling to him.

I got up and walked to the foot of the stairs and saw that oh so familiar sight making her way from atop the landing that meant I was going to be here for a long minute.

"What's up sleepy head?" I quipped. "An hour, huh?"

"I'm *so* sorry H," she conveyed, apologetically, "I fell back asleep. You still need me to come with you?"

"Uh, *yuh?"*

Her face lit up when she heard my answer, "Ok, I'll get dressed."

She was panicking. At the time I hadn't given it much thought, but this was her first oversight slash fuck up if you will since I hired her. Working after school and keeping late hours for both me and Kate had her understandably exhausted.

"Nana. *Na-na,"* I paused to make sure I had her undivided attention, "calm down and take a shower and all that good stuff. *They* will wait?"

Her panic disappeared as he managed to calm her fears and reassure her that he wasn't going anywhere, that she couldn't help but appreciate him and smile.

"Ok, I won't be long," she said, and ran up the stairs, past her mom and shouted, "not *too* long!"

Then I heard the bathroom door slam. It was a bright and sun shiny Saturday in May and we were heading to P's house in Westchester this morning for a meeting. I was supposed to call Anastasia last night to let her know my plan got changed, but I was sort of in the middle of a Kate and was understandably distracted. Seeing as how I sprung it on her last minute, I guess this was her righteous ball busting unbeknownst to the facts, so I kept quiet and waited patiently. Anastasia came back down about a half hour or so later and found her mom and I getting acquainted and she did not look happy.

"Hi, honey," her mom said to her, giggling, "*¡Él es tan lindo* and really funny!"

"Yeah, I'm sure he is," she grumbled. "Let's go."

I looked at Sophia whose facial expression said it all as Anastasia headed to the door urgently and I got the hint and responded, "Sophia it was very nice meeting you."

"Likewise," she stated confidently. "Please don't be a stranger and enjoy your day."

"You too, now."

She added, "Please, take care of *my* child."

When I stepped outside after assuring Sophia that I would, her little girl was already parked at the curb waiting on me. The car door was lifted by the time she got there, but she wouldn't go in. She wanted me to assist her and I chuckled. It would appear that every time I see her, she has a fresh installment of *Katherine Summers' Debutant Etiquette and Ball Busting Techniques* to try on me. I stared at her as I walked up to her.

She grilled me, "I thought you were in a rush?"

"Look at who's *Miss Bossy* this morning?" I quipped. "Didn't you slow shit down when you overslept, sleepy head?"

"Whatever," she barked, totally annoyed with me.

"May I, Miss Movado?"

Overnight I was witnessing the culmination of all my spoiling of her being thrown back at me. She was trying so hard not to smile, but I won. She grit her teeth and took my hand and got in and seeming to have recovered from her brief crisis, decided to entertain me. I got the thought that maybe I needed to lose money and interrupt her sleep more often- maybe not so much.

"This *is* nice!" she complimented as she fumbled in her bag for something.

"Thank you, Na," I said as I pressed the ignition. "This is still the same car you've been in a couple of times now, you know?"

Her mom stood in the doorway and waved, and Anastasia paid her no mind and smirked at me as we pulled off.

"Yes, I know. How much did you pay for this?" I looked at her, as much as I could while driving and she reiterated, "I'm supposed to know *everything* about you, remember?"

I smiled at both what I saw and what she said and replied, "Half a million."

"Shit, on a car?"

"On a work of art."

"Work of *art,* my ass! You can't hang this car on your wall!"

"It's road art."

She gave me the stare first and then her sharp tongue followed, "You bought this to get women, didn't you?"

I smiled and replied, "The kind of women this car can get me, there's a strong likelihood I don't need."

She retorted, "I said *get* women, not *keep* women." I laughed and she laughed with me and added, "That would be a dick move."

"Yes, Nana. But you do know I'm rich, right?"

"I know," she confirmed. "I don't know how *much,* but I know."

"So, you want me to drive a frigging Camry?"

"No," she smiled, flirting with me, "I like this… it suits you."

I nodded my head at her clever quip, "Righteous."

"So, what did you and my mom talk about?"

"You," I responded, "her *favorite* subject."

"Yeah, right," she rebuffed the thought. "If I was my mom's favorite subject, she…" Anastasia stopped in the middle of her sentence and her facial expression went blank and her gaze fell, "never mind."

I let it rest again. I know pain when I see it. Sophia wasn't fooling me with the doting mom routine she was running while Nana was getting ready. Nana had her father's eyes, based on the picture Sophia showed me, and of course her exotic beauty based on how close she spoke with me. She also took her height and her body. They were damn near twins except Sophia was a shade lighter with a little birthmark on the right side of her chin, which was even lighter. They both wore their long hair in a ponytail, and I loved their nails. Clear and simple. French. Sophia didn't hit on me or anything, but then again, we had just met. She was the *original* beauty though, but why she was still single escaped me. Maybe Nana's attitude was a nig killer or maybe she just liked to play. I mean, she was grown. At face value, I couldn't tell you what was amiss. Her house was neat and clean, and Anastasia was well raised, so exactly what was their issue? I'd have to wait to find out. I know Anastasia wasn't happy with her mom talking to me, at all. Nana wasn't selfish but she wasn't sharing me either. I wondered what else this twin beauty didn't want to share. On the drive out, my girl had dug into her seat with her dark shades on, which is what she was looking for in her bag and blasted the radio listening to shit that if it was up to me, these motherfuckers would still be working a job. Who the fuck made them rich? Black radio. Once upon a time, they helped build us up but now, I don't know. It was tragic. This shit sucked! The beats are timid, and the lyrics are bullshit. It's a sonic lobotomy for black people, man. That shit ain't scarin' off no invaders? Nonetheless, it was *her* day and she was enjoying being free. Every guy we passed wanted her, and every woman who laid eyes on her was jealous. I was rich and she was with me, so that made her a rich *bitch,* and she embodied it.

"Black man, how are you my brother?" asked the one and only, Phillip Kassa Michael, as he greeted H at the top of the steps to his front door as H exited his Lamborghini that he so generously parked next to Phillip's Bentley.

"Righteous!" H laughed and responded. "Where the fuck behind God's back is this motherfucker? Dude? My GPS said, 'Fuck you! You on your own!'"

"Ha-Ha!" P bellowed with pride.

"Look at the fuckin' agriculture you got up in this bitch, and shit... *Massah!*"

"I'm livin' nig, off the earth! Can't truss them crackers!

"Rule #1, baby! Look, your driveway alone is the length of a city block?"

"I know. I need the head start should the fuckers breach my perimeter!" he joked, then paused as I held her hand and she stood and turned to face him. "Anastasia, I don't believe we've met?"

P had a phat ass house out in Westchester and why shouldn't he? His businesses were doing well, and the man got vision like an X Men, and like we planned it in Vegas, it was all up from there. As he said, *"Our ancestors are steady trying to wake us up but nigs is lovin' the sleep!"* It was too cool out to me, so even though the pool is heated, I didn't tell her to pack a bathing suit. No matter, if she needed one, I knew homeboy had plenty of spares and the day turned out to be warm after all. Nana entertained the option while she admired his home, which was big, yet cozy, but not ostentatious. He was successful and comfortable and enjoying it without beating you in the mug with it. After breakfast, she did opt for the pool and a black *Burberry* bikini, to my chagrin, while P and I settled in for our first of several conference calls of the day. Black didn't make the trip due to circumstances out of town, so it was just us, with Star, Griot, Asay, Milk, she was on the call, Decisive from his fishing boat, Sly while on a continental mile calling every partner, boys and girls, as we were checking in on everybody making us money, while Vetty and Amanda held court. When we were done, a couple of hours later, I asked for some privacy and went outside to have a talk with Nana. She teased me while she swam with her arms outstretched treading water. I asked her out of the pool, then walked away to

269

take a seat at a table under the shade of the umbrella and wait for her to join me. It was then that she gratefully watched me gaze at her slowly get out and drip dry herself over to me, seemingly cold, yet only I was shivering, and with her eyes never leaving mine.

"Girl, put on a robe," I said as she took pleasure in the way she was making me feel. "In fact, put on *two*." Nana delighted in my fantasy but covered herself as I requested and took a seat across from me at the table, "We need to talk."

"Ok."

"A little while ago, I lost some money, the biggest amount since I began the company, and it caused you some unnecessary duress and for that I apologize." I watched her as she listened attentively and I explained, "The reason you were in crisis aside from any personal unresolved emotional concerns is because you had not been read in on the details of me or my company. That shit ends today. I am very happy with you Nana and your loyalty to me and most importantly your honesty with me," I said as I watched her begin to get emotional and her big beautiful brown eyes began to fill. "Na, you're a beautiful person and a-" I paused slightly, "a very fine young woman and I want you to know how much you mean to me."

Her eyes filled and began to tear. I did not console her because she was no longer *just* a teenager to me, and it was necessary for her to get through this. There was a box on the table that she had paid no mind to until I brought it to her attention by pushing it in front of her to open.

"Babe, this is for you."

Her eyes widened in her surprise to receive a gift from me. I waited for her to open it and then I explained its contents.

"I want no secrets between us, so moving forward what I know you'll know and if you don't know, it's not yet *time* for you to know. You now have access to me 24/7."

She smiled and wiped her tears. The first box she took out was a new phone and she got all excited.

"That phone rings when this one," I said as I pulled out mine, "rings." I'm putting you between me and the world. Except for my daughters, my sister and Rebecca and maybe my wife one day, who knows, if I get my shit together, no one can reach me directly. They must go through you to get to me. If Rebecca calls, you *must* pick up. Is that clear?"

"Yes."

"Righteous."

"What about Kate… and your mom?"

"My mom tends to agitate me, like my house, and I gotta keep focused, and Kate- that's you, so she goes through you too." This confused her. I could see it on her face, but I was emphasizing a point, "Now, I know you're in school, so the system won't be efficient yet, but this is my commitment to you," I said as her eyes filled up again. "For now, just forward the calls and we will test the shit on our days off."

She nodded and I motioned for the next box. Anastasia liked this gift and was curious.

"A laptop?"

"Yes. I hope you love it as much as your new tablet. Glenn hooked this up! It's got state of the art blah-blah and more blah, super thin and all that good shit, but the *important* thing is that *this* is *company* hardware giving you access to my business, so you know what I know. It's password protected, which our phones generate for access to sensitive info. This is my private information, Nana, and I'm trusting your judgement. Please be careful?"

"I will."

H nodded, "Next."

She dug in the box and took out two credit cards.

"The regular one, yes, that one," I said as she held it up, "is a bank card where your pay is going to be deposited. This account due to my relationship with the bank, has zero fees."

Anastasia asked, "You opened an account for me?"

"Amanda did. She'll explain." She nodded and said, "Thank you," and continued to listen, "The next one is a *Black Card*. It's a company credit card and it has no limit."

"Oh wow? I've heard about this," she said. "I didn't know it was true. But don't you have to be like *super* rich to get this?"

"Eh, or super stupid. You gotta have enough, which brings me to my next and final topic, my wealth. Curious," I asked, "how much do you think I'm worth?"

"Honestly boss, I don't know," she exclaimed. "I have no concept. I figured you got baller money. You got those Lambs and properties and businesses and God knows, Kate ain't cheap and neither are you?"

We laughed.

"Kate's actually my least expensive bill if you can believe that. She's her own *independent* woman."

"You mean what she wants from you is not your money. What's the deal with y'all anyway?"

H paused and reflected and answered, "Hmmm, we will get to that. I'm taking care of you now."

Anastasia was flattered by his attention to her and asked, "So... how much *are* you worth?"

"Let's log in and find out, shall we? Now you can change all of this info later but for now your username is: *Abeja Reina.*"

"Queen Bee," she said, softly and gazed at me for a moment.

"Ok. Password?" she asked.

I responded, "The date that I hired you."

Anastasia's big beautiful brown eyes filled up and then they started to rain. She got up and ran around the table to me and as I stood up, she hugged me. I consoled her while she poured out her heart to me and trembled in my arms releasing some of those unresolved emotional concerns.

"I'm sorry, babe, are you ite?" She nodded yes, with her head buried in my neck, gripped in a choke hold like her life depended on it. "It's alright. I got you."

She remained silent except for some sobbing, sniffling and an occasional nodding. I gave her all the time she needed and held her tight and when she was ready, she let me go and I straddled the bench and she sat across my lap.

"You're gorgeous, you know that?" I said as I kissed her on her head, and she chuckled.

"You've told me," she stated and hugged me tighter.

"You remind me of-" He stopped abruptly and whispered under his breath, "Siren."

"Who?" she asked, and he ignored her. "What?" she asked, again.

"No one," he answered, sighing. "Babe, what are you crying for?"

"You wouldn't understand," she replied, as if doubting his ability to appreciate the role he has played in her life in the brief time that he has known her.

"Probably. I wouldn't mind hearing it though. You wanna try me?"

She lifted her head and gazed into my eyes. I wiped her tears with my fingers, then she put her head back down under my chin and said, "I realized today that my father ain't shit. He left me when he left my mom and he never looked back. I was six. It's as if I paid for *her* sins. I didn't do anything wrong to him."

"Wow? I'm sorry to hear that."

"He broke every promise he ever made to me because he didn't want me. I never mattered to him."

"I'm sure that's not the case, babe. Sometimes these things get... what the fuck, *complicated.*"

"Didn't your father leave you?"

H hesitated but answered, "Yeah."

"How old were you?"

"I was three and a half."

"Was that also complicated?"

H chuckled softly, "No, malicious." He reflected and said, "I'd like to think he is a one in a million asshole, you know?"

"Sorry, mine was the second."

"I dig," he conceded. "Was it an ugly divorce?"

"I don't think so. I know he didn't want custody. He just wanted to pay child support. I *know* what you're thinking," she said, like she's had to defend it all her life, "I *am* his child."

"I see that, you've got his eyes."

"I hear that a lot from my mom and from my family... *when* I see them."

"Can I ask, what happened between the two of them?"

"My mother said he found a trick and left but I know my mom is a bitch, so I never believed that."

"Harsh, but ok? What do *you* think happened?"

"I'm not sure. I just know it happened after I got sick," she said as she snuggled closer to me, which I took to mean that she didn't want to talk about it anymore. I had learned a lot today and straight from her. She trusted enough to discuss a subject this painful with someone she felt close enough to. Me.

"Eh, you'll be ite."

"Are you?"

"H grinned some more and replied, "Yeah, let me get back to you on that? You wanna finish login in?"

"No, I'm fine."

"Yes, Nana, you are."

The rest of the day I enjoyed her having fun. She was enjoying her new phone and interceding on everyone's behalf. She grilled me on every number in the bitch, adding to her inventory of my history. She was safe with me, I guess because she felt a part of me and a part of *my* family. She enjoyed being at P's house in the open space and the freedom it gave her. She had been cooped up too long both physically and emotionally and releasing all those hang ups just made her radiate with joy. She was like the second coming of Rebecca. Her smile was radiant, and her laughter was fuller. Her big beautiful brown eyes were brighter and more optimistic. I just enjoyed her having fun and now I understood why, and I accepted it.

"You sure about her?"
"Hers was the strongest of all. I'm done."
"Hmmm. Ok, shuga. I'll see you Thursday."

Nana and I left for Queens listening to that fuckin' radio again the whole ride back and the only thing that made it bearable was the joy on her pretty little face. *'Daddy is my bitch'* as my youngest would say was the song Nana might as well had been singing when we arrived at her house later that afternoon.

"This really means a lot to me, what you've given me, and I'm not talking about the stuff either. I mean your trust and you believing in me. I promise you I won't let you down."

I saw her getting emotional again, "Hey, stop that. No more crying ite, *ever.*"

"Yes... boss," she chuckled and said, gazing into my eyes, "I just really appreciate it?"

"I know babe, and you earned it and," I said as I held her chin up, "I haven't given you anything you didn't deserve. You're worth all of it to me?"

"Ugh!" she exclaimed, annoyed as her phone rang interrupting her moment with him and when she looked to see who was calling, she became completely disinterested.

"Who is it?"

"One of your exes."

"Which one?"

"Does it matter? She an ex, and I'm not answering it."

I chuckled softly and asked, while she paid me no mind continuing to compose herself, drying her eyes and wiping her cheek, "You gon be ite?"

"Yeah, I'm good."

"That's different?" I celebrated to myself, "Cool!"

With a nod Anastasia indicated to me that she was ready for the world, so I got out and opened her door for her and walked with her, up her walkway to her steps. She hugged my neck tight and kissed my cheek and without a word she went inside. When I got back in the car I thought, *"You know, maybe I'll stay at my fuckin' house tonight... a six pack. Yeah, that'll numb the pain."*

"Hi, honey, how was it?" Sophia asked as she was coming down the stairs. "Did you have fun?"

"Yes, mom, I had a really *great* time," Anastasia replied, realizing that her mom had just left her perch in the window where she obviously saw her kiss him.

"Wow?" Surprised by her enthusiasm she replied, "Aw, *mi hija,* I'm so happy for you! Do you want to talk about it?"

"Maybe later?" replied Anastasia, fueling her mother's curiosity.

"Ok, I cooked if you're hungry," she said, fixing Anastasia's hair on the stairs.

"Maybe later."

"Hmmm, what's in the bag," she asked, noticing it was wet.

"My bathing suit."

Sophia looked again with her interest piqued and uttered, "Oh?"

Anastasia relishing her moment of glory responded, "I spent most of the day swimming in the heated pool while H had his conference calls."

"Oh, you did have fun, didn't you? I can put it to dry for you if you want," she offered.

All day Anastasia had been served and paid homage to from H to his partner to his house staff to the onlookers they passed on the road and all whom she met or laid eyes on. She was their *"Abeja Reina"* for today, so why should her mother be any different?

"That would be great, mom," she said as she gave her the bag and Sophia saw the scant contents and gazed at her daughter. "Thank you!"

Anastasia continued up the stairs into her room and shut the door and immediately got on the phone with Raphael to tell him about her day. Sophia could hear the laughter and commotion from the spot where she left her.

"… and I got some toys! I got a new phone, so I can reach him with no more issues. You should have *seen* this crib!"

There were still some unresolved emotional issues to cry out and until then she would have to head to the laundry room to serve her daughter. When Anastasia was done talking to Raphael, she took out her new laptop on the bed with her and finished logging in and scrolled through the company menu. A password was required for access beyond personnel and company PR, and she remembered.

"It's password protected, which our phones generate for access to sensitive info…"

Anastasia took out her new phone and looking through it found an app that was also password protected. She entered her sign on info and it generated an alphanumeric code. She entered that code into her

277

laptop, and it granted her access. What she saw was unbelievable but not confusing, after all, she was an economics major. She scrolled down the various accounts until she came to a line that read: *Total Net Worth.*

"Oh... my... GOD, H?"

"Sometimes I worry about him, Kate. He gets down on himself like he can't get over some pain or something."

"He had it rough, kid."

"Shit, didn't we all?"

"Not his kind of rough, sweetie." She cautioned, *"You and I may never understand his kind of rough. Different world... well, at least for me?"*

"You know what I mean?" I said.

"I do. As great as you think he is, he isn't infallible, you know? He has his own way of dealing with his hang ups. Pouting is one of them, sulking is the other. Shit, it's his favorite along with the occasional tantrum and breaking shit. If I'm nearby, I'll go over and perk him up and he'll perk me up too, or three-"

Kate could insert a sexual innuendo in a bible verse. She was so lucky. I picked up the TV remote and pointed it at her and repeatedly pressed the "OFF" button as she spoke.

"Honestly, I think I get the better end of the deal?"

"Oh, God."

"I end up feeling much better than he does!" she said, cracking up.

"God, Kate," I tried to get the thought out of my head, *"off!"*

Kate paid no attention to me. She was so free and beautiful *and* crazy. I envied her style and spirit with her sexuality and how she could share him the way that she

278

did. The more he wasn't exclusive to her is the more she had to have him.

"You know he doesn't stay down for long, right?" she asked, lowering her head and moving it to make eye contact with me and confirm that fact. *"You do know that?"*

Kate's hair was in a ponytail just like mine. Her French manicure tips were square with white in a *"V"* shape and mine were white straight across. Around her neck was a custom diamond given to us by him. Kate wore the diamond pendant to the diamond charm bracelet I wore, and Amanda wore a pair of diamond earrings. Yvette wore a beautiful diamond choker she received not long after she started with us and on Rebecca's right finger was a rock that made us all jealous.

"Yes."

"Good. Once he recharges, he will be back to his normal, lovable, odd self again." She scooped her bowl and put her arm around me, and I laid my head on her shoulder and she said, *"Thank GOD he doesn't drink or do drugs! We'd all be fucked! Sorry, sweetie."*

Footnotes

Pg. 23 *"No digas eso!"* - "Don't say that!"

Pg. 41 *"Dios mío, él era tan lindo!"* - "My God, he was so cute!"

Pg. 195 *"Debes ser sordo."* - "You must be deaf."

Pg. 195 *"Te prometo que no soy."* - "I promise you I'm not."

Pg. 217 *"No sé qué pasa con su dinero,"* - "I don't know what's up with his money,"

Pg. 217 *"vete al baño"* - "Go to the bathroom…"

Pg. 217 *"Esto es lo que quería. Gracias."* - "This is what I really wanted. Thanks."

Pg. 240 *"¿Claro mis amores?"* - "Are we clear my loves?"

Pg. 240 *"Se bueno, boss,"* - "Be good, boss."

Pg. 255 *"Dime, ¿cómo hizo esto?"* - "Tell me, how did he do this?"

Pg. 264 *"Aye Dios mío, ¿qué es ahora, mom?"* - "Oh, my God, what is it now, mom?"

Pg. 266 *"¡Él es tan lindo!"* - "He's so cute."